NO TELEPHONE
TO HEAVEN
DAVID WORLOCK

David Worlock took a History
degree at Cambridge and
became an education publisher.
His involvement in this
field in Nigeria provides the
background to this story. His
subsequent career took him
into digital information and
the strategies and technologies
being deployed to create future
information market places.

David Worlock is the author of
a memoir, *Facing Up To Father,
The Pleasures and Pains of a
Cotswold Childhood*.

NO TELEPHONE TO HEAVEN

DAVID WORLOCK

Marble Hill

First published in 2024 by Marble Hill Publishers
Flat 58 Macready House
75 Crawford Street
London W1H 5LP
www.marblehillpublishers.co.uk

A CIP catalogue record for this book is available from
the British Library.

ISBN: 9781738497027

Typeset in Abobe Caslon and Blakey Slab
Printed and bound by IngramSpark
Text and cover design by Paul Harpin

To Anne, whose strength
and patience was so vital to the
completion of this book.

CONTENTS

INTRODUCTION

CYRIL FAGUNWA TRACED a line in the dust with the toe of a dust covered shoe. He felt ill at ease. He'd been with the police for 12 years but here in Lagos, in the last two years, things had been different from his experience in Benin. This of course was partly because he came from Benin and he understood how people there thought and spoke. The whole world was here in Lagos and when it came to these company types he felt ill at ease. Especially when one of them was British. They worried him, even a young one like the one standing at the corner of the little lane in front of him. Not very distinguished looking. When they are young, all these European faces look the same. He felt they were full of unanswered questions, and that he in particular was poorly equipped to understand those questions let alone answer them.

Yet, he acknowledged, for three people thrown together by events at nine am on this Lagos morning we're going to have to ask and answer a whole lot of questions, and he was the policeman and so they would expect him to take the lead. The Nigerian guy looked so sad. He was middle-aged, heavily built, and by his facial scars Cyril knew that he was Ibo. He cleared his throat and summoned up all up all the things that he had learnt from his instructor in police college and from watching detective films on television. He rehearsed what he would say when they got started.

Now, gentlemen, I need to know all that you can tell me about the deceased. Where did he come from?

Do you know who his parents are and how we can contact them?

Cyril realised that he had dozens of questions to ask. The important one on his mind was how these people would react: would they accept his authority? This was the first real murder he had tackled since joining the Lagos force. Normally he got domestic violence, or bar fights leading to violent death. So why had the Detective Chief Inspector given him this job?

Murder was the nature of things in Lagos. Cyril was a detective inspector, and so he had a greater sense of the hopelessness of things than most members of the Lagos force. When he had checked in this morning at six am there been 17 reported murders in the book from midnight. So normally the first job you did as a detective was to try to identify the body. But this case was different. These two corporate characters turned up at central police headquarters only a few minutes after Cyril had rung the office in Ibadan, where, from the name tag that he still wore, it appeared that the dead man worked. Given this town was 70 miles to the north, Cyril found this very odd. Neat, though, he thought, turning the line in the dust into a circle. If everybody wore a company name tag then identifying bodies would be a simple formality. Apparently, when he had phoned the main office, the two men had been in the company compound in Lagos and had been alerted by colleagues. This meant that they could identify the body and, to Cyril's way of thinking, this made things delightfully easy. Sometimes identifying the body took weeks.

They waited around in this dusty lane in what was already a very hot day in the Lagos slum of Mushin for forensics to finish their work. That in itself was something different. Most cases that Cyril handled did not have forensics. Most detectives on the force thought that they were a nuisance and it was certainly true that they always slowed things down. At the moment, after spending ten minutes erecting a blue plastic tent over the body and fastened it closed, they had gone inside. This left Cyril and his two witnesses on the outside, with nothing at all to say to each other prior to the identification of the body.

When the murder was reported, it was reported as a ritual murder. Cyril was reputed to know all about these: he came from Benin. Every time there was a Muti killing or something to do with a Shango cult, it got pushed towards Cyril. It was useless to point out that he was Efik and did not know any more than anyone else. He was born in Benin city and therefore, according to the superintendent, must know about such things. It was also a conviction of Cyril's that the superintendent did not much like him and that this was probably why he was assigned to this job in the first place.

And the fact that there is a company and an Englishman involved, he thought gloomily, means that I am a sitting duck if anything goes wrong with the investigation.

The sound of the zipper on the tent broke into these thoughts. Femi from forensics peeled off his gloves as he stepped outside.

"It's a very neat piece of work, Cyril, and you are probably looking for a ritual killer who is also a medical student practising the sections!"

There was a laugh from the inside of the tent and the second forensics man emerged. "Died just before midnight, in case you were wondering, inspector, and

3

probably undisturbed because this path only goes down to the mosque so no one came down here until morning prayers."

Like a good actor, Cyril knew that he was being given a cue and it was time for him to get on stage. "Now gentlemen, I have to ask you to identify the body and to confirm that is it is the same person as the individual whose name is on the name tag."

He ushered them inside the small, baking hot, airless and blue tinged space. The Nigerian went first, and Cyril heard him gasp and retch and turn to rush back past the other two as Cyril stood there behind the Englishman. They heard the Nigerian being sick in the lane. But the Englishman was calm and seemed to be taking it in his stride, although as he turned to Cyril his face was a mask of sadness.

"This is Marcus Diello," he said, and his shoulders sagged as if to express the utter hopelessness of the situation.

"Thank you," said Cyril, "and does your colleague agree?"

The Englishman looked towards his colleague who nodded, and then looked back. "Yes, he agrees."

Cyril then placed the identification form on the top of his notebook and invited them to sign. Once he had the forms in his pocket he felt a little more confident. At least he had something to put into the file.

Cyril now turned to his two witnesses. "I know that you are just work colleagues and not relatives, but can you tell me anything about his family and his parents? Obviously we need to contact them urgently, and since they are not resident here in Lagos, I need any help you can give me on that."

To Cyril's surprise, it was not the pale young Englishman who had signed the form as "Henry Kettering" who responded, but his older Nigerian companion, who signed as "Philip Nkworu."

"Marcus is a highborn Hausa. His father is the head man of the Hausa community in Ibadan. Our chairman is his close friend which is how Marcus came to be working with us as a trainee accountant. No doubt the chairman will have spoken to the family already and I'm sure that we should hear from them very shortly. They will want to reclaim the body for immediate burial."

Yes, Cyril thought, that could be a complication. But he put it behind him for the moment. "If he worked with you in the Ibadan office, what was he doing down here in Lagos and wandering around in the middle of the night?"

Now the Englishman took up the responses. "He was very devout and we think he may well have gone to the mosque for late prayers. The day before yesterday we had a great party at our office to celebrate the fact that he had passed his accountancy exams, and that the company was offering him a job as a manager, in charge of our warehouse at Apapa in the Lagos docks."

Cyril sighed. He knew exactly where the docks were and he did not need any geography lessons from an Englishman. So he paused for a moment and pretended to write a lengthy note in the notebook. Then he turned back to the older man.

"And now, Philip, isn't it, exactly what was your relationship to the dead man?"

Philip screwed his eyes up for a moment as if there were some dust blown into them. Then he said, "He was so young when he came to join the company that we all felt a sort of responsibility for him. I suppose I became what they call a mentor, sort of father figure. We got into the habit of discussing problems. Things were complicated for him. His family was very protective. There was a feeling he should return to Kano and join the military, like his brothers. It was a sort of family tradition. For some reason I think that he felt that someone like me, an educated Ibo in his fifties who had survived the war, might have a different angle on life. So when he wanted to test the things that were said at home or amongst his Hausa friends, he came to talk to me over coffee, two or three times a week. I came to think of him as I do my own children."

At this the older man broke down and leant against the top of the wall with his head in his hands. Cyril felt that he had no choice but to turn back to the Englishman. "And you, Mr Kettering, what was your relationship with Marcus Diello?"

The Englishman had been listening closely and attentively to Philip's responses.

"Please call me Henry," he said. "Everyone does and it does make things easier." This was said in such a simple and unaffected way that Cyril almost reluctantly found himself warming to the young man. "I was simply his friend. We played squash two or three times a week. We always sat at the same table at lunch. We were close in age and neither of us knew anything about the publishing business. I only left university a few months ago, and as you have heard he was an accountancy student. But I have never met anyone with such an open and enquiring mind or such a gift for friendship. In the last few months we formed a strong bond, and he even took me to his family home for a meal only a week ago. I am deputy to the chairman and his assistant so I organised the leaving party two nights ago at our offices to celebrate his new job. I had a very smart black attaché case sent out from our London office as a going away gift for Marcus and I am very worried that he might have been robbed for this. Please tell me if you have found it. I have checked at the compound where he left his suitcase before going to the mosque, but there is no sign of it there."

Cyril did not feel that he was quite in charge of the police interrogation. Witnesses were not expected to question him, or entertain theories about where the dead man had been going, or the motives for the murder. So he ignored the information about the attaché case, and simply commented that he would ask at the mosque to see whether Mr Diello had been present there that evening.

Now he told his two witnesses, "I need to know what your movements were since you last saw Mr Diello and then I need to know a little bit more about your company and your relationships to it and Mr Diello."

Having delivered himself of this, Cyril felt happy. That should keep them busy, and damp down this tendency to speculate about what their friend might have been doing in this dark Mushin slum in the middle of the night.

Cyril indicated that Philip should go first, and after he had blown his nose and composed himself a little, he told Cyril that their company was an education text book publishing company. As soon as he mentioned the name, Cyril recognised it. In his mind's eye he could still see the red covers of the Readers in his primary school in the village just south of Abba where he had lived as a child. For a moment he experienced a warm distracting glow but was forced to start taking notes again as Philip recounted his role as editorial director. In answer to a question from Cyril, he said that he employed staff from all over Nigeria since they published in twenty-eight different languages at primary school level. Clerical staff were mostly Yoruba from Ibadan and the villages around it. In this respect Marcus was no exception. In Philip's view, there was no one who disliked Marcus. He did not seem to spend a great deal of time socialising outside of work, and normally returned to his family compound as soon as work was over. No, he did not drink and he did not take drugs or smoke ganja and he did not gamble. So if he was so good, wondered Cyril, what on earth could be the motive for murdering him.

Here Henry interjected, and Cyril looked at him balefully. If this man had been a Nigerian, and if he had been trained in police college as Cyril had been, the punishment for interruptions had been a sharp rap on the knuckles with an officer's swagger stick. But this was just a thing, you could not stop Europeans from speaking whenever they felt like it. Then you had to address the question, which was in this case Henry turning the question on motivation back on him and asking what was the normal motivation for a ritual murder in Nigeria? That made Cyril impatient once again, as he said the normal motivation for a ritual killing was to perform some religious rites.

"Surely," Philip said, "if you were going to do black magic of some sort or another or worship a Shango cult, then you would take away the bits that you took out of the body, not leave them alongside the corpse in a methodical line just as if they were being presented on a butchers' block or anatomists' table."

8

This caused Cyril to sigh deeply, and reflect that since he did not know the murderer he did not know what his motivation was, or whether he had been disturbed at work This would be the subject of the investigation, but that investigation could not begin until both Henry and Philip had answered his questions to his satisfaction.

He saw the two men exchange a glance. Then Philip politely asked him to please go on with his questions, and Henry turned slightly away from him as if trying to master the discipline required not to interrupt. Cyril felt that he needed to know more about the company, and particularly about this powerful chairman who had been mentioned earlier. Philip smiled for the first time and asked if he meant the chief?

"Chief Samuel Mydogun. Yes, I did."

Before he became chairman of the company the chief had been commissioner for economic affairs for the province. And having said that everybody knew him, Philip also commented that he felt sure that the chief knew the police commissioner extraordinarily well.

Wasn't this just typical, Cyril thought. Not only do I have this English man to cope with, but now a hugely influential political figure through whom complaints about my performance will go to the commissioner faster than bullets. This just confirms why I was given this job. This is a no hope case, since not only is it never going to get solved, but the risk to the life and limb of the police investigator is clear at every point.

Cyril turned to Henry and asked him about the chief's relationship to the dead man. Henry paused for a moment and said that he was more like a father with a son. He spoke about the relationship between the chief and the dead man's father, how he had persuaded Marcus to try a career in publishing, how the company had sponsored Marcus to go to the accountancy college, and how proud both his real father and the chief, his surrogate father, had been when he passed his accountancy exams and became a manager in the company. How both of his fathers had been there to present him with his diploma and to give him a going away gift that the company had selected, this attaché case already mentioned that had been acquired in London and flown out for the purpose.

Cyril made a note. This attaché case must mean something, because it kept coming up in the conversation.

The Lagos sun seemed concentrated on this narrow passage way. It was hard to think. Police headquarters was hardly a cool, air-conditioned paradise, especially when the power packed up, but all of a sudden he longed to be back there, away from the scene of the crime. Away from these two difficult witnesses, who could testify to the identity of the dead man, but who seemed determined to fog his brain with all sorts of information that did not seem relevant to why the man was there and why he was killed. He guessed that he had brought it upon himself by seeking some background on the murdered man, but now he had quite enough to fill the file. He concentrated hard on his notebook for a moment, and then turned back to Philip.

"I get the picture of why the dead man was in Lagos. What I do not get is why he was in this narrow alleyway in a slum area where, from your account, he is unlikely to have known anybody."

He said this forcefully so that Philip, and by extension, Henry, would stop thinking of fresh questions and start thinking of his questions. They looked at each other, then turned back to Cyril. It was clear to him that neither of them had a clue.

"So if I suggested that he was here to say his prayers in the mosque at the end of the alley, would that sound like his behaviour?"

Both men nodded. "Exactly like his behaviour," Henry volunteered. "He was very dutiful in his religious observances."

Philip agreed, and said that he may have missed evening prayers because he was travelling, but would have come to say his prayers somewhere before the end of the evening.

"So how did Mr Diello know about this place?"

The two men looked at each other once again. Clearly they had no idea. Cyril felt that he was back in charge once again. At least he was beginning to impress these two educated and sophisticated men that there was some point to following police procedures. He himself had learnt this at police college from Mr Braithwaite. Mr Braithwaite had been a detective inspector with the Cumbria police before he was seconded to Nigeria. They only had him for two years. He got malaria and went home. But Cyril had been hugely impressed with his gravitas, as well as his procedural notes, and it was this that he tried to bring to his enquiries.

In Cyril's mind, suspicion was turning into certainty. The murder was one thing. In most of his cases, where everybody knew the victims of domestic violence or a fight in a bar, motive and means were normally clear. It was catching anybody in this vast city that was impossible. Here, by a stroke of luck, the man was wearing a badge, his workmates had arrived quickly and he had been identified. But that was all.

So the police commissioner and the detective chief superintendent, with all their experience, had said to themselves, "No hope in solving this case. The company involved is prominent and run by a Yoruba chieftain. So let's send Fagunwa to investigate – if he makes a mess, we can send him back to Benin City where he belongs and it won't look so bad for us."

Cyril forced himself to think about Mr Braithwaite.

"So do you have any idea where Mr Diello might have heard of this mosque, or who might have advised him to come here?"

Again the two men looked nonplussed. Philip thought it might have been the gate man at their compound. Henry just shrugged and said he knew very little about the religious observances of his friend Marcus, but he would have thought of him worshipping at some central mosque in downtown Lagos rather than here. Philip argued that this mosque was much closer to the compound than any of the central Lagos mosques, and it was fairly late in the evening when Marcus had arrived at the compound. Cyril considered that a speculative debate between two people who didn't know anything at all wasn't likely to get him to any rapid conclusion.

"So did Mr Diello have many friends in Lagos?"

Again, the mute but expressive glances between the two men. Philip volunteered that he did not think that Marcus had ever been to Lagos before this visit. Henry said he knew that Marcus often went to his grandfather and extended family's home in Kano, but he had never heard him speak of coming to Lagos. Cyril thought gloomily about the parochialism of Nigerians. Very few people travelled anywhere except back to their home state. So they know the place where they are, and the place where they come from. Just like me, he thought. He knew Benin city and Abba and now some parts of Lagos, but the idea of going as far north as Kano was as remote as going to Ghana. It would never happen. He looked back at the two men.

"So what did you expect him to do once he had reached the compound?"

Philip said that he would have eaten, since there would have been a meal waiting for him, and then gone to bed. Henry believed that he would have wanted to revisit the plan they had made for the reorganisation of the management of the warehouse.

"Marcus was due to go to the warehouse the next day to familiarise himself with the current working procedures, and the chairman, accompanied by me, planned to have a meeting with him there later in the week to go through the first steps in improving the way the warehouse was running."

He then explained that this was important because until the previous year the whole company had been sited in Apapa above the warehouse, but since they had moved to Ibaban the warehouse had been under-managed, and there had been problems with distributing books arriving by ship to the various places where they were needed in the country.

Philip joined in. There were also problems with stock control it appeared, and it was sometimes hard to know how many copies of which textbook they had available. Henry agreed that this was one of the issues that he and the chairman had identified, as well as the fact that the textbooks were in twenty-eight different languages, and no one in the warehouse spoke more than two or three of them . At which point Philip added that the delays in the docks because of the Nigerian cement crisis added to the management issues in the warehouse.

Cyril ground his teeth and raised his eyes to the heavens as he thought for a way to refocus these two on the fact of the murder. He guessed that they would rather talk about anything else, but he had to drag them back.

"Did the dead man have any enemies, and can you imagine who would want to kill him?"

Both men almost laughed. Henry repeated that he was absolutely certain that Marcus had no enemies in Ibadan, let alone in Lagos. Philip, with a Nigerian consciousness of who might or might not be enemies, was more thoughtful. He said that there were always people who would try to promote violence between Nigerian ethnic groups. Marcus was an offspring of a great Hausa family. He might be a target for inter-tribal bad feeling, or indeed for somebody trying to get at his father or his grandfather personally. How did that explain the nature of the killing? he wanted to know.

This is better, thought Cyril. At least they've stopped talking about warehouses. But now, I have to stop them getting back to asking me questions.

So he told them that the issue he wanted to explore was not how the dead man was killed, but why. He accepted Philip's points, but the issue that then arose in his mind was who knew that Mr Diello was travelling to Lagos and who knew that he had left the compound after his arrival there the previous evening.

"Can you now tell me who knew about his travel plans?"

Henry thought it was a question of who didn't know, as far as the company and its employees were concerned. They all came to the party in Ibadan to wish Marcus joy in his new job and to see him off. Philip said nobody would have had an exact idea of his travel schedule, although probably members of his family might know that, and the gate man doing security at the compound would have signed him in.

Cyril agreed that he would have to go and talk to the security man. He wrote it down in his book. As he did so, the image of the body on the pavement kept coming back to him. Surely they had been right in their earlier discussion? It was a really strange ritual murder. In his head now he had the image of all those organs lined up on the right of the body. One lung, the liver, kidneys. Cult murders were done to harvest those parts and offer them to the gods. So here he had the murderer not taking them away. Was he disturbed? Or was this an attempt to make something look like a cult or ritual killing, when in fact it wasn't? As if he was reading Cyril's mind, Philip now asked another question. "He obviously did not make an appointment to meet his murderer, so do we really think there's a ritual killer who is looking for someone to murder and bumps into Marcus by accident?"

Cyril knew that he was on dangerous ground here. So he said that he was not really an authority on Muti killings. His superiors had sent him out on this case since he came from a district that was famous for them on the other side of Nigeria. This stopped the conversation for a moment. As silence hung in the still, humid air, Cyril found his mind going back to his wife and his little children in Benin city. What was really stopping her following him to Lagos? She must know how lonely and difficult he found it, a man who had loved being with his family, living in the police barracks with no company except raucous young policeman.

She said that she and the children could not afford to come across the country, but he knew that was not really the case. She did not know enough about their finances to know if they could afford it or not. The truth he felt was that she did not wish to live away from her mother or her family, and she did not wish to bring her children up in Lagos. So he had just begun to rehearse in his mind why he himself had come to this stinking, corrupt city when the Englishman broke into his thoughts again.

With his face screwed up in painful recollection and concentration, the Englishman was saying something that seemed to be very important to him. He was talking about the organs – somehow they couldn't get away from this topic – and asking which organs, and why those organs. Cyril found himself flipping back in his notebook where he'd written down a list of organs, and now he was reading them out, slightly surprised once again that the interrogation was going so badly out of his control.

Heart, one lung, kidney, liver, spleen, genitals. As he read he found that he too was wondering, Why just one lung? And why in such a neat line and why on the right hand side of the body? He looked up at the Englishman. He knew that they were both being forced to follow a story, but neither of them knew what it meant or where it was going.

Cyril shrugged and looked at his two witnesses as dispassionately as he could. He would tell them that they would have to come into the central police station for further questioning, and that they should bring identification. At that point he would ask them to sign a formal statement, and if they had any further recollection of events which might materially help him to catch the killer, or killers, then they should get in touch with him immediately. He should have the forensics report in two or three days. As he looked over their shoulders he saw that the forensics team had removed the body while they were talking, and were now packing up the blue tent. Soon the little alleyway would be clear, only the blood on the pavement and in the guttering to show what had happened here.

Cyril asked politely whether he could give them a lift in his squad car. He guessed that they had come up from the compound, but he did not know whether they had been in a taxi or a company car. The question got Philip moving. He put his hand on the Englishman's shoulder and said, "No, of course we have to tell our driver, John. He will be shattered."

Cyril asked if the driver had been a close friend of the dead man, and Philip said that John was everybody's friend, and the confidant of everybody who rode in the back of his vehicle. He was really the chairman's driver, but he also drove Henry almost everywhere because the company did not consider it safe for the Englishman to drive himself. Cyril nodded at the wisdom of that. Philip then pointed out that Marcus and indeed himself were often passengers in the same car, especially going between Lagos and Ibadan. Just as Marcus was the friend of all of them, he was a special friend of John, who was closer in age to him than anybody else but Henry.

At this point Cyril felt that he should really talk to this John character while he was still around, and he followed his two witnesses down the narrow alleyway to where the black Peugeot 606 waited, with a young man leaning on the bonnet with a very bored expression.

"Excuse me a moment," said Philip, before Cyril

could take proper control of proceedings, and he walked around the vehicle, took the young man by his shoulders, and addressed him rapidly and forcefully in Ibo. Philip was explaining about the murder and the need for John to answer some questions, but as he did so, the young man sagged, cried and fell forward onto the older man's shoulder. Cyril felt this was getting out of hand and that he must intervene again.

He stepped forward and introduced himself to John. He asked him to compose himself, and remember whether he had heard anything about the intentions of the deceased in regard to things he might do or people he might see in Lagos.

John said that as far as he knew Marcus had no friends or contacts in Lagos. Probably his family had many contacts in the Hausa community, and his father had probably directed him to visit one of the leading imams in the city, but he did not know which, and he certainly did not know why he was here in Mushin, which he himself would not visit alone for any religious observance. In his view, anyone who could kill Marcus was drugged or mad or drunk or all three, because this was a good man, and an innocent man. If, he said, Cyril was half a policeman then he would get after the killer straight away, with a machete, and leave him on a pavement in many more pieces than the murderer had done to his poor friend.

Then he flung his arms around Philip once again and sobbed uncontrollably, shouting out in Ibo between bursts.

There was no more to be said. Cyril turned away and went in search of the squad car. As he did so it came in search of him, and he climbed gratefully on board. He sat in the front passenger seat observing the three men, still clasped together, as he drove slowly away. Here was one of those crimes he would never solve. That was why none of the so-called best detectives on the Lagos force had been sent out to try. Yet failure here would hang around Cyril's neck forever, and while the others were out bringing in local gangsters, or receiving heavy dash for not bringing them in, he would be left with this one.

Let's just suppose, he said to himself, that I did find out who committed this appalling murder. It would turn out to be some associate of some high-ranking person, some rich man, or somebody who in any event I was not able to touch or arrest. It's hopeless. I might as well go back to Benin City, live with my family, and solve breaking and entering mysteries on half the salary that I get now. He stared through the windscreen with such intensity that his driver did not dare to interrupt.

CHAPTER 1 CYRIL

IT WAS AN hour before Cyril was back at police head-quarters, an hour of slow chugging through heavy traffic across the bridges and onto the island and then into police headquarters. It was cooler there, and although the deep suspicion remained that he was being set up in a hopeless investigation and would be the ultimate recipient of blame when nothing tangible came of it, he did feel that he needed more time with his two witnesses, perhaps with the chairman of the company, and certainly with the young Ibo driver whom he had met fleetingly at the end of his initial investigation.

Any other thoughts were dashed from his mind by a message to "put his head round the door of the DCI's office," and when he presented himself at that door he found his boss in a smiling, friendly mood.

"I understand you made a good start on this job, Cyril. We all know that these murders are the hardest to crack, so any progress you can make will be welcome. But for the time being, please confine your enquiries to the man's family, friends and associates. Sometimes these ritual things create unwelcome ripples of their own, so any suggestion that there is an element to this that is sectarian, religious, tribal, or anything else is now outside of your remit and I will handle it directly. And please be very careful in talking to the chairman: he has powerful friends and we do not want anybody investigating us while we are investigating a murder. So try to build a picture of the dead man in his environment and let's see where that takes us."

Cyril asked, "What if that takes us nowhere?"

"Then we close the case. There are plenty of things we can solve without worrying with the things that we can't, and some things are just too complicated. So I give you three weeks to sort this out, and if we have nothing by then, we shall close the case and move on."

Cyril stood there contemplating a question left in the air, but not for long, since he was instructed to close the door on his way out and get on with things. As he wandered along to his desk on the third floor he became even more thoughtful. Helplessness and hopelessness were qualities that he was used to in a criminal investigation. Let's face it, he thought, most Lagos murders go unsolved, he knew that, but he knew his boss very well. He detected that there was a nuance in what he had just heard which was new. His investigation was to be limited; leads were not to be followed up if they took you into difficult areas. He could understand this, and on the surface it seemed very sensible. Although Philip had suggested that there might be something deeper in this, no evidence at the scene suggested that. All that the DCI would have known was that a death had occurred that might or might not be a ritual killing.

The worm of suspicion that had wriggled in Cyril's mind before he went out to the scene of the crime – that he was specially selected to take the blame for something – was wriggling again. This time it was the idea that the DCI knew something that was not being shared with his investigating officer, and that he was taking steps to ensure that the investigation was fruitless and could quickly be closed.

Three weeks! The thought reverberated around Cyril's head all the next day until he got a message that Henry and Philip would be coming into the police station as instructed, and their chairman was coming with them. In the meanwhile Cyril was busy with the corpse. His initial thought had been there should be a post-mortem, but the DCI's office dismissed the idea as time-wasting, and then was reported as saying, "After all, the killer seems to have done most of the dissection for us!"

Cyril got little support from forensics. They pointed out that the body was thoroughly drained of blood, and in the heat the organs had dried out almost completely. Perhaps they sensed the mood of investigatory reluctance as well. Apart from some interesting comments on the knife that was used, which was not a regular surgical instrument but something with a serrated edge, they had little more to add. And when, in the late afternoon, the dead man's family arrived from Ibadan, and applied to the commissioner to release the body for burial, the DCI agreed without even consulting Cyril.

Then it came to him. Three weeks time. That was when Festac began. It was due to be the greatest event in Nigeria in 1977. Cyril could not remember the first Festac: it had been held in one of the former French colonies a few years previously to celebrate black African culture. Cyril saw it as a sort of Olympic games of music and dancing and writing and poetry. Police involved in crowd control and traffic management, as if anybody could manage the traffic in Lagos, were already getting special training. Cyril had seen briefing notes that said Lagos would have over 15,000 visitors, many of them performers, and a good number of them would go north to Kaduna for a special durbar celebration there. So that was it: this nasty little murder needs to be swept under the carpet before we meet our international guests in three weeks time.

Cyril could see how important this would be to the military government.. Only ten years had passed since a disastrous civil war. The politicians clearly wanted to put on the event which showed a united Nigeria capable of hosting a great international gathering without any untoward incidents, and especially incidents which might make the guests question whether the tensions that caused the war had been permanently overcome.

"I could tell them that very little has changed and very little will change," mused Cyril.

He concentrated instead upon the interviews due to take place the following morning. Indeed, he was looking out of his window when the company car drove into the car park. John the driver got out first, opening the passenger door, helping his chairman out and rearranging the huge flowing robes that Chief Samuel Mydogun was wearing. Then Philip and Henry joined him on the pavement. Cyril was fully prepared to hate this chief. They were all the same, these Yoruba. His old teacher Inspector Braithwaite had said that they were "very old school tie".

Cyril knew that he did not mean that many of them had been to the Dennis Main grammar school in Abeokuta ("We did our learning under the Lion rock" as the commissioner always joked about the school that he too had attended). He was referring more broadly to the Yoruba love for their clans and tribal subgroups, for their hereditary offices and privileges, and for the mysterious class structure which created alliances between one chief and another. Chief Sam was certainly a powerful chief and as he now swept into the building, word of his presence went around and Yoruba officers of all ranks rushed downstairs to pay their respects. When Cyril arrived, the scene in the lobby looked like one of those sessions where a chief arrives in the village and "sprays" the crowd with small coins which the urchins fight for in the dust while the grown-ups admire the chiefly mannerisms and generosity. Whether the assembled policemen would have fought for small coins was something that Cyril could only speculate about, but their faces shone with real appreciation at having such a great man amongst them.

Yet as Cyril came out of the lift, the chief raised his head and caught his eye.

"The man I have come to see and the man I must see first is Inspector Fagunwa. Kindly introduce me to him."

The crowd opened up and beckoned Cyril forward, where he was met by a firm handshake.

"My name is Sam, and I am chairman of the company where our beloved colleague, Marcus Diello, worked. I've come in to help you in any way that I possibly can, and I have brought with me my senior colleague, who you have met already. We are at your disposal and united with you in our urgent need to catch the individual who did this."

This was not at all what Cyril had expected. He thought that the chairman would go to the commissioner's office and that he would be called when all the social meeting and greeting was over. He had not even checked whether the interview room was vacant or occupied, but with relief he found it empty and ushered the three visitors inside.

Cyril had a list of questions that he wanted to ask, but he could see that the chairman wanted to speak. He was so impressed by the man's introduction that he decided to defer to him.

"I want us to start in the way we mean to go on," said the chief. "We three loved this young man. We made up a collective David to whom he was Jonathan." (How often, and how inaccurately did the Old Testament come into Nigerian speech forms, reflected Cyril. Those missionary schools had a lot to answer for!)

"My company and I are happy to offer a reward for information, but this may give you too many false leads to follow up so I place this possibility at your disposal if you wish to use it. I should also say all of my colleagues are completely open for your questioning, as are all of our warehouse and office staff. We are determined to see justice for Marcus and we will work with you to get that done in every way you ask."

Cyril asked a few questions about where the chairman was in the critical time-frame and what he knew of any enemies Marcus may have made. The answers were very much in line with his colleagues at the murder scene. The chief was a corpulent man in the Yoruba chiefly tradition, and by the time he had answered the questions his face was glistening with perspiration. Cyril knew that he was looking at an honest face, and when the chief said that he really should go now and greet the commissioner and the DCI, it was clear to Cyril that this was a statement of fact and not an attempt to intimidate him.

And so he found himself once more with Philip and Henry. After going over the previous ground again – Cyril always felt that it was good procedure to see if people told the same story twice – he asked them if they had any better idea about why Marcus had been out that evening. Philip said that he had questioned the gate man at the compound once again, and had confirmed that

Marcus had asked where the nearest mosque was, and that the gate man, who was not a Muslim, had told him that he thought that the nearest was in Mushin or in Ikeja.

"Any idea why he needed a mosque so close to the end of the day?"

"I think he wanted to purify himself," Henry answered. "Marcus took things very seriously. You see, we had already worked out that we were overstaffed in the warehouse. He knew that his early weeks of work there would lead to the removal of several jobs, and the redeployment of several people. He took these interventions into peoples' lives very seriously. He told me that he prayed for good judgement, and for the lives of the people affected by his work."

"I think this is exactly right," continued Philip. "He would have wanted to make sure that he was in a state of grace when he made his decisions, and that everybody appreciated that they were guided by his God and his sense of justice."

"Well," countered Cyril, "we have several Muslim colleagues, in our HR department and elsewhere, and they don't always behave like this."

"Then you don't yet understand Marcus: his religion was everything to him and was entirely fused with everything he did," said Philip. "He would have wanted to get the moves he made exactly right, to take into consideration the feelings, the families, and the impact on the lives of the people he was moving or redeploying. One of the reasons why we all warmed to this young man was his caring and considerate nature."

There was a short silence after this. Philip and Henry appeared to be contemplating the colleague they had lost and Cyril felt reluctant to interrupt them. At the same time, he thought bitterly, there was no one in the Lagos police detective section whom he could describe in similar terms. He wondered if years of policing knocked decency out of you, or whether the Yoruba detectives that he so despised were simply born without the capacity for consideration for any but their own.

The silence was broken by Henry. "He was so concentrated, you see, on getting this right. It was his first real job. I know that part of him was terrified: he had never managed anybody, never given orders to anybody, and he never had authority over anybody. These all weighed heavily. Would people from other parts of the country, older people who in his own village he would be paying respect to on account of their age, accept the things that he asked them to do."

"And then there was the language thing," Philip added, suddenly emerging from his contemplation. "Of course his Hausa was perfect, in fact he sounded like a politician or an army general! And his English was really good, since it was the language we used in the office and which he used in college. But he was worried that his Yoruba would not be good enough. He said to me that he sounded like a small child and no one would respect him."

"He was worried that he had almost no Ibo or Efik," Henry said.

"So I told him that he should behave like the English do: if someone does not understand what you say in your own language simply say it more slowly and much louder!" put in Philip.

Cyril tried to sum things up. "So I have a picture of a rather nervous young man setting out on his first job with all sorts of worries about whether his performance will be good enough. Do you think he could have sought advice or guidance from someone that night, or did he go to the mosque in Mushin for any specific non-religious purpose?"

"Not a chance," Philip said. "I think he went to relieve his mind."

"Probably because he could not sleep for excitement and worry," Henry said, completing his colleague's sentence.

"So I must conclude from the way you look at things," Cyril continued, "that he left the compound without telling the gate man where he was going and without taking a car, so he went by taxi or bus to the nearest mosque, and as he reached it or left it, he met a person or persons unknown who murdered him and left him looking like a medical school dissection class."

"Was he actually seen at the mosque?" Henry interjected.

Cyril frowned. Once again he experienced the English tendency to speak when an idea arrived in their minds, and he felt the need to remind them of what was going on here.

"This is a murder enquiry and I am investigating police officer. I ask the questions and you, the witnesses, provide the answers. Is that clear?"

"Yes, of course, and we are only here to help," Philip said quietly and respectfully, "but actually what is the answer to the question?"

Cyril was placated. "Well, we have established that the iman went home in the early evening, and the gate man closed the mosque at midnight to say his own prayers and have something to eat. He unlocked the door again after an hour. Neither man saw any strangers that evening, no one who is not a regular member of the community came into the mosque to pray. The gate man has given us details of everyone who came to prayers between 10 pm and midnight. We are interviewing them now."

Cyril paused and looked at both men. He saw grief and incomprehension but he did not think he was looking at the faces of people who were holding back a great secret.

"When we first met in the lane the other day," he continued, "you told me that you could not think of anyone who might want to kill Marcus Diello. A couple of days later, has something else come to mind? Please share it now if it has."

At first there was silence. Both men looked at each other and then back at Cyril. Then Philip cleared his throat.

"You must forgive me. I lived through the war and the atrocities that preceded it. I was there in Enugu when we opened the cattle wagons, the railway carriages and saw what had been done to our relatives."

He choked and broke off. Then he looked down as if the answer was under the table.

"I carried the body of a pregnant Ibo woman off the train, her throat cut and her belly slashed open with a machete. She had bled to death on the journey. I can no longer be surprised by anything that my fellow countrymen do to each other in the cause of politics or tribalism."

He sat there shaking his head as if in disbelief that anyone could any longer be surprised by what Nigerians might do to each other in any cause.

Henry leant over and put a hand on his older colleague's forearm, and then moved it upwards to grip the still shuddering shoulders. Cyril decided on a tactful line.

"Well, that was a terrible time for all of us. I was interned in Port Harcourt and that was not pretty, I can tell you. But, surely, we cannot suggest that someone was attempting to create inter-tribal friction without at least some tiny piece of evidence? No message or leaflet or insignia was left at the scene of the crime which would suggest one of the extremist groups – and I acknowledge that those groups do exist and in their minds are still fighting a war from ten years ago."

"I agree, I agree," said Philip hurriedly. "But every time something like this happens, I am back in the horrors of 1966 and 1967. My generation can never forget, and I know it was tough for all those caught up in it too. But are we really still left with the idea that this was the accidental encounter of a homicidal medical student with a pious young trainee manager?"

Cyril knew that there was not much more that he was going to get out of this discussion, so he told the two men that he was going to hand them over to his sergeant who would record all their identity details, and then take down a formal statement covering their two conversations, both at the crime scene and here at the station. He expected that this would take about an hour and after that they were free to go, but he cautioned them to stay in the area of Lagos and Ibadan until the investigation was complete.

Cyril was glad to be out of the stuffy interview room. For some reason it did not enjoy the benefits of air-conditioning, and the lazy fan had not prevented the room from getting very hot. But still it was fortunate that the fan remained moving during the meeting: it was a rare Lagos day that did not have one or more power cuts. One of the world's biggest oil producers and we still don't have an oil refinery, he thought cynically.

A glance out of the window reminded him of his next assignment. While the great chief was with his Yoruba peers and his sergeant was taking down evidence, he had an opportunity to talk to someone who saw everything. In a few moments he was greeting that bright young driver who was lounging against his vehicle in the shady part of the police headquarters car park.

"John, good to see you again. Is this a good moment for me to have a word and re-introduce myself?"

"Well, I already know from the other day that you are the policeman who is looking into the death of our dear Marcus, and I do hope that you will bring his killer to justice – it is the least Marcus and his family deserve. I was at the funeral yesterday and cried with them."

"Did you get any idea that the family has a malicious enemy who would try to do this to them?"

"No, I certainly did not. They are peaceful people, mostly devoted to their own community. They are devastated, deeply shocked, and only asked me whether I thought this had happened because Marcus had gone out of his community and was working in a company with so many different people from all over Nigeria."

"Did you tell them that there were people in the company who didn't like Marcus and didn't want to see him succeed?"

"No, I did not. In fact it's always been exactly the opposite. We love the boy, he was like a mascot, and for most of us the symbol of everything that is good and honest. We make school books: there are so many dedicated people in our offices who just want to make this place better. And we don't exactly get paid as if we work in an oil company. There are a lot of good vibrations in this company, and Marcus was very representative of them."

This conversation set Cyril wondering. Very few drivers that he had known in Lagos, and certainly not those who drove police cars, thought in such a philosophical way. John was clearly an educated man, but he was doing a job which in the Nigerian hierarchy was a fairly lowly one. If he was to trust his judgement, then Cyril wanted to know a bit more about him.

"Where do you come from John, not around here, I think?"

John broke into a broad smile. "Certainly not, Mr Nosy Policeman! My name is John Williams and I come from a village near Ikot Ekpene. My parents were Ibo and are both now sadly dead. My father was killed in the war and my mother starved to death while keeping me alive in the Biafran Enclave. Philip found me, dying on my dead mother's lap. His mother looked after me, he educated me and I do not wish to work with or serve anyone else. You must know, Mr Policeman, how rare decency and honesty are in a postwar world. I think it would be unwise to walk away from those qualities once you discover them in the sea of degeneracy and corruption that is Nigeria today!"

There was a sort of challenge in his voice, as well as a long, lingering sense of loss and misery that Cyril was familiar with and which he knew was a long-term residue of that dreadful war. But he felt that he was getting somewhere, and he reflected that drivers overhear everything, and that this was one pair of ears that might make some sense of things overheard.

"I quite understand, John. I too was born in your part of eastern province, although I left long before the war. What I want you to tell me now is whether there have been things going on in the company which would have been disturbing to Marcus. What are the policies or activities that he opposed or did not like? Did he have enemies who were jealous of his relationship with your chairman and his senior colleagues?"

"If there were any enemies, then I never heard of them," came the reply. "Actually, Marcus and the whole company were in a state of euphoria and excitement. You heard about UPE? We are working so hard to deliver this no one really has time to think, let alone bicker! This is a huge national project and we are one of the few groups of people who can make it happen for the whole country and the children of tomorrow. Marcus was caught up in this like the rest of us."

Cyril thought this might well be true. UPE stood for Universal Primary Education, one of the great postwar innovations designed to bring free state education to every child up to the age of eleven. Funding this from the oil money and ensuring that everybody got a textbook in their own language in a country with over 300 distinct dialects and some 50 distinct languages was the problem that Cyril read about every day in his newspaper. There were apparently only four big publishers and the leaders, like John's chairman, complained most days about inefficiency in the ministry, uneven distribution of funds, and problems with creating books in languages which had never yet been printed on the page. So he thought it might be best to change tack.

"Williams is a slightly strange name for a man from Igboland?" he asked

John, who had now taken a seat on the bumper bar, smiled up at him.

"It's a very special name. If you had lived in Abba for a long time you'd have probably known the story behind it."

"I left when I was six and the family moved to Warri. As I was telling your colleagues, I was interned in Port Harcourt during the war, or at least at the end of it. So this is a famous name where are you come from, is it?"

"Indeed it is. It was my grandfather's surname. My mother was his daughter, but she kept the name when she married because her mother's bravery meant so much to her."

"Got it! I remember this story. Your grandmother was one of the women in the Abba market! She was one of those who refused to pay their increased market taxes, way back in the past? 1918? 1919?"

"Yes indeed. She was only 20 but she was strong and resolute as are all of those other Ibo women who managed the farms, the finances, the trading, and the families who lived on the yam farms cultivated by their husbands. And they still are a tough breed: you should meet Philip's mother!"

There was silence from moment while both men contemplated the awesome powers of Ibo women and the matriarchal society from which they came. Then Cyril resumed:

"As it was told to me, the British garrison at Port Harcourt marched up to make the women pay at gunpoint?"

"Exactly, and they took up their positions in the market square with bayonets in place. Then my grandmother and the other women marched on them, stripping to the waist and placing their bare breasts upon the point of the bayonets!"

"And so the soldiers retreated?"

"Well, it was after the first big war in Europe and most of the soldiers were raw recruits in the Royal Welch Fusiliers. My grandfather was 19. Anyway, he told my mother and she told me that he joined the army to fight the Germans and not to stick knives into women. Apparently, he was so struck by my grandmother when she stared him down that a few days later he ran away from camp. He had to be carefully hidden to prevent the British from capturing him. He would have been shot as a deserter. Instead, he got adopted by an Ibo village and a wonderful Ibo family and they turned him into a brilliant yam farmer."

"Amazing story, John. Now, if you hear anything which you think might help us to capture the killer of your friend then you will please let me know?"

The young driver nodded slowly. "I know that you have been asking a lot of questions about Marcus. All the answers that you are getting paint him as a real goody goody. If he had any secrets to hide, we certainly did not know them. He was very young. No war made him rapidly mature. Instead he had a very protected upbringing. You can believe the chief and Philip: they are dead straight. I know the Englishman less well, but I really like him, and if the chief trusts him, then I do as well. And I am happy to keep in touch and tell you what I know whenever I know it."

Perhaps influenced by the exchanges of confidences and stories, Cyril added a final comment: "They are saying here at HQ that this investigation must be over in three weeks. For Festac? Or maybe something else?

Anyway, this was a crime that must not be buried prematurely. I may need to be in contact with Henry and Philip without it being obvious to others. Can I rely on you to be my messenger and can I rely on you to tell me anything that I should know that comes to your ears?"

John had stood up as this was being said, and he did not directly reply, but he extended his hand, took Cyril's and shook it firmly. As he did so, Cyril saw the chairman and his two senior managers leaving the building by the main door, and he walked around the other side of the building so as not to bump into them again.

He felt really pleased that he had made light of the fact that they would stay in touch and were establishing a relationship that might prove very valuable indeed.

CHAPTER 2 HENRY

MY NAME IS Henry Kettering. My name is Henry Kettering. My name is Henry Kettering.

I have lost count of the number of times I have said my name to police sergeants, to reporters and television interviewers in the last three days. Despite the number of daily murders in Lagos city, the circumstances of the death of my dear friend Marcus Diello seemed to attract media attention. But the how and why of this dreadful crime is as much a mystery to me as to the people asking the questions. Yet as our investigating inspector remarked, three days is a long time in the Lagos news cycle, and today the pestering seems to have stopped. By tomorrow, dear Marcus will have been forgotten in terms of the public interest, but I shall always remember that I could not go to the funeral and I shall never see the face of my dear friend again.

The stupid thing is that if he were alive I would be trying to explain all my feelings to him. In six months we had become friends who shared everything, the sort of friendship I longed for as a boy at school and at university and had never found. I thought I had it when I first met Mary and took her to the college May Ball. University proved too busy, too frenetic, to allow me the confidante that I desperately needed. When I was a boy I used to tell everything to my mother. I was the youngest, you see, and my siblings were not always sympathetic to my problems and issues.. So here I am, all alone in the middle of Africa, away from home for the first time. I could genuinely talk to Marcus, and he, I really believe, could unburden himself to me. He told me so much in the process. I know that some people reading this would think that young men with backgrounds so different and cultures so distinct would find it hard to come together in this way. I feel that because we were so different, we could not be rivals. We could not make judgements because we had no cultural context about each other's lives. It was easy for us to share everything and talk endlessly. Now I have lost him in this mindless, arbitrary way. This piece of paper will have to serve as a confidant for now.

I feel a sense of duty. Or is it a sort of responsibility? What if I died tomorrow? In colonial history, being sent to work for the Empire in the gulf of Benin was a sort of death sentence. Three out of five never returned. I would not want to die without leaving behind a record of real regret. I have done two things in the last year of which I am deeply ashamed. I do not know what will happen in the next few weeks and months, but I would like to think that, if I died, someone would find this and realise that I knew that I had done wrong and was very sorry about it.

My name is Henry Kettering. I was born in a small village between Much Wenlock and Bridgnorth in Shropshire. My father is a farmer, a product of many generations of Ketterings farming in south Shropshire. My mother is a farmer's daughter. I have two older brothers, Dick and George, and a sister. Elizabeth is five years older than me, and is married to Harry, a farm manager.

I'm telling you all these things because they are the context to the series of decisions that I made in the middle of 1976, and which have brought me to this point. If you asked my brothers, especially George, they would tell you that I was a spoiled brat who never did a full day's work in his life. They may be right. I certainly hated the twice a day slavery of the milking parlour, and I could not imagine growing up to live a life so constrained by routine and the deadening feeling of being strapped to a perpetual motion machine more powerful than oneself. Yes, I loved the country and I loved the animals, especially the pigs. but I never believed, from my earliest days, that I could cut it as a farmer

To the jeers of my brothers, my mother floated the suggestion of further education. She saw me as an agronomist, or as a real estate agent. Clean hands and regular hours, jeered George. My father's response was equally blunt. His object, as I saw it, was to get all his sons into farms of their own in the locality. His working life of paying off his mortgage would then be repeated in their lives. Success.

But not for me. There is no need here to rehearse the long and bumpy road by which I moved from the local grammar school that went back to the Tudors, and then on to the scholarship to Pembroke College, Oxford. And no one who has read this confession so far should be surprised at the family derision when I turned out to be – an historian!

The misleadingly simple truth was that I had pursued the things that I enjoyed. I loved history. I strove to get to the place where all the famous historians that I had heard about worked, and I would gladly have stayed there for the rest of my life. But, the middle of the 1970s were unkind to innocent would-be postgraduate students, especially if, like me, they did not get a double starred first. By the middle of 1975 it became clear that I had to find a job. It had been obvious to me for a decade that I could not return to agriculture, and justify the dismal jibes of my brothers that I would never find sustainable independent employment. Equally, my father had decided not to fund me at university, and that I had a full state scholarship, as well as a college scholarship, vacation work, and getting used to making a little go a long way, had been the way my life had been lived.

It was at this point that things began to go wrong. One afternoon, browsing the notice boards in the University careers' office, the attractive and friendly young woman behind the desk asked if I would mind helping pin up more cards with job opportunities. She gave me a stack of cards and smiled at me, and as I pressed the pins into them to fix them to the pin board, I browsed through them. Suddenly, one caught my eye. I saw the words: "researcher… British High Commission… Short-term contract… premium rates." I stuffed it into my pocket while glancing at the girl at the desk to confirm that she had not seen me do it.

So, you see, I began with a deceit and then there was worse to come. When I looked at the advertisement back in my room it said next to nothing about what the job involved. I imagined that being a researcher meant working in a dusty archive somewhere, so on the basis of nothing at all I wrote to the London address (I remember that it was the British Council in Spring Gardens) and put my name forward.

And that, crudely, is how I came to be a spy and how I came to be in Nigeria. From my little deceit in the careers' office grew the monstrous lie that I came to live there. And I did not even know how to be a spy, or what my paymasters wanted from me. I came to fear that my very presence in the country might be to act as a distraction for other people so that the real activities of my masters would go unnoticed. I felt that I was somehow

40

implicated in the awful plottings of MI6 and the CIA in this country without really knowing anything about what was happening around me. I became obsessed with the idea, for reasons I will explain later, that something I said to Marcus drove him to the place where he died, and that his death itself was somehow linked to what my employers were doing. I had no proof of either, of course, but that did not decrease the worry, the stress, or the guilt.

I am leaving this paper in the security box in my bank in Lagos. I do not know how to direct the bank when it comes to giving this paper to someone on my death. But, make no mistake, I am involved up to my neck in something desperate and I do not think that I shall survive it. Indeed, part of me thinks that the death of Marcus was a warning to me.

A reader of this note needs to know what happened at that job interview. I was met by an amiable Englishman of the old school, George Mainbrace, who I learned later was a cultural attaché at the British High Commission. He scared me at the beginning when he said that I was his only applicant from Oxford ("although we take young men from both universities, I normally recruit from Oxford: Balliol Man, don't you know? Came down myself in '51." He told me, somewhat alarmingly, that he knew my history tutor very well and had been in touch with him.

"Vouched for you, dear boy, said you were just the sort of fellow we were looking for, for the type of things we wanted to do."

This it appeared was quite enough. The interview was taking place in a private room in a London club in Pall Mall and while we soon settled into a facile English conversation about weather and schools and the likelihood of retaining the Ashes, it was not hard to sense that we were waiting for something. Someone, in fact. A burly American now exploded through the door. He demanded to know why he had been kept waiting, shook the tie he had been requested to wear ("You limeys! Wouldn't wear that to my ex-wife's funeral!"). He then bustled over to me, introducing himself as Cy Sackler. He said he worked for the US Embassy in Lagos as an oil economist. They seemed, even then, to be an odd pair but they clearly knew each other very well and worked together regularly.

Cy led off with a lecture about the oil industry, the emerging importance of Nigeria, and the need for energy security in underpinning democracy and freedom across the world. I actually recall him saying, "I am a Texan, and I know about these things." Then George, and nobody named George could have been more unlike my brother, talked about Festac. I could not see how these things were related and indeed my future employers seem to have had rather different conceptions themselves. George kept saying that all the visitors coming to Nigeria to celebrate African culture gave other countries an excellent opportunity for observation and infiltration, and they wanted someone at the Festac to watch and monitor. and they could not do the job themselves because the people who needed watching would have friends who knew who George and Cy were and where they worked. Cy on the other hand seemed to be saying that the festival would distract everybody, and give me, as the researcher, an opportunity to see if there are people about the country making enquiries and forming connections. The threats that they wanted information about were never quite described, but from the number of times words like "Russkies", "commies" and "Chinks" came into the conversation it did not need any imagination on my part to guess.

It was when they told me about the cover under which I was to operate, that my interest in what was being said began to warm a little. They said that they had spoken to the chairman of one of the country's leading publishing companies. He was a right-thinking man who agreed with them about the threats to democracy. He also agreed that the individual appointed to this job should not work in the British Council, the High Commission, or the US Embassy. If the individual worked in the publishing company itself, and attended all of the Festac events naturally ("This company has the contract to publish the creative writing book which celebrates African contemporary writing at the festival,") then no one could question his credentials. The chairman of the publishing house was worried however that if he gave a functional job to the individual appointed, then that individual would have to show that he knew something about publishing. It was therefore decided that the cover job should be assistant and deputy to the chairman, so that nobody could ask any embarrassing questions. After all, who would expect the chairman's assistant to know anything about anything, they joked!

The conversation swiftly moved on to terms of employment and money, and the picture they painted was really very good. I was hooked already. I knew that as soon as I told my mother that I was going to be deputy chairman of a publishing company, wherever it was, and whatever it did, all the arguments in the family about the wasted education with no future would disappear. It meant that I could return to Shropshire with status, and it bought time for me to discover what I really did want to do. If anybody asked questions, I only needed to quote a salary level far in excess of what my brothers could earn to settle the matter.

So I said yes. I know how rash this was. I had little idea of what my interviewers intended, or what they might be likely to require of me. It took me months for the penny to drop that I was actually going to be some form of intelligence agent. It certainly did not occur to me that the work might compromise me with my friends, or at some future point force me to break my word and go back on solemnly taken legal undertakings. If I did not have the intelligence to work any of these possibilities out then I wonder whether I was in any sense "the man for the job".

But Cy and George seemed delighted. They clapped me on the back and said that I would fit into the "team" splendidly. And that I would love that chief when I met him, he was a "grand guy" and one of the most influential people in Nigeria who could introduce me to everyone and everybody. And it was such an exciting place. Lagos was the "busiest capital in the world". Port Harcourt was "just like Austin in the old days, abuzz with money and enterprise". There would be some preliminary training in the UK, "getting the hang of filling in your expense forms, dear boy," and then I would be off to Nigeria in September. The idea was that I should have six months on the ground with the publishing company, making connections and finding my feet before Festac itself began.

I was right about one thing. My announcement, when I had the offer in writing two weeks later, silenced all critics in Shropshire. It was a satisfying moment. They all had to shut up and sit down. I got lots of satisfaction as well in writing to J Walter Thompson to tell them that I would not be pursuing a career in advertising, and the same to the Midland Bank. I was given an allowance to buy tropical kit, and my mother and my sister having sewn Cash's name labels on every garment, drove me down to Gatwick to get on the British Caledonian flight to Accra and Lagos and say goodbye. I remember sitting on the aeroplane with a glass of champagne feeling happy and excited. My faith in the security and secrecy of my assignment was only slightly shaken when the courier with the diplomatic bag sat down next to me in the first class compartment ("Hello, old boy, I am the Queen's messenger,") and asked if I was Kettering, a new boy for Lagos. Then he told me that he had access to the passenger list, so it seemed odd but okay.

The date of my arrival in Lagos was a real introduction to Nigeria, in several different ways. Murtala Mohammed International Airport was under a military curfew since another imminent coup was suspected. Our aircraft was surrounded by tanks and armoured cars, but the courier pointed out that the guns were pointing away from us.

At the airport I met two men who had a very great influence on my life in the coming months. If this paper is to be a useful record of what I think actually happened, then I must start by saying that as I came down the steps from the aircraft I was greeted by the man who I now regard is the most honest and forthright Nigerian I have met. He was a great mound of a man, not particularly tall but wide and thick. Whenever I see him standing somewhere, dressed in his usual robes, which reach down close to his ankles, he reminds me of a shrub, or a small tree, so firmly does he seem to be planted in the ground. When his moon face lights up in a great smile, which it did repeatedly in conversation, and when he hugged you or clapped you on the back or pumped your hand, the power of Chief Samuel Mydogun seems to vibrate through you. He had a rare ability to inspire loyalty and affection. After I had been in the company a few weeks I heard an employee refer to him as "not just the chief, but our chief". Superficially he seemed to be very keen, as many of his fellow Yoruba chiefs were, on rank and privilege and robes and tribal ceremonies. But I know now that these things are to him a childish delight, and underneath the child is a shrewd judge of people and a natural negotiator and dealmaker. Typical of Sam was the way he turned to the military officer who stood next to him, and who turned out to be both an old classmate and the military commander of the airport, and said, "This man is coming to join us as my assistant and deputy. And you will witness what I say when I tell you that I am the first chairman of a publishing company in Nigeria to have a British Oxford trained scholar working directly for him. Imagine that."

With Sam's officer friend acting as a military escort we very soon got into the airport arrivals hall, and queues of passengers from the flights that day gave way when Sam's friend said "VIP". In fact we had reached security, where the longest queues were situated, and I was just coming up to the desk when a voice said, "Can I help you with this?" The voice was loud, authoritative, and had a sort of rasping quality. It did not sound as if it was asking you a question as much as giving an order. We looked round and saw a tall thin-faced soldier wearing a beret and fatigues, but with no insignia or rank showing. But I knew he was important. Our officer saluted him, and Sam introduced me in a far more subdued tone than he had used out on the tarmac. The new man said that he was in charge of security, and it seemed proper that I should get through the airport quickly and start my important work. He took my passport from my hand and pushed it across the desk to the security official who had been about to reach forward to check it. I recall that the official's hand was trembling as he took my passport, and as he did so a swagger stick descended with force on his knuckles.

He pushed the passport back to me quickly. "In these matters, my new military acquaintance said, "speed is the operative word, I think."

He then marched past the security desk and every other desk until we reached the carousel where my luggage was circulating. Here our a little party of four paused and the tall man bent forward and told me that I had seen how efficient Nigerian airports could be. Under the guidance of the chief, he knew I would come to love this great country. Then he took his leave of us.

I remember saying how impressed I was by airport security officers as porters summoned by Sam retrieved my luggage. My two companions shook their heads. "That was not airport security at all. That was Baban, the head of national security. The most feared man in Nigeria." Sam's military friend escorted us to the chief's car, and as we climbed aboard remarked on the statistical chances of meeting a man like that at a place like this on one's first trip to Nigeria. The chief's young and cheerful driver whose name I learnt was John, said that if he had met Baban the first time he came to Lagos then he would've gone right back home immediately! As I relaxed in the backseat of the air-conditioned Peugeot 606, cooling off after the hot airport arrivals hall, I felt a quiet sense of triumph. Here I was, in a new country, starting my first job.

I apologise if this account of how I came to be in Nigeria has proved long and too convoluted for you as a reader. But it is so important to my testament. This digression has been necessary. I want it to be understood that from that first day two critical forces were at work in me. From the beginning, and increasingly as I reached the office in Ibadan, I liked the way that Sam worked and I found myself getting really interested and involved in the publishing issues. From October, the following month, there would be 17 million children in Nigerian primary schools, of whom 13 million had never seen the inside of a school before. We would be giving them the first book that they had ever held in their hands. Who could not be inspired by that? That same day I realised that it was possible that George and Cy had it all wrong. Even after these early encounters, it was beginning to dawn on me that the Nigerian government itself might want to have its future decided in Nigeria and not manipulated by British and American interests. I could see why the Nigerian government wanted to educate all of these young people who had never received a free education before. I wanted to help. At the point of my arrival the country had been independent for 15 years: as I started the intelligence part of my work I was already disenchanted with the idea that the Nigerians needed to be told what was in their best interests.

So I was hugely confused. I started to write this record when my confusion was at its height. After my friend Marcus had been killed my feelings about this strengthened. You see, I told Marcus something that he should not really have known, and, if anything, that is the crowning mistake, an error so gross that I now tremble when I think about it. But I wasn't thinking then. I was too full of my growing confidence, the feeling that I was finding my feet in Sam's company, beginning to be useful, and finding new friends and building relationships. So I blurted something out and it may well be that this killed the first real friend that I ever had.

If you are to understand this then I think you need to know a bit more about the company and about Marcus himself. In the first place, I soon realised that the company was a powerful team of two. Sam managed the Ministry of Education, the state directors of schools, and the important people who influenced the Nigerian school curriculum. The editorial director managed the editors and the authors and made the books. He also managed their production, which was currently being done mostly in Hong Kong since a combination of Universal Primary School Education (UPE) and Festac had eaten up the printing capacity of the entire country. The editorial director was called Philip Nkworu. His office was the beating heart of the company. He had 45 people drawn from all over Nigeria, speaking all the major languages like Yoruba, Hausa, Efik and Ibo as well as countless local languages. These men and women were experts at translation, transliteration and localisation as they worked at high speed to produce ranges of readers and simple science and maths textbooks that not only fitted the Nigerian curriculum but also looked and sounded as if they came from the local culture in which the schools were set. And as soon as we got together Philip began to use me as a reference book, sending editors to talk to me about the nuances of a translation of the theory of Pythagoras from an English text into Hausa and so on, and I really enjoyed it.

When it came to morning breaks, or lunch in the canteen, or a drink after work I often sought Philip out, and I think he did the same to me. Sam was mostly too busy for either of us, and besides the company he had official duties of a tribal nature that took up a good deal of free time. He explained to me that he was peacemaker in the Yoruba tribe centred on Old Odo, a town which was a few miles north of Ibadan. Apparently it was famous in Yoruba culture since this was where the Hausa invaders from the north were halted as their horses were unsuited to fight the Yoruba infantry at the tree line. Well, the disputes were different these days and from his description I gathered that Sam was a sort of psychiatrist, arbitrator and social worker rolled into one.

So I was thrown much more into Philip's company. It was not long before I was learning about the disastrous Civil War of ten years previously and the shadow that it still cast over Nigeria in 1976. The mental wounds that remained were obvious, and I came to know how deeply they had affected Philip. We talked a lot, in those early days, about Nigeria. Because of, or even despite, the Civil War, he felt about tribalism the way I have come to feel about class distinctions in England. I did not wish to be anywhere near people who judged you by your school, or your accent, or the wealth of your parents, and Philip did not wish to be near anyone who did not value people for their brains and their contribution rather than their state or their language or their facial scars. We fell into an older/younger relationship: when we disagreed, he said

I would learn better when I grew up, and I said it was surprising that he had not learnt better by the age of 103!

It was because of him that I got to know Marcus. Sometimes when I went into the canteen I saw that Philip was already at his usual table, but with him was a young man in a long white gown, and the two were in intense conversation. I always pulled back, afraid to intrude, but one day he beckoned me over and asked me to sit down. He introduced me to Marcus, who, after a few pleasantries, left us. Philip then told me about Sam's great project. As in many Yoruba towns, Ibadan had sections devoted entirely to Hausa or Ibo people. Sam had met the imam of the mosque since they were both on the local economic reform council. Through him he met Marcus's father, who was the head man of the Hausa community. The two men had evidently bonded, though a period of years had passed before Sam was trusted and allowed to bring one of the younger sons of the head man into his company as a trainee.

I, an Englishman with no more sense than he was born with, crashed into this delicate web of political and social interests with a story that may have caused this very innocent young man to lose his life. I find it hard to think about it, let alone write it down. In the first weeks of my stay in Nigeria my relationship with Marcus grew very slowly. He loved numbers and should really, I think, have been a mathematician. I hate numbers. But we had things in common, and these started to come out when he sat down beside me in the canteen when I was reading a letter from my mother. I started to explain that I had never felt that I fitted into my family context: I saw his face light up as I tried to explain this.

"Neither do I," he said. "All my brothers want to

be imams or soldiers. Businessmen are despised. They say no one will want to marry me. They say I am letting down the honour of our family."

As you can imagine, from that day onwards we had a great deal to talk about and we explored the subject until it became one of the bonds that created a truly special friendship. Yet, if what I fear is true, and if I said something that led directly or indirectly to his dreadful death, then I think that I would come to a point of desperation. My failure in England, my deceit, my running away to Africa - all this, I felt, would be capped by finding my role in bringing about the death of someone who had reached out to me as he had. I suppose he represented to me all that was good and young and hopeful. I had not known him very long, and perhaps I did not know him fully, but when I first started writing these notes, I did so because I was in agony. Later, as you will see, it became easier, but at that point I was becoming paranoid. I thought that if I wrote it down there would at least be a record and one day everyone could know the truth. Looking back, I see all of the confusions of an inexperienced 22-year-old in a different culture mixing with people that he was only just getting to know. I remember that my great fear then was that people would think that I was unaware of the mistakes I had made, or did not regret the things that I had done. None of that was true. The weeks after the death of Marcus were miserable but I could not let the mask slip in the office – or indeed elsewhere.

One day in those early weeks I was called down to Lagos to meet with my secret masters. I had not seen them since I had arrived in Nigeria. This time we met in the US Embassy, and after a while Cy called in another man, called Vance, to give us what he termed a "sit rep". George Mainbrace, I remember, looked bored and played with his pipe for most of the meeting. There was a screen and a slide projector and lots of graphs and fig- ures. And then I sat bolt upright when a face came onto the screen and it was a face that I recognised immediate- ly. It was Baban who made such a huge impression on me at the airport and whose aura of malevolent violence was immediately recalled by his image on the screen.

I think that George noticed my reaction because he said, "We all do well to take note of him, Henry. Many of us think that he is the most dangerous man in Nige- ria."

"Or indeed, in all of Africa," Cy interjected. "We believe that he directly engineered the succession to the presidency after the end of the last military government. We think that when he went on the Haj a few years ago he established direct links with the Saudi Oil Minis- try. We know that he is negotiating for Nigeria to join OPEC. We are now fairly certain that he has established close links with Gazprom and the Russians."

Sensing perhaps that I was feeling a little lost George leant over and said into my ear, "The Haj is the pilgrimage to Mecca which all good Muslims like Baban seek to accomplish in their lifetime." I nodded, although I knew this already, as if I was grateful. Then Cy resumed.

"Our analysts" – here he nodded at Vance who smiled in a tight lipped sort of way – "are saying, and of course they don't tell us where they get this stuff from, but they are saying that Baban is planning another coup. He doesn't trust the officers of his generation who he went to Sandhurst with, but he would like to bring in a younger group who would be more dependent upon him.

53

They say that although he has been traditionally the ally of the Hausa interests, he is going to throw them over and work with tribal interests in Cros Rivers and the Delta country. The most powerful guy in those parts is the current chief of staff, who is also his great friend and brings Yoruba interests with him. All this is according to the analysts, who are wrong as often as they are right!"

This pronouncement gave rise to another thin lipped smile from Vance.

"Well, if that is to happen, Henry," said George, "then it could well happen during Festac. The troops will be on the streets, ensuring public order in Lagos. It would be easy to seize some of the major public buildings, the radio station and, of course, the Dodan barracks. Some of the festival organisers may be tipped off in advance, and as you go about the festival site you may spot things before we do. Of course, we are taking steps to prevent this happening, but since we have had two coups in the past five years it is hard to argue that it is unlikely.

"If he does succeed, then it changes political life here completely. The Hausa have no real economic power, the north is poor in agricultural terms and projects to grow cotton and other crops by irrigation have been expensive and had a high failure rate. Without the political power that comes with a strong representation in the military, the northern states would find it hard to get their share of the oil money. It would be a calculated gamble to desert his northern friends and the traditional rulers up there who make such a fuss of him, but Baban is nothing if not the political poker player."

The meeting went on, and I recall that we looked in detail at the movement to create more states in order to divide more equally huge revenues now flowing from the oil industry in the Niger Delta. I recall George saying firmly, "When I first came here the country was divided into four provinces. By the time I leave there could be as many states as in the USA, as each district declares that it is a completely distinct area so it can create a state and then go for its own slice of the oil revenue cake."

When I got back to Ibadan the only thing lodged in my head was the idea that the military regime was about to fall. I was used to governments changing, but the biggest revolution I had seen in my life was when Harold Wilson became prime minister. We were now talking about change on a totally different scale. It was obviously in the front of my mind when I saw Marcus drinking tea in the canteen. I thought he looked worried and thoughtful, and when I sat down beside him, I asked him what was on his mind. Apparently his father had been meeting with other Hausa leaders in Yoruba land. There were rumours of an attack upon their tribal ghettos. A senior member of the Diello clan, a relative of his father, had driven down from Kaduna and met them. Marcus did not know what it was all about. But his brothers had told him that his mother and his sisters had been told to be alert and ready to pack and move back to Kano instantly. He looked up at me with a face begging for reassurance. But I had signed the Official Secrets Act, and I had given undertakings at every meeting that I had attended that the information I was given should be held absolutely confidentially. There was no way in which I could tell him anything.

So making all the allowances you like, I am still at a loss to explain coherently, why, within five minutes, I was warning Marcus of the danger of a coup. Of course I said nothing about the source of my story, and I was at least cautious enough to stress to Marcus that the story must not be traced back to me in any circumstances. Even as he did so I knew that his promise to me, as a good religious man, was more likely to be honoured than my undertaking to the UK government. By speaking to Marcus, I knew that I was putting myself into a very false position, and yet I did it all the same.

In the moment, I got my reward. The gloom that had settled on Marcus dissipated immediately. He could see how my story of the coup plot could link and explain all the rumours that he had heard. He said that nobody liked Baban, who was not a Hausa but came from a smaller northern tribe related to them by way of the Fulani language. He quickly saw the danger to his people: just as people had feared the Ibo before the Civil War and risen up against them in the townships when the war began, so the same thing could now happen to his people. As this realisation came, he became more agitated until he finally stood up and said, "Henry, I must get back to the township and tell my father this. I will not involve you, but I cannot stay here if I have information that he needs to know, and that confirms many of our worst fears. Baban is evil, and we have to speak with the Sultan of Sokoto and the Emirs so as to snuff this out before it starts. I will respect your confidence."

And with that he was gone.

I know that I've done wrong, but I could not turn back the clock. I regret to say that I soon put it to the back of my mind. Because I was staying in the hotel next door to our offices in Ibadan, I tended to work late. There was so much to do. Unless somebody had arranged a party, of which there were many, I often had my dinner brought over from the hotel so that I could work on the logistics of distributing millions of books in a huge country with very inadequate communications. I cannot say that the conversation went out of my mind, but my real sense of guilt about what I said did not develop until much later when I realised that what Marcus knew may have been a factor in the circumstances that led to his death.

Even after the murder the issue did not quite crystallise until that evening, sitting in silence with Philip, I suddenly heard him say, "He was not murdered for money. He may have been murdered for his religion, although I do not think he had yet reached the mosque, or to create tribal tensions. But the only thing we have not yet discussed is whether he was killed because he knew something that he should not have known."

Of course, I shot upright and was all attention. Yes, he did know something he should not have known. Immediately, I saw it all before me. I saw him contacting his father and saying that he had confirmation that down in Lagos they believed that a coup was coming, led by the man that they did not trust, and it was a danger to them all. There would be spies in the councils and in the clans and in the families, and word would get back to the plotters. And those plotters, if they felt endangered by the source, would do what was needed to shut it off. They would not know where Marcus got the story, but they could make sure that he did not get any more stories. As soon as this idea entered my head, I felt as if I myself had stabbed and eviscerated Marcus. Despite what was on my mind I had to be fully attentive to the chairman, do the work of the publishing office, and my duties to my secret employers, and although I was now ready to go down to Lagos and live in our compound there during the Festac events, I did so with a heavy heart. If that harassed inspector really wanted to know who was responsible for the death of Marcus within the next three weeks, he need look no further. It was me.

CHAPTER 3 PHILIP

PHILIP WATCHED AS the worker ants laboriously carried sections of leaf towards the nest, the guards, positioned on the flanks of the column, taking in the whole scene. He tried not to move at all. Getting down here to his own village, 26 miles east of Enugu, was an anticipated pleasure. His mother was the centre of what was left of the family. Village life meant a great deal to him, and he often said that if you had a problem and could not work the thing out, then you needed to take it to the village. Yet this was a way of recording the prewar world. In truth, he found it difficult to think of anything when he was actually in the village, other than the missing people and the huge difficulties of those who remained to remake their lives in the absence of so many.

Only a third of the people in the four villages grouped around here had survived the war. He saw the starvation and suffering in their faces, even though almost ten years had gone by. Ten years! Even after 100 years, he thought, you would still see the marks of war here, but then perhaps it would not be in the malformed bones of the children who would live through the great starvation, the limping, limbless, struggling men with haunted faces who struggled in the yam gardens to feed their families and raise a crop to sell.

He had stopped in the market at Enugu on his way to the village so that he could tell his mother that he was coming. There she was, behind her stall in the usual place, ready to trade with her goods on the trestle table in front of her. But he saw her before she saw him, and the distant look in her face recalled a look that she shared with so many around the market. It was a reminder that everyone in Ibo land walked in several worlds: the world of today, the world that they lost, and the years of the complete degradation of a human society. Philip imagined that he still went east to the quiet of the village to think about his problems, but in fact in the village he could only think about the problems of his people.

His people. He wondered once again why he felt guilty and responsible . Like many another survivor, he felt guilty that he was not dead. After all, his father was dead and his brothers were dead, and he knew that he should be there in the village shouldering some responsibilities. Yet there was no job in the village that would earn the salary that he could earn in publishing. Although he knew how economically important his contribution was to keeping his mother's household intact, he could not sit on the step of her house, watching the ants, without that guilt welling up inside him.

He had no dependents in Ibadan, and he and John Williams, to whom he was a sort of surrogate father, lived simply. It was right that the bulk of what he earned came here. This old home of his with its happy memories of childhood did indeed ring again with children's voices. But it was like an orphanage. At the end of the war his mother had taken care of seven children whose parents did not reappear when the enclave around the towns and villages was opened and the full extent of the dead and dying was revealed. Once his mother had sheltered some, others soon joined. Now the old house contained a boisterous crowd of boys and girls. The result was more like a school. Games and fights and noise were cheerful - if you did not know that your mother was the only mother that they would ever know. A few minutes ago Philip had heard her come into the house and resume her task, from instructions on washing to preparations for the evening meal. He loved the sound of her voice when she was taking charge: the orders came like bullets from a machine gun and soon kids were flying in all directions. Impelled by such an order, little Ade came out on the step and looked at him dubiously.

"Mrs she say I to run to the store for cold Star beer for you, if you want."

"Yes, I want. And what shall I be when I have drunk the beer?"

"You will be Starbright for life, Mr Philip," said Ade, dashing away on the errand. Philip smiled, thinking that the kids knew more about local advertising slogans from the radio then they did about the contents of his books. He was proud of his Ibo books. If the promise of the federal money came through, they should sell three million copies of each of his Ibo Mbu series in the two Ibo states during the drive for Universal Primary Education. The manuscripts that he had driven across the country to pick up would help make that happen: it was not something that you could entrust to the federal post office. The local newspaper frequently had stories of postmen burning the mail rather than delivering it.

When the beer arrived, its bearer produced an opener from a pocket in a ragged pair of trousers. When the cap was removed, Ade looked relieved and satisfied.

"Not shaken, Mr Philip?"

"Thanks, and well done."

So he could help to make sure that Ade and others could read and write and learn some basic mathematics and science, and also speak to other Nigerians in their own languages. It was slow, but research that he started in the company demonstrated that these books were beginning to help teachers and, through them, their pupils to achieve this, though on a limited scale.

On his way out of Enugu, he had passed the railway station, and of course he had looked away. Now, sitting on the step, he took a deep swallow of beer, and he was back there, on that platform. He heard the steam trains. He saw the cattle wagons being opened. He saw the bodies lying there, men, women and children, the old and the young. Limbs hacked off, pregnant women cut open, dead children thrown in upon their parents. The distress and agony on the platform was unbearable. The women screaming and tearing their hair and clothes, the men running to and fro, shouting and crying and not knowing what to do. The dead brought no message, but everybody knew what had happened. The citizens of Kano in the north had returned the Ibo ghetto in their city to its homeland.

It was always the same when he came home. It just took a sight or sound or a person to take you back ten years in an instant. What hope was there, he wondered, of rebuilding anything until everyone who had experienced what he had experienced was dead. The federal government talked about reconstruction and reconciliation and used the example of the American Civil War. He found their trite sentiments insulting to the dead. Yet, here he was, trying to do his best in the only way he could for other children, since he had lost his own, of another generation who would grow up, hopefully, to be Nigerians.

Had he ever been a Nigerian? He wondered if anybody in his generation could say truly that they had been real nationalists. Locality and language came first. It was not as if the people who lived there had created Nigeria. Its borders were defined by the power struggle of the British and the French 100 years before. Its name was the bright idea of the governor's wife on a boat trip up the great river.

Of course, the British were to blame. Philip knew all about colonial exploitation, and he could see that the country had not been created for the sake of its indigenous peoples, but more as a sort of administrative convenience. He had experience of the British as colonial rulers, so he knew in real life they seemed as powerless and as guileless as all the rest. You could say that about the Hausa. Philip took another swig of beer and grunted to himself. If the past three weeks proved anything, they proved that a Hausa man could be an innocent victim and an Englishman could prove to be a friend.

When he first saw the body of Marcus lying there, laid out, eviscerated, looking more like a waxwork than the vibrant young man he had known, all the images of the terrible savage war that he had survived ten years ago flashed before his eyes. As he leant against that wall outside a little tent erected by the police, his mind had been walking through the enclave after the surrender. The bodies laid out for a burial. The starving huddled in front of their pathetic imitations of tents. Just as his eyes had searched for signs of life and recognition in Marcus, so his eyes had searched the living and the dead, looking for his wife and his two boys. Looking in vain, and perhaps that was better. Philip could not really tell. Was it better to hope or to have no hope? While he had spent several years half anticipating that the three of them would one day walk into the village – people had turned up, unexpectedly, having been presumed dead in the enclave – that hope had gradually diminished to nothing. But then, he himself had never returned to live permanently in the east.

Another swig of good cold beer. He must go and visit the friendly Dutchman who ran the Star brewery in Abba. Meanwhile, the ants marched on, and his mind turned to his own feelings of guilt. Of course he should have died in the enclave. It was not enough that he did not believe in the war, and that he was fully aware of the role of his own leaders over many years in provoking and creating the conflict between peoples. When it came down to it, his helpless people had been butchered, and he should have stood and died amongst them. Small wonder that he only drove east these days on business, and to check up on his old mother. His chairman, Sam, saw how simply he lived and knew that he sent almost everything that he earned back to the village. Both men acknowledged that all the salaries of all the Ibo executives working outside their own homeland, together with the federal reparation funds, and all the state oil revenues, could do nothing to heal this generation's scars from the conflict that they had survived. Survived. That was the word that choked him. Since the war, only his belief in education had kept him going. Was it enough? Even Universal Primary Education? What sort of country, even a better educated country, could be built on the back of so much senseless, murderous inhumanity?

Then there was his mother. She would listen placidly when he poured out his guilt and frustration. When he asked her whether she ever felt guilty or questioned why she had survived, she simply said, "Because I was needed. You see, I am here doing what I am doing because I am needed. It is enough." Then she would lean across and put a rough hand on his. "You should count your blessings, as we all should". So he would ask her what her blessings were and she would smile and say, "All these children now who need me, enough yams to sell in the market, and my good son who supports us all."

What were his blessings, he wondered. He certainly never enumerated them for his mother, and she never asked. Yet in his own head he counted them all the time, like the rosary beads that they used at the mission where they had christened him. He felt that it was those priests who had started his urge to learn and then to educate. Was that a blessing or a curse? It certainly felt like a blessing at the present time, since it had got him onto the teacher training course at Jos, and then into the business of writing textbooks, and then into employment as a publisher's editor, and now into his present position.

Since the job in Ibadan had emerged he had not had much time for sitting on doorsteps drinking beer. He had been as industrious as the ants. Every week it seemed that his chairman came back from the federal ministry with yet another contract for course books, or translations. The latest was to create reading books in the Kanuri language, printed for the first time. Just imagine he thought, the excitement that English people must have felt when they had seen their language in print in the 15th century. Now that moment of revelation was coming to Bornu State for the very first time, and he was to be the magician who raised the curtain on this new age. Surely that was a blessing?

And surely Sam was the blessing behind this blessing. Philip realised that he had never seen his patron down-hearted. The man was an optimism mill. And more than that: he was a rare manager who did not see drawbacks before he saw ability and application. He had encouraged and helped develop Philip's career at a time when many from the east were finding it hard to get jobs in the west or the north. The clue to Sam was, Philip realised, he loved to be loved. Sam was now in his 60s, very conscious of his status in Yoruba society and his role as an adviser to tribal chieftains. But while he obviously loved the gold threaded robes and the lavish agbadas, they clothed a man of very serious intent. While he loved winning new publishing contract opportunities, he also wanted to create a company that could fulfil them, and to do that he self-consciously recruited talents from right across the country. Philip's own editorial unit had 19 different tribal identities in 45 people, as Sam was proud to tell visitors.

Philip felt a sort of affection and regard from Sam that he had not felt since his own father's death. He felt that warmth on each of the many times he was entertained in the Mydogun family home, but it was more than the hospitality to a close colleague. He felt that Sam saw him in some ways as a deputy, sometimes as a confidant, and even sometimes as a sort of son. Philip recalled a moment when he walked into Sam's family living room while there as a guest one day, and discovered the chairman, laid out on his back on the sofa, with nine shouting, brawling, laughing and screaming grandchildren crawling all over him. As they pinched and tickled a noble chief completely robbed his usual dignities, Sam had looked up and said, "I am an old Arab dhow in rough seas in the Gulf of Benin and they are trying to bring me into safe harbour in Calabar!"

He was certainly blessed by that relationship,

thought Philip. There were others too. His mother always anxiously asked if he was meeting interesting women, but he never had anything positive to report in that direction, and he did not think that he was really ready for that type of relationship. When he first arrived in Ibadan Sam's wife had found him a housekeeper /cook, and shortly after that his spare room was taken up by John Williams the driver. Was that enough, in terms of company, Philip often wondered, and after he had wondered, he immersed himself in the work once again.

Sam had asked him to keep an eye on Marcus, and for both of them the young Hausa boy had become something of a project. He could see that it helped Sam to have the young man training to be an accountant in his office, and in time, as Marcus passed his exams, taking over some of the financial functions of the company. What he soon realised was that Marcus had much more to him than merely a head for figures. He wanted to know everything, how everything worked, and where the problems and issues presented themselves. He had a quick understanding and made some very interesting observations. Philip thought that within six months of the young man's apprenticeship beginning, he was making sensible suggestions for improving the business processes, and Philip would encourage him to discuss these with Sam. Philip had little spare time, and Marcus went home to the family compound for prayers in late afternoon, so they tended to sit together at lunchtime and talk. Philip thought sadly that he had never expressed to Marcus the pleasure he took in these conversations. The thought that now he never would was another burden.

Philip shook his shoulders, as if he was releasing a burden. Think positively. Having known Marcus was a blessing. Certainly he had no other relationships over in the west which came anywhere near to this friendship with Marcus. John was his lodger and in some ways his responsibility. He was enjoying the company of the young Englishman who had just joined them but while they had shared some confidences he could not really say that he knew him, as yet. He had certainly never met anybody quite so naive. He could not have known less about the world if he had come straight from a yam garden in Umuahia. It was interesting, though, the Englishman had bonded so quickly with Marcus. Maybe they recognised each other's vulnerability? Sam had said that Philip should look out for the Englishman just as he looked out for Marcus, and obviously the chairman found it flattering to have a British assistant, straight from Oxford. It had occurred to Philip that maybe this had been a strategy for getting him cheap, because he certainly did not know anything about Africa, or about books.

On the other hand, it could be a strategy by the parent company in London to infiltrate someone to report back to them on the way things were going: if Universal Primary Education really did come through in the way the federal government envisaged, the publishers would get very much larger very quickly, and maybe this appointment was a way of protecting their investment. Philip thought of it from many different angles, but it still didn't quite make sense. Yet Henry was really quite nice, polite, and obliging. He learned quickly and seemed to want to concentrate on the one area no one else wanted much to look at: the business of moving millions of books from Hong Kong to Nigeria and from the airport to the schools in the provinces. It was a major logistical

problem, and an urgent one, since the company warehouses were already full, and there was no spare warehousing in the country which could take this volume of
containers. Philip liked the way that Henry had found a
problem nobody owned and had taken control of it, just
as he like the way Henry had involved Marcus in the
costings and the route planning and the delivery cycles.
At the moment it was a big game being planned on wall
maps and black boards, but Philip knew it was shortly to
become a serious project.

So, in his mind, he told his mother, I do have some
blessings to count, and some of them are really important,
but into the middle of them a man with a knife has struck
an awful blow, and taken my dear Marcus out of this world
with a sudden finality comparable to the way my sweet
and wonderful wife Adele and my two lovely boys were
extinguished. Just as with the war, he thought, there are
no immediately identifiable villains. It will be something
if I could point that poor policeman in the right direction
but what can I really say to him? Philip knew that he had
never seen anybody threaten Marcus, and indeed knew
almost nothing of his life outside work. There was no reason to believe any threat to the boy came back to work or
through work, and Sam had indicated that he was as lost
as anyone else in trying to find an answer.

Philip looked at the ants and the methodical col-
umns that streamed on regardless. Maybe he should try
to be as methodical as the ants. Who could want a young
Hausa boy in his early 20s , a newly qualified accountant
working in his first job, ritually killed? While he watched
the ants, and took the last mouthful of beer, Philip enumerated all of the possibilities that he could think of in
that moment.

First on the list must be a straightforward ritual murder. The murderer was harvesting human artefacts for a ceremony or a sacrifice. Marcus was just in the wrong place at the wrong time. Pure accident. But why was he there? Why didn't the murderer take away his harvest? And why did this seem so implausible? Philip put this at the head of his list. Was there some great dynastic issue in the Diello family and he had been murdered as a result? This seemed unlikely: the family's main centre was in the north and Marcus was far from the centre of power. And ritual murder in this context? Very unlikely. What if this was an anti-Muslim murder? It was near the mosque, but again, why the ritual? Okay, Philip thought, let's try a different tack. The ritual element troubled the police inspector, who plainly thought that it was strangely done and strangely not ritual. Was that the intention? Was the murder presented in such a way as to distract any investigators and lead them off in the wrong direction? So was this a sham ritual murder made to look like a new ritual? In which case Philip thought, a much wider list of potential murderers became available. Someone might be wishing to stir up tribal or inter–regional conflict. Since colonial days these things had happened, Philip knew, but normally they were related to some form of political movement or action.

Nobody had left a message or a slogan at the murder scene. And although he had not looked very thoroughly, he had seen no mention of a political dimension in the press coverage. Philip could not believe that someone who had gone about this work so carefully and had performed such a precise and difficult operation without raising any alarm in the immediate vicinity had not done this for a purpose. But what purpose? Philip felt baffled.

He had all the pieces of a jigsaw, but they were all parts of different pictures.

Philip knew most apparently unprovoked attacks were usually rooted in family or tribal disputes. If those were dismissed, then you had to look to the police, or the army or the government for a reason, or sometimes to commercial rivalry. He felt he could dismiss the latter: there were three big publishers in Nigeria, and all of them were racing , with full order books, to fulfil the requirements of UPE. And if you wanted to strike a blow against the company then surely you would attack Sam or, indeed, Philip himself? Finally, everything in the Nigerian world came down to oil. Oil and land deals concerning oil. Oil and exploitation rights deals concerning oil. Yet so far as he knew Marcus had no connections with the shady world of oil. Nor did he have any connection with the people outside Nigeria who wanted to manipulate the country. He knew no Russians or Americans or Chinese. His murder was so bizarrely remote from anything that was happening in the Nigeria of 1976. While there was undoubtedly an explanation, when it was known would people would nod and say, "Of course, it was obvious. Why didn't we think of that?"

At this moment he didn't have a clue.

Voices indoors called, "Dinner."

He had stiffened as he sat on the low step. He staggered awkwardly as he regained the perpendicular and brought his feet back together. Looking down, he saw that to his distress he had dragged one of them through the column of worker ants. All was mayhem. The guards were rushing in all directions. The workers had dropped their burdens and were directionless. Philip said, out loud "I am so sorry I did that." Then, leaving the chaos and confusion that he had caused, he went in to share dinner with his mother and the orphans.

CHAPTER 4 CYRIL

CYRIL TRACED HIS finger along the dusty flank of the squad car. He was waiting, and he did not like waiting. When he really wanted his sergeant, that individual could never be found. Otherwise, the man was hanging on his shoulder, awaiting orders and instructions that Cyril was not ready to give. The relationship was a difficult one. His sergeant was bright, energetic, and keen to learn. In other circumstances he would do well. But not here. Cyril recognised the man's problems. He was 24, which was problem enough. He was Igibio, forwarded from Calabar – the first promotion scheme from minority tribes had many victims – and Cyril knew that his sergeant would get nowhere without an influential patron or protector. Not Cyril, obviously, but a Yoruba officer on the fast promotion scheme. The man's problems were compounded by the deep initiation scars under his eyes. Not of course that lots of people didn't have scars. These were just the wrong ones.

Then there was the dust that irritated Cyril. If he had been asked to name Nigeria he thought, he would have ignored the river. Very few people ever got to see that, or certainly not its mile wide stretches as it flowed towards the sea. He would have called the country "Dustland". It was the most pervasive thing in Nigeria, barring only the insects. The choking dust of Lagos, laden with petrol fumes and the outdoor cooking efforts of a million homes, shacks and shanties, the layer of grime covered everything and everybody. Now, in the capital of Dustland, he needed to come to a conclusion.

He had undergone a troubling interview with the DCI that morning, and he was under instructions to brief his sergeant on it. What would he really like to do? He looked around surreptitiously. He knew what his children would want to do, far away in Benin City. No one was watching in the car park outside police headquarters. He quickly drew a face, added curly hair, and wrote "Clean me" underneath it on the driver's door.

He finished with a flourish and not a moment too soon. His sergeant came up panting, telling him that he'd been looking everywhere for him.

"Do you remember you told me to try to find out how Marcus Diello got from his company compound and into Mushin on the night of his death?"

"Yes, but we really need…"

"Well, he took a taxi, and I have the taxi driver here for you to interview!"

This trumped all other matters, even conversations with the DCI. Cyril put his own business on hold, praised the young man and asked how he had come by the driver.

"Well, I started with the compound gatekeeper. I wanted to know if any of the pool cars had been driven out that evening, and he said that none of them had been moved after Mr Diello came down from Ibadan. So did you see Mr Diello leave? I asked. Well, yes, of course, he had. Mr Diello had talked to him in his hut, wanting directions to the nearest mosque which would still be open for evening prayers. Then he asked him to call a taxi. He was surprised when one came almost immediately. It was not a taxi from the cab rank by the bus station, which is where he had called to get one. It was a yellow taxi from the city centre, and a man got out and beckoned Mr Diello, and he got in with him and they drove away. So I think this taxi driver can tell us something."

"Excellent, excellent work," said Cyril. "How did you find the taxi driver?"

The sergeant explained that he had driven over to the Island because he thought that the yellow taxis only use the stands outside the Ikoyi Club and the hotel that stood behind it. So he had asked the drivers on the taxi stands, and eventually found one who admitted to taking a ride that evening at about 11:30 from the club to the compound.

"It took some time, inspector, because they all wanted to know how much they were going to be paid if it was them who took the ride! When I told them that no one was going to be paid, but the man who took that passenger without admitting to me that he had done so was going to be arrested, I got some grudging cooperation. That's why I was so anxious to bring him to you, sir, since I think it will need a 20 naira note even to get him to tell you his name, so perhaps it is best if you manage the interview."

Cyril shrugged. It was ever thus. Inspectors carried petty cash for these purposes. Every transaction required "the dash", an inescapable fact of Nigerian life since the British had begun the practice of paying premiums to secure monopolistic trading positions amongst the tribal chiefs. The passage of the small change from hand to hand was now as natural as conversation itself and the sliding movement of the note, or the clink of the small coins, seemed to have become the simple gestures of greeting and politeness. Certainly no one would open his mouth to a policeman without such a payment. Cyril also quite understood not only did his sergeant not have an allowance with which to pay dash, every naira of spare petty cash that he had while trying to live on subsistence wages in Lagos was destined to be sent back to Calabar – come and live and be at rest as the missionaries' acronym instructed.

The interview room at Lagos police headquarters was misleadingly named. It was actually a cell, a large, full one, for a sort of reservoir of humanity whom the police wanted to question, but did not have time at the moment. Cyril liked this aspect of it. Witnesses tended to be much more forthcoming after an hour or so in the interview room. Especially, as today, if there was a considerable crowd inside it.

His sergeant beckoned to a constable, who unlocked the door. Then he pulled at the shirt of a tall man with a distinctive paunch standing close to the inside of the door. The man needed no second invitation. He stepped out of the cell with alacrity and was hustled by the sergeant across the room to where a chair and table were ready for the interview. Cyril appraised him carefully while his sergeant took down his name, his address, and the details of his taxi license, including a check on whether it was up to date. Now that he was free of the "interview room," the man seemed anxious to talk and finish things up as quickly as possible. This was only reasonable, thought Cyril.

The taxi driver addressed his sergeant first of all: "There is nothing wrong with my license. Is bang up to date. And is no crime to take a fare from the club. Ask anyone. I am always there. Regular. So what do you want with me?"

Cyril felt it was time to intervene.

"Well, we can waste a lot of time here. We can play games. We can start talking about all the crimes that you have committed. Who knows a Lagos taxi driver who does not have a criminal record? Or we can sit here and talk about the passenger in your taxi that evening. We need to know who he was, but this is not bad business and you will not get into trouble if you tell us anything that you can remember. Indeed, we could be very pleased."

As he spoke, Cyril's hands rested gently on the edge of the table, and the taxi driver's eyes remained fixed on the folded 20 naira note he was tapping on the table top.

There was a pause, and both Cyril and his sergeant looked intently at the man.

"Ibrahim," he said. "His name is Ibrahim."

"How do you know he was called Ibrahim?"

"That was what his friend called him when he came up to the car outside the compound. 'Hi, Ibrahim,' he said as he got in. Then I took them up to Mushin and I drop them both outside of Oladipo's bookshop. The one called Ibrahim paid me and then they both walked away."

"Did they go into the bookshop?" asked the sergeant.

He got a derisive look in return. "Bookshop all closed up that time of night!"

Cyril intervened again. "Have you ever seen this man before, in the many times that you have waited outside the club and the hotel?"

Now the bank note slid across the table under Cyril's hand, and as he raised his hand the driver's hand swiftly replaced it.

"Oh yes, many times. From the club, not the hotel, I think."

Cyril was now tapping a second note.

"So we need to know where you took him?"

"Central Mosque, sometimes. Dodan barracks. I always thought he might be a soldier, but no uniform."

"Thanks for your help. My sergeant will see you out and will come and visit you in a few days. He will have another note for you if you have remembered anything else about this man. Meanwhile, please do not mention these questions to anyone, especially if they ask you about your visit here. Tell them it was about your licence, which is out of date. If I hear that you have spoken about our talk, then we will take away your licence and you will never drive in Lagos again. Understood?"

The two men nodded at each other and the sergeant took the witness to the front door of the building.

When he returned he was full of questions. "Surely, sir, we should've asked him more about where they went? And what's this business about not talking? Why are you saying that?"

Cyril put his arm round his young colleague's shoulder, and without answering marched him out of the room, up the stairs and into the inspector's office. Once there he closed the door carefully and switched on his elderly and noisy fan. Over its rasping sounds, he said, "Maro, I hope I can call you by your first name? I have your career in mind as well as my pension. Before you brought that fellow in, through good routine police work, I was called upstairs" - and here his eyes gestured upward through the ceiling towards the seventh floor - "and I was told in no uncertain terms that I must move this case to the bottom of the file and concentrate instead upon that long list of murders perpetrated in the course of burglary or infidelity. Killers as we know that we will never catch!"

The sergeant looked down at the floor, as if the

answer to the puzzle lay beyond his knees, and then looked up at Cyril.

"But you went on investigating?"

"Thanks to your good policing – and I did try to protect you if anybody asked any questions."

"Okay, so I can figure this much out. You think that you were told to as good as drop this investigation because there is a connection here to the federal military government. Because this man who was with Marcus Diello was also a visitor regularly to the federal government barracks. Getting to know too much about this thing could be dangerous for both of us, you are saying. But what on earth do you think this is all about, inspector?"

"Not a clue, Maro, not a clue! But I would certainly like to find out, and I'm not very appreciative of being told to drop things. I feel that we have been warned and therefore we must now be very careful. If we decide to follow up on this lead that you have created, we have to cover our tracks. But I can tell you one thing: I am going up to the Ikoyi club and I'm going to find out exactly who our friend Ibrahim is. I don't know yet what excuse I will use. I would like to know if the caretaker at Oladipo's bookshop saw anyone late that night. I suggest that you might like to do that. Tell the man we are investigating car thefts or something. And Maro, you do have a choice: this might be a very good time to request a transfer back to Calabar, and I will understand completely if you want to opt out of doing anything else on this case. I only ask you not to write up the notes."

The sergeant smiled. To be told not to write up his notes by a man who told him to do the opposite every day for the previous six months was quite strange, and quite funny. He stood up and turned towards the door. He was still smiling when he said to Cyril, "I am on my way up to Mushin. First time you ever said anything sensible about my notes."

When his sergeant had gone, Cyril switched off the rasping fan. It had served its purpose in an office building where everything was overheard. His enthusiasm for trying to move this case forward, which had increased when he saw that he had the support of his sergeant, had been stoked up by the reluctance of his superiors to allow him to get on with it. Being able to trust his colleague would make things very much easier. The problem was, they had very little to go on. They knew that Marcus Diello had made his late night journey in the company of somebody else. They knew that this person was a Muslim, and most probably a northerner, maybe a clansman or relative or childhood friend of Marcus? Clearly Marcus had received a call, which is why he had gone out to the gate to meet his visitor, but he had not simply told the gate man to call the taxi. Instead he got into it and went to a very suspicious part of Lagos night town. Narcotics, women, gambling, alcohol? All of his good friends in the company painted a picture which did not admit of any of these things.

Cyril knew the area well. The light railway line ran between the houses and across the square in front of the evangelical church. On the far side was a narrow lane running up to the mosque, the lane in which Marcus was found dead. On the nearside, around the bookshop, was a cluster of other shops, but none of them was likely to be open at that time of night. If you were looking for a drink or female company, this was not the part of Mushin that you would visit first. People might take you back there to a shack that was used as a temporary bar room, or a gambling den, or a brothel. Cyril knew from his own experience that any evening of entertainment here began on the main road under the bright lights in the bars and restaurants for which the area was famous, not in its hinterland. Unless Maro picked up a significant clue regarding the destination of the two men, the only thing he had to go on was a name: Ibrahim. Yet, if he walked through the door of the Ikoyi club and asked the secretary if he knew the man , he would create more questions than he could answer, and those questions might go back to the DCI, who would wonder why he was there at all, as would the commissioner. Especially the commissioner, who was widely known to be a club member of long-standing.

As he drove back into town, over the bridge and through the latticework of approach roads around the lagoon, another thought struck him. He needed to inform the two witnesses who had identified the dead boy. He had to demonstrate that something strange was going on regarding the way his superiors were handling this case. Their chairman was an influential Yoruba figure who had much more access than Cyril to the people who made things happen in the Dodan Barracks and at police HQ. Of course, this powerful chairman would undoubtedly be a member of the most influential club in Lagos. What if he could be persuaded to ask the questions that Cyril hesitated to ask?

Cyril parked in the hotel car park and walked over to the club entrance, still in two minds. Go right in and ask the questions that needed to be asked, or wait a while until he could try to manoeuvre a much more influential questioner into place? In the event, his questions answered themselves. Outside the club, in a group of other drivers, stood the very taxi driver who he had interviewed earlier. From the way that he was waving his arms and making his points, Cyril imagined that he was either retelling his cruel mistreatment at the hands of the police, or narrating how cleverly he had extracted banknote after banknote in dash from some village idiot up from the midwest who did not understand streetwise Lagos boys. In any event, he froze when he saw Cyril, who beckoned him to come over, while all the other drivers carefully retreated to stand beside their vehicles.

"There is just one other thing you can help me with, my friend," Cyril began, noting from the man's face that he rejected the implied friendship but certainly did not want any more trouble, or another excursion to police headquarters. He nodded curtly. But Cyril noted that his palm was open when the policeman deposited a handful of small coins into it as they stood side-by-side. Cyril closed the man's fingers over his palm, and held his hand, not so much with friendship in mind, but because he did not wish the man to know how much or how little money was in the palm until the questions had been asked and answered.

"I want to confirm your story. Introduce me to a porter, a bellboy, a commissionaire, anyone who can identify who got into your cab that night. I see that someone comes out with each guest and opens the taxi door before they drive away. Who did it that night? And who is reliable, and would know, and would speak honestly to me?"

He squeezed the hand a little tighter, and the man winced as the coins bit into his palm.

"Abel, you see him, boss? Over there, moving that luggage?"

Cyril looked. The porter wore the top half of a uniform coat, and a pair of shorts underneath. Still holding the driver's hand, he marched him across the pavement to where the porter was standing.

"Do you know this man, Abel?"

The porter looked at the taxi driver for permission, and when he received it by way of a nod, acknowledged that the two men were acquainted.

"So do you remember putting someone into his cab just before midnight, two days ago?"

Again the glance requiring permission, again the nod giving it.

"Yes, sir, certain sure, I know him, yeah. He young man, but already member here two, maybe three, year. And he know everyone!"

"Does he have a name?"

"You know, sir, how dangerous is names in Lagos?"

Cyril grumpily surrendered his hold on the taxi drivers hand, and produced a 20 naira note in the other hand.

The porter looked around carefully, and moved closer to the other two before he said, in a whisper, "Kabeysi, Mr Ibrahim Kabeysi. He's fine man. You like him, sir!"

Cyril nodded, and turned away. Now at last, he felt he had something to work on. By the sound of the man's name this might be another northerner, like Marcus himself. He needed to research young Ibrahim and then to talk to him in conditions that didn't have a police interrogation flavour to them. He needed to approach the man indirectly. If Ibrahim was alarmed, and reported things to the police commissioner or anyone else in authority, then it would be clear that Cyril had contravened the spirit if not the letter of the instructions from his DCI. That spelt trouble. Cyril needed help, and he had a very good idea where to get it.

CHAPTER 5 HENRY

I CAN'T REMEMBER where I was when I got it but I do remember being surprised by the inspector's message. I realised it was really important for Marcus to have a swift burial according to the traditions of his people. At the same time it seemed to me very strange that there was not going to be an inquest or any laboratory or forensics work. Once the paperwork was done, everybody at police headquarters seemed to float off doing other things. Philip and I went back to the compound in silence, but no sooner had we got there than there was a call from Ibadan saying would we find a hearse and get the body there for burial next day. So we did all this. Apparently, it was the chairman intervening and wanting to get the body to Marcus's home and family without them having to come down to Lagos to identify him. At this point, I still supposed that the inspector in charge was being supported in a full and proper investigation of the murder. In those early months of my learning something about Nigeria and its culture, I did not understand the way people reacted to disaster, or the short nature of the news cycle. In some circumstances, the death of Marcus might have led to sectarian or tribal violence: he was buried a day later and it was out of the news cycle in 48 hours. I think now that the people I met in Nigeria are much quicker to take acts of vengeance when they see, or appear to see, immediate cause and effect, and much slower once an event is over and they know that they have to live with its consequences.

But in any case I was glad to have something to do.

I wanted to go to the funeral, but the chairman told me that was impossible. With Sam's big paw on my shoulder, I understood that I would be out of place, and indeed he himself would not go: "It's a family affair now, Henry, and we must learn to grieve in our own way."

Our chairman's way of grieving was, as ever, to be hyperactive. I was put to work drafting a "Marcus Diello Memorial Scholarship scheme" directly aimed at replicating his recruitment and keeping his name alive. Philip was kept busy by being sent east to sign publishing contracts with Anambra state and collect manuscripts. He was instructed to do his duty and visit his mother at the same time. But it was only a couple of days afterwards that I had a message from the police inspector who was investigating the murder. While our official work as witnesses was now over, he would appreciate an early meeting with us once both Philip and I were back in Lagos. As it happened, I had received a request from my secret employers at the High Commission and the US Embassy that they needed to see me again, so I was anxious to get down there. As soon as I heard that Philip had arrived back, I sent John the driver to see him, and we arranged to see the inspector on the Monday morning.

It was so good to see Philip again. I could tell he felt the same. We hugged each other before we realised that we were doing so. It was amazing to me, having never experienced it, how a traumatic event bonds people. I was beginning to feel that he and the chairman were my real support in Nigeria – a sort of proxy family – while my employers and their concerns seemed unreal and stranger and stranger.

I went into the US Embassy first thing that day. I told Philip that I was running errands for the chairman, and he of course believed me. Here was another thing: I was beginning to resent living the lies that my cover story entailed. This briefing meeting was built around "persons of interest you may encounter."

I remember that there was a Russian archaeologist who was part of a team working on the Jos plateau site, and the leader of a Chinese technical team working on a satellite station in the north. George clearly thought this was a waste of time.

"For goodness sake, Cy, he's not going to see any of these at Festac! I am sure they will be more interested in the sex clubs rather than the traditional Efik dancers!"

But Cy did insist and we ploughed through a lot of grainy photos and brief biographies on the screen before at last we came to a face that I did recognise.

"Yes, I know that we have discussed Baban before, but I feel that I should encourage you to keep him in front of your mind."

George was less enthusiastic, but his American colleague went on, "I have added in here a few of his known associates, on the grounds that you may bump into one of them before you see their master himself." Another face and biography came up on the screen. "This is Ibrahim Kabeysi. We know there are links between these two men because we have seen the flow of money between offshore accounts which we identify as belonging to each of them. We are anxious to know what the business is that they do together. Ibrahim has a high on the hog lifestyle, spends a lot of money and seems to know everyone. The rumour is that he is an arms dealer, but for whom we do not know."

I recall looking blankly at the screen. The list of things that they did not know seemed to be endless,

finding out those things did not seem directly connected in any way to anything that I was likely to be doing
during Festac. George was right, and I was beginning to
think that the role they had designed for me did not fit
the requirements they had set out in London. With that
realisation came a feeling of relief: I could go home as
soon as my contract was over without feeling that I had
let anybody down.

Eventually, even Cy tired of his slideshow, and
having confirmed the events that I would be attending
after the opening ceremony at Festac, I hurried out of
the building and took a taxi across town to the police
headquarters. Philip was waiting outside. We were a few
minutes early, so we sat in the car in the car park with
the doors open and John and Philip chatted about their
trip east. John told stories about the wonders of Philip's mother's cooking, and the glories of egussi soup. He
had us all smiling when he described how quickly Philip
fell back into the disciplinary routines laid down by his
mother. Philip nodded in rueful agreement, but then it
was time to see the inspector again. We tripped into the
building and the same airless room with its creaking fan.

At first I remember thinking how pointless this
meeting was. We seemed to rehearse the same old
ground. No, there were no grudges against Marcus. No,
nobody wanted to kill him. No, it was inexplicable that
he should be involved in some form of ritual murder. No,
he had no enemies. So then we started on his friends.
Cyril was anxious to quiz us about who else besides us
two were particularly close to the young man. Who did
he go to visit? Neither of us could remember him ever
going to visit anyone or indeed leaving the office except
to go to his college classes. And then, just as I was get-

ting bored and tired of all of this, the inspector dropped a thunderbolt.

"Did he ever mention a man called Ibrahim Kabesi to you?"

I was too shocked to speak, but Philip replied for both of us. "I never heard the name, did you, Henry?"

I shook my head. Philip continued, "Did he live in Marcus's village? He sounds like a northerner to me."

Cyril was looking at us both intently. "No, this is not a local or family contact. But we do know that Ibrahim knew Marcus, and that they spoke on the night that Marcus was killed. Sadly, my investigation is being discontinued: it must end before Festac begins. Such public interest as there was has now died down completely, and the authorities here are anxious not to have the newspapers full of lurid stories of ritual killing while the town is full of visitors. I am sure that this man's name is the last clue that I have. We have precious little information about the man himself other than the fact that he stays at the Ikoyi club and is often in the hotel."

The three of us then lapsed into a difficult silence. Cyril was leaning forward with his arms resting on the desk, and at one point put his head in his hands. Then he looked up, and said: "Philip, Henry, you realise that I have put my job in your hands. I should not have told you what I have just told you. But from now on the amount of investigation that I can do will be strictly limited. I was told on the first day that it was confined to family and friends, and I get repeated reminders from the most senior sources here that spending time on this investigation, especially if it moves outwards and touches major institutions or senior people in the community, will not be permitted. I feel very sad to say it, but if anyone is likely to find out who killed Marcus Diello and why, then it is you two, his closest friends. If I can help you unofficially in anyway – a look at a criminal record or a check on a license plate, although most of those are made in Lagos – then call on me. My sergeant can help a little as well. But officially we are now diverted to other duties."

Then he closed the file, picked it up and put it under his arm while shaking our hands. As we all left the room, Philip and I said not a word until we had climbed back into the car, quite devastated to think that the investigation was over, and telling John all about it and registering his shock at the same time.

It seemed like only moments later that we were back in the compound. The chief had come down from Ibadan and beckoned us into the lounge, requesting a briefing on our session at the police station. His reaction to the news that the case was closed was predictable. "I shall be on the blower immediately to these people. This decision must be overturned. Indeed more senior detectives should be put upon this case. I will speak to the commissioner!"

While Sam went off to break windows in high places, Philip got a couple of beers from the fridge in the dining room and we sat in the lounge and drank quietly. It wasn't too long before our chief returned, looking somewhat crestfallen. I went out and got him a beer, and when I came back he was explaining things to Philip.

"I can't understand it at all. The commissioner says he cannot help. The orders to cease investigation come from above him – he says from the most senior people in the administration, people close to the president. He says it's because we do not want any stories of this type circulating during Festac, but I know this man. This is not the real or only reason. There is something else involved here. I have known the commissioner since he was six years old, and I can feel the embarrassment in his voice. He is hiding something, and he always found that hard even when we played in our primary school under the Lion Rock in old Abeokuta. I know that something is wrong and he cannot tell me about it. In the meanwhile, what can I tell the family? I have agreed to meet them at the weekend after prayers, and at the moment I cannot think of a single thing to say which would make any sense to a grieving mother and father."

I had never seen Sam looking like this, his face drained and grey and tired, and the life and energy gone from his voice. Philip and I were a match for him in disillusion and depression. We were certainly sitting in silence when John came in. He was loaded up with clean towels which he had brought back from being laundered and which he was about to place in the bathroom. He took in the scene in a moment. Putting his towels carefully on the coffee table he perched himself on the arm of the sofa. When he spoke, it was in a soft voice. I remember that he did not shout at us, but his words were completely effective in waking us from a stupor and persuading us of the need for action.

"This is sad, so very sad. The events that we have witnessed, the death of our dear friend. And sad too if we must record that the three cleverest people who I've ever known cannot do anything about it. The inspector may be right: his work has been blocked and he can go no further. But you are not blocked. You have powerful minds, strong determination, and excellent connections. You do not just owe it to the family to get to the truth of what has happened, you owe Marcus justice. That doesn't mean revenge. The world will deal with the people who killed Marcus as they deserve. Just as you owe to him it to demonstrate what we all know, which is that it did not happen because of any fault of his or because he was involved in shady dealings in politics or business. You owe it to Marcus, and so do I, and I will drive you to the ends of the earth if that will help you!"

It certainly did. And within moments we were planning our next move. Philip recalled that the name Ibrahim Kabeysi should be our first point of research, and the chief asked how we knew Ibrahim. Then we realised that we had not briefed Sam on this aspect of our meeting with the inspector, and by the time we had explained all of that, the chief was telling us that he knew Ibrahim, that they were members of the same club, the Ikoyi.

"He is a very civil and pleasant young man, and I have always been told that he is a dealer in Fine Art and archaeological artefacts. He seems to have lots of money, and he must have very good connections, because getting export licenses to take African art out of the country is very difficult indeed these days."

I suggested that we might look for some of the people who did deals with him, and then Sam said we needed a strategy and we needed dinner: so he got up to book a table for three at his club, and asked John to get the car ready to drive us there.

By this time the chief was a man transformed. The energy had returned, executive decisions were being made, and he was certain that we would end the meeting with a strategy. As we walked over to the car I put my hand on John's shoulder: "Thanks, friend, that was just what we needed!"

It was early evening when we rolled up outside of

the club. As we did so, the chief issued executive orders. "John, take this dash" – he unfurled a bundle of 20 naira notes from under his robe – "and talk to the drivers and porters. They are the most knowledgeable people on earth and you will find out a great deal about our man from them. Philip, do you know where the library is? I am sure there is a record of every member in the archive and the archivist will show you if you say that you come from me. And Henry, you come with me. We will order dinner, and while it is being prepared we can question the club secretary in his office. Philip, join us there when you are ready. Let's go!"

Ever thoughtful, Sam pored over the menu, explaining the content of Nigerian dishes to me until he felt we had a satisfactory blend of Nigerian and European food. He pointed out the table that he wanted in a secluded corner, he ordered some French wine and then marched off in search of the secretary. That individual was found in his office. He was wearing a European suit and tie and, like other aspects of the club, would not have looked out of place in Pall Mall.

The chief came straight to the point. "I have some questions to ask you. I am thinking of doing business, publishing business, with one of our members. I know him slightly because I have met him here. But I do not know very much about him, and I do not wish him to know that I was asking questions about him. So you will be discreet." The club secretary looked the model of discretion. He nodded vigorously. Clearly he was not going to do or say anything which upset the chief.

"Now, the man I am interested in is Ibrahim Kabeysi. You know who I mean?" More affirmative nods. "I want to know everything you know about his background, his friends, his family, his business activities, or anything that would tell me whether he is trustworthy or not. Think about your answer carefully. If I do business with him and he proves not to be trustworthy, then it will all come back upon you. I am the chairman of the club appointments committee that reviews senior staff appointments and salaries. Please bear that in mind. My deputy chairman and assistant, Henry Kettering, is here to take notes and record your responses. He has an Oxford degree in history, you know."

I shifted in my seat and felt a little of the club secretary's embarrassment, but nothing like the pain which was now flitting across his face. Fortunately for him, he got a moment of recovery time, since there was a knock on the door, and Philip entered. He was carrying a sheaf of papers and looked excited.

"Come and take a chair, Philip. Club secretary, this is my publishing director, and he is also anxious to hear your response to my questions."

After these words there was a long silence. Then the wretched man, who by this time I had begun to pity a little , began to mumble and was soon being encouraged by Sam to "speak up." After a stuttering start, he did.

"Well, chairman, like yourself, Ibrahim is a valued member of the club, and very popular, especially with the younger members. He is generous in the bar with drinks, you know, people generally like him a lot. Also he travels abroad quite a bit, so that younger members recognise him as a cosmopolitan Nigerian citizen. He knows a lot about wine and food."

"Stop this drivel, man, start on the credit rating. Should I trust him? Who does he know? Who should I speak to if not to you to find out more about him?

"Of course, sir, I was coming to all of those things. Ibrahim comes from the north west, I believe. His people live not far from Sokoto. I have heard it said that they were in the import and export business." "Be more precise if you please. Importing what? And to whom exporting?"

"Peppercorns, I think I heard, across the great desert. A very important resource in those parts. Camel trains to Timbuktu and that sort of thing. At least, sir, this is what I gather from other members."

"What does Ibrahim himself do? And how does he make so much money doing it?"

"He tells me that he is an art dealer, and he specialises in Nigerian ceramics. He supplies these to museum shops in Europe and the US, and to fashionable interior designers. He buys in Zaria and Jos, he says, but I hear from the drivers that he goes all over the country. In fact he seems to have no home but stays mostly in the hotel next door. He pays his bills here promptly and is not in arrears."

"So who else can I ask about him? Who does he have lunch and dinner with when he's here in the club?"

The club secretary was looking sulky and dejected. He clearly thought that he had said enough. "I do not know all the people he sees, sir, and I do not think I should be talking like this about another member."

"I'll do the thinking while you do the talking," came the reply. The poor secretary could see that he had to put some sort of answer in place or this could go on for a long time. When the reply came I felt that he was giving away as little as he possibly could.

"Ibrahim has a girlfriend, and she is a friend of my wife. I'm sure she will not mind my saying that her name is Bimpe Ojo. As I am sure you know, Ibrahim was once a captain in the army, and an officer on the general staff. He meets often here with another member, Captain Dauda. I know that they are good friends because they celebrate their birthdays together, and many other army officers joined them."

Even Sam seemed satisfied with this. "Well, club secretary, I must thank you for your help. We will pursue our enquiries and hope that we can do business with Ibrahim. In the meanwhile, silence is golden. Words in the wrong place, my friend, are very expensive and can cost jobs. You will remember that, won't you?"

We moved swiftly across the hall on leaving the secretary' office, and Sam headed straight for the dinner table. A man on a mission, with a knife and fork at the end of it. Our first courses arrived as we did, and words were redundant until we had eaten, and Sam had drained a schooner of wine. He then looked round at us, with his normal beaming smile restored to his face.

"Well, gentleman, I thought that went rather successfully, didn't you?"

I replied that it depended what you meant by success. All I could see was that we had gathered a few more clues to follow up and we still didn't have much solid information. I was left with the feeling that the secretary knew a lot more than he was saying, and was somewhat reluctant to tell the full story.

"Yes, Henry, yes indeed," said my leader, "you have it precisely. He feels that he has bought us off with some information that we could have got easily elsewhere. The fact that we were heavy with him and have sworn him to secrecy will mean that he spreads the word that we are anxious to find out more about friend Ibrahim.

This should bring all sorts of people to our door!"

Philip and I exchanged glances of amused puzzlement. Speaking for myself, I had certainly not imagined that this was the motivation for the chief's approach to the interview, yet at that moment it seemed obvious to him. Well, I thought, he knows these people far better than I do, and if he says that is what will happen, then we should just wait and see. I still had an uneasy feeling that we might have closed a door by our treatment of the secretary, rather than opened one. Even if the chief was right that the secretary would now go and tell other people about our interest, just because we had so firmly told him not to do so, it did not follow that those people, and in particular Ibrahim's friends, would come and talk to us. I didn't see the logic, and neither, clearly, did Philip.

Meanwhile, the chief, in his self appointed role as chief investigating officer, was heading in a different direction. "Now this girl, Bimpe, did you get to find out more about her, Philip?"

Philip had his mouth open and was about to speak, but Sam continued, "I must say, the name seems familiar to me. Are we talking about the young woman who manages the flower shop at the hotel? If so, I get on really well with her. She selects splendid orchids for me to take home to my wife and I am very grateful to her when I forget, and she comes over here to the club to remind me. I can hardly think she is mixed up in something shady, but I can quickly find that out."

Philip was back into the conversation as soon as these words were uttered. He was clearly trying to head off the chief from further investigative work, and he now produced a bundle of papers and put them on the table in front of us.

"The thing is, chief, that the relationship of this Bimpe and Ibrahim maybe a bit more complicated than we thought at first. I really wonder whether the first approaches to her should be made not by us but by our police inspector. Surely the commissioner would not object to him talking to a flower shop girl? You see, I did find something new about her and a few things about Ibrahim. Unfortunately, the archivist is away sick, but I was able to persuade his assistant to let me look at the club records. The note on Ibrahim is very short indeed."

He waved one of his pieces of paper at us. "I have brought a photocopy. What it does tell us is that he went to school in Zaria and that he attended the Military Academy in Kaduna. Nothing much else I'm afraid. So then I looked at the club newsletter, and flipping backwards through the copies on the library desk, I found that three months ago Ibrahim held a party here with that same Captain Dauda that the club secretary mentioned. I've brought the newsletter, and here you can see photographs of the two men together welcoming their guests."

We all craned forward and I got a glimpse of two young officers, in full uniform, raising a glass of something or other, as if they are making a toast while welcoming their guests. Dauda, on the right of the picture, has a glass in his right hand while his left rests on the forearm of the guest who he has just greeted.

"Jehoshaphat," shouted our chairman. "Look at that!"

We all peered intently. It was clear to me immediately that Sam and Philip were seeing something that I was not.

"I recognised him immediately, and so did you. I only saw him once, when he came to the office, but you must have seen him more often." The remark was addressed to Sam who nodded in reply.

Philip continued, "So when I saw these three army officers were all such good friends, I looked up the class of 1971 the Kaduna Military Academy. Here is the class list. It includes all three of them. While Ibrahim went off on a different route, the other two went to Sandhurst and came back to the federal army as captains."

"Well, you did an excellent job in your new detective role," said Sam "and I think we should promote you to inspector immediately."

By this time I was feeling a little left out. I had no idea what they were talking about.

"Hey, wait a minute, who is this army captain that you have identified here? I'm getting lost," I said.

Philip turned in his chair and put a hand on my shoulder. "You were not to know Marcus had two elder brothers. One is an army captain, while the younger is the man we recognise in this picture."

Since none of us wanted to draw conclusions from the simple presence of the three men in the same picture, or build a conspiracy theory upon the fact that they were all obviously close friends, the table relapsed into silence. Sam paid the bill and we left the club. We went through the swing doors at exactly the moment that all the electricity on the island went down, and we stood together in a little huddle on the pavement in the clammy warmth of the Lagos night.

I remember the chief remarking that he knew one of the senior engineers on the electricity board, also a club member, and he said that they were having difficulty in reducing the outages to less than six hours a day, partly because of the rapid growth of the city, now over

5 million souls, and partly because of the illegal wiring everybody used to get round the meters. Just when we were looking round the car park to see if we could see John, the Peugeot came in sight, lights flashing, and we climbed gratefully into its cooler interior. But John was not in the mood for a quick drive home. He was a man with a story to tell.

"You will never guess where I've been, boss! I've been over the bridge and down into the Festac village. You guys took so long to eat that I had plenty of time to see every taxi driver, porter, commissionaire and every other hotel employee who works outside the building rather than inside it. I'm talking to these folk, and they made me know that there was a man who did work there but doesn't any more, who I really needed to see. This one big important man. He is promoted to be superintendent in the gatehouse of the festival village. and, I am telling you, he needed to be seen. One very important man. Uniform jacket. Stripes on the sleeves. Epaulettes. Yes sirree, he needed to be seen."

John was convinced that he was the man of the hour, and he had news that would not wait.

"Well, it happened like this. Everyone I spoke to outside the club and the hotel told me that this one person could help me. So I asked them why. They said because he owed his promotion to this new job to Ibrahim and some army officer friends. Apparently, he did them favours. Now you are going to ask me who these friends are, and what the favours were. Well, I can't help on the favours. But if that was army officers, I am betting it is women in the rooms in the hotel, cheap drinks, and ganja to smoke. It is not hard to guess this, since this is what army officers normally do."

Philip interrupted him. "Well, John, I for one am much more interested in who his friends were rather than in the sex life of soldiers."

I heard John giggle in the darkness of the car. Then he said, "Don't you worry my friends! You gonna get the whole story, told my way, with all the frills. But you've got to wait until we get home."

At that moment the headlights lit up the gate man raising the barrier to let us into the compound. I remember thinking we were coming to the end of a momentous day.

CHAPTER 6 JOHN

JOHN LOOKED AT the writing in the dust, both on the bonnet and the boot of the car. "Clean me" in English and in Ibo. Except that the Ibo version, had both a spelling mistake and a grammatical mistake. "Cleaning is me." Was this what that jokey policeman thought was funny? All those people from the Delta thought they were so funny. The joke here was that the fresh Lagos breeze coming up from the lagoon would soon cover the message with a fresh layer of dust. John and his boss had a tacit agreement. John only cleaned the car on Sunday mornings, when the chief, his wife, and his children had to be taken to church. This cleaning was performed for the benefit of the chief's wife and her status in the Yoruba community. Otherwise, it was a waste of water.

Switch off and settle down to wait. This was something John was very used to doing. This was the life of a driver. Its rhythm had very quickly become his rhythm. He could not quite remember how many years it was since he came to the west, following Philip. Making that journey had been the one thing that he had set his heart upon. There was nothing left of his old life in the east after the war. There was nothing about his new life that he disliked. And waiting was easy.

He was not a great reader. Philip had encouraged him, and was always giving him things to read. Yet his favourite book at the moment was a car maintenance manual, though not from the chief's relatively new car either. It was about very old car called a Lagonda. He had found it in the office. Apparently the chief had one once and this was all that remained of it. John had seized upon it, and now he could spend hours, taking it apart in his mind, and putting it back together again. It was a very old car, but the instructions were simple, and, he thought, very beautiful. Like a sort of mental jigsaw puzzle.

As he sat there, he wondered if you grow out of these things. The chief was always saying things like, "It's his age" or "They will grow up". He had said it about Henry only the other day. John found this hard to understand. He had no real way of calculating his own age. When Philip had lifted him out of the death and destruction of his world and his family, it had taken months of patient nursing to bring his body weight back to near normal and for his consciousness to recognise the security and safety of his new position. He had attached himself himself to Philip and to Philip's mother, as if they were the family that he had always known, and indeed, during the recovery period, he could scarcely remember his life before his rescue. When he had hesitatingly confessed this to Philip, the older man had put an arm around him, and told him that the doctors from the UN medical mission who had examined him in Enugu had said that while the trauma that robbed these children of their childhood, it also robbed them of the terrible memory of what had happened to them. John thought this was true. He knew people who had bad dreams about the war, but they had mostly been older than him.

But how old was he? He supposed he was in his early 20s. Yet, he could not prove that. All documentation had disappeared.. He had no known relatives, no elder brothers or sisters. The other day, he had a really interesting talk to Henry about this. He saw that there were advantages and disadvantages on either side. And he wondered all the time about his mother and his father. He knew that his mother was dead, and he also thought that Philip's mother, busy as she was with so many deserving cases, could never quite be a mother to him.

It was Philip himself who he had fixed upon in those early days, and now, ten years later, he was still desperate to stay close to him, to support him and to be within range of his support. You see, he rationalised to himself, even if my real father were to walk up to me in this car park in the next five minutes, he would still just be my father. But Philip, he selected me. He chose to save me. I will never know why, and maybe he does not know why either, and maybe why does not matter here. But I do not know anyone else who was chosen in this way, and it means a lot to me. I have to stay very close to him because I need to protect him. Mostly from himself. He is a wonderful man, though I wish he would not work so hard. But he is also an idiot and not very clever at looking after himself. He thinks everybody deserves a chance and has the best intentions. I agree on the first bit, but not on the second. He is also hopeless with women. I know that I should be so much better, if only life would give me a chance in that direction.

So when he came west, I was very unhappy. I begged his mother to let me join him, and eventually she got it. She saw that I could look after him and make sure he was safe, and since he was not going to have another wife like the one he lost, it was better for all of us that somebody did this. So she let me go. Because I was around Philip, I met the chief, and the chief liked me too. He also saw that I liked cars, and he asked me if I could drive. I said, "Yes."

Well, I looked at the way Philip drove the car, and I knew I could do better than that."

The chief stared at me and said, "John, are you old enough to drive?"

"How old do you need to be to drive?" I said.

He told me, and I said that age - and that age was the age that restarted the clock of my life

Philip and I once had a real argument about this. He thought that I was at least three years younger than my ID and my driving license say, but I told him that the difference is that living with him ages you faster than a normal life would. So he smiled and it was a really good moment and he pretended we're having a boxing match and he cuffs me around the ear and I come in close and I'm punching him and every little punch is saying, "Thank you, thank you, thank you."

So we go on, Philip dedicated to saving the world through education, and me with my three jobs.

John recognised that he really did seem to have three jobs at the moment. Driving the chief was easy. so was working with the housekeeper in Philip's home. Looking after Philip himself had never been more difficult: he was so cut up by the death of Marcus, and if truth be told, so am I, John thought. I cannot show him just how much I feel it. To me, it is another huge blow, no reason to it, like the war itself.

The first thing was to get him through the next few days. Then John recognised that he had to fulfil duties to the chief. After all, he thought, he is our boss. I know that he cares for us because I hear what he says in the car. Why, I wonder, do people think that when a driver takes the wheel in his hands, he closes his ears at the same time? I can't figure that out. But I know that the car is a sort of school room: this is the place where I am learning.

Now there is this extra job, this job of sorting out who killed Marcus. And why? I hear everything in the car, and I may be the only one who understands everything. That jokey police inspector suspects that there is something shady going on behind all this. That is why he is trying to be so chummy-chummy with me, writing on my car as if we are all jokey boys together.

I think they are looking at it from the wrong direction. Each of them has a story in mind, and each of them is trying to fit what happened into that story. But I don't have a story, I just have a Lagonda car manual. It will be simple to sort out this murder. Once we have all the pieces, then we can fit it together with the simple precision with which that car was built, and then, in the headlights, we will see the murderer.

One of the real frustrations of being a driver was hearing all the conversations in the car and not being able to contribute. John felt with certainty that he saw as much if not more of the picture as anybody else. That's why it was frustrating to see them sitting around in a circle in the compound with their heads in their hands.

I do like Henry, he thought, remembering that clap on the back. He sees me as part of the team, and not just as the driver. The same goes for the chairman, and for Philip, but one is my employer, and the other is my sort of father, so that is very different. Henry is valuable just because he does not see with Nigerian eyes.

John was pleased when his passengers returned. Crossing onto the island, where the Ikoyi club and its hotel were situated, his three passengers chattered animatedly about the various things they were going to do in the club. He too had his orders. He parked the car, and when his friends had gone into the club, he sauntered over to the taxi drivers and porters sitting on the pavement outside the door of the club. John was soon leaning on the fence between the club and the hotel. It did not take long for the chairman's dash to begin to open mouths. Soon John knew that he needed to contact Benny, the taxi driver who had been taken down to police headquarters. Then he learnt that after the interrogation, Benny had suddenly got a prestigious new job.

"He on the gate now," he heard, "down at the Festac village."

"He is one important man now."

"Dash so big down there, he soon build a village of his own."

It occurred to John that the only way to test out these theories was to go and see for himself, and knowing how long the chairman's dinners took to consume, he knew that he had plenty of time to do so.

The traffic around the festival village was much greater than it had been on the roads coming into town. The village was already almost full of performers and artists who had arrived for the opening, due in a week's time, and by a miracle of organisation that John knew was not very common anywhere in Nigeria, let alone Lagos, the village was almost finished. Builders and carpenters seemed to be at work on some of the two and three floor blocks of flats in First Avenue, but all of the bungalows seemed to be finished and the streets were thronged with happy Festac crowds.

John parked on the Badagri Road and picked his way through the puddles, a reminder that the village had been built on a drained swamp, until he got to the first gate gatehouse. There he found two clerks, sorting out passes and allocating accommodation, and behind them, a man who looked as if he might be in charge.

"Is there a man here called Benny?" John asked. "Can I speak to him for a moment?"

The supervisor, who had been leaning over one of the clerk's desks, looked up.

"I am Benny," he said, "But I cannot speak now. Man, we have real problems here. The people coming in droves for houses and passes. We need to check they are okay on our lists. But the list is alphabetical, we have many thousand names, and these people come from all over. We cannot even spell their names."

"Ask them to write down their names," John said, "and to come forward in groups, letter A followed by B and so on. Then one of your men can check the name against the list, and the other one can do the pass and accommodation."

"It's good thinking, man," said Benny and got his officers organised along the lines of what John felt was fairly obvious advice.

After a few minutes, Benny was able to turn back to John. "How can I help you? You certainly helped me so let me repay the favour."

"I want to talk to you about Ibrahim Kabeysi. I am told you are a friend of his."

Benny turned away immediately. Over his shoulder, he said, "I got too much work to do here to be gossiping with guys like you. Who are you anyway? Who said Mr Ibrahim was a friend of mine? He is one very important man. He put me here to do this job, and when the festival is over, he say, I can have one of the bungalows. Not just a flat in the duplex, mind you. A bungalow. He pointed one out on Third Avenue. I am not going to talk to you about him, not anything about him. Who sent you here anyway?"

Benny was still not looking at John, and was concentrating on, apparently, checking the work of his subordinates. John knew that the stack of 20 naira notes in his pocket would be useless. Whatever Benny knew, he was clearly going to hold onto it, while the idea of that bungalow filled his mind. John thought that he either had to walk away or play all the cards available to him. So he took a deep breath and responded.

"I know that when you had a taxi, you drove Ibrahim. I am also a driver. I drive a great chief. He is boss of one of our biggest companies. He is a chief in old Owo and you should respect that. As a Yoruba man, you must respect it. My chief walks close to your Alaafin. Surely you must respect the greatest Oba in Yoruba land? My chief is a great chief, and a rich businessman, and he was schooled at Dennis Main Grammar School, Abeokuta, where his classmate was our police commissioner. This is not a man for you to cross. If you make me say his name out loud then it will be shameful for you and for your children and for all who hear about it in Yoruba circles. So, if I ask you to say what you know, then you must say it."

Benny has now turned back around to face John. But there was no sign that he was impressed by Sam's great credentials. Indeed, if anything he looked slightly relieved.

"Hey, man," he spat back, "why are you troubling me. Your man is no match for my man. Your man is some pygmy! Why should I be afraid of him? I drive Mr Ibrahim to the Dodan. He used to be a military man himself. He is close, so close, to these people in the barracks who are calling themselves the top brass. Why, I have had people in my taxi and with Mr Ibrahim, who are bigger than your chief. And you cannot threaten me with the police because I am finished with all that."

John suddenly loved his Yoruba neighbours. They loved a good story and they loved to boast. The next question was easier.

"Well, I think you should be afraid of my chief and his friend the police commissioner. Nobody can ignore the police."

"But I can. It's unreal, man. They sent people to get me. They took me to police headquarters. they put me in a stinking cell and questioned me. Mr Ibrahim, he got me out. I am under his protection. The police, they wanted to know about some boy that Mr Ibrahim and I picked up from his compound, and Mr Ibrahim said they had no right to ask me who I carried in my taxi. Nothing happened anyway. We only went up to Mushin. We stopped outside the bookshop and they got out. And the brother of that boy, he was there as well. Mr Ibrahim, he told me, there were no problems. So there were no problems."

John knew that he just had to keep this running. "So aren't you just the clever guy, you can see who is brother to who at one glance?"

Benny sneered back. "I knew it was the brother because Mr Ibrahim said it was the brother. And I seen him before. He is in my taxi. In army uniform, he is one big officer, and I know Mr Ibrahim is one big officer when he is in the army too. They are best of friends these two, and it is typical of Mr Ibrahim. He's so kind. He is bringing the baby brother up to see his elder brother. Nothing to do with what the police are saying. They are talking murders and things. I am seeing no murders. Just two brothers."

"Just how kind and considerate is your Mr Ibrahim. My guess is you had to go back up there to pick up these people late in the night? Always the way with these people, eh? As my chairman is always saying, I should sleep in the car outside where he is having dinner, so I can be ready to take him home again. I can eat my dinner in ten minutes so who knows why he takes two or even three hours?"

Benny was anxious to underline the difference between a driver and a taxi driver.

"No, no, he don't do that. Mr Ibrahim said that his friend would send for an army car when they left, and that I should go home now and get some sleep. You see, considerate man, Mr Ibrahim. and, although it is late at night, there are always places to eat in Mushin, and the two brothers, so keen to see each other, and dancing on the pavement and clapping each other on the back and hugging each other. I am sure they were going to eat somewhere so I was glad to go away. Then, after the police pushed me around, Mr Ibrahim said I deserved something better. He said his friends, and he has lots of friends, man – his friends would find me a job here in the village because they had the federal government contract to run all the festive things. So here I am, and now, you see why I cannot tell you about Mr Ibrahim, because he looks after me."

Just then one of the clerks announced "D" and another group edged forward for passes and accommodation. The announcement triggered a memory in Benny.

"Really grateful for your good idea, man. But sorry I cannot say anything about Mr Ibrahim. Yes, he really good to me."

John turned to go, nodding his thanks to Benny, as he did so, but he had only just stepped down from the gatehouse when Benny called after him.

"Hey, man! If you want to know about Mr Ibrahim, that is his company moving in to the shop over there. They sell masks and other things. Traditional things for tourists, would you believe it! You can ask them and see what they know."

John said thanks to Benny's retreating back and crossed First Avenue to where a truck was unloading crates and boxes outside the corner shop.

The road was even muddier on that side, and the workers were not carrying the crates into the building, but stacking them outside. John presumed they did not want to get the floor muddy so without going in, he looked round the door. A young woman, with her back to him, was trying to arrange a cloth on a long trestle table.

"Can I help?" he called.

Without looking round, she replied, "Only if you take your shoes off."

John pushed his trainers off and left them on the step. He moved to the other end of the trestle table, helping to straighten and smooth out the cloth as he did so.

"Ikot Ekpene?" he asked.

She looked up and smiled in welcome. "Are you our expert on Efik weaving ? The weavers in Ikot sent some notes, but I am having real difficulty in turning those" – she pointed to some papers on the other trestle table – "into labels for the exhibits. I have these two wonderful tablecloths, and four wallhangings in one of the crates."

"Sorry to disappoint you," John smiled back. "I was just passing by and saw you struggling. But I did go to

Ikot on a business trip to Bonny and I do love this work."

"Well, in that case, thank you kindly," came back the reply. "I think this weaving is second to none, and it is typical of my boss that we have these splendid examples to show here. If you like them that much, you can always buy some of them at the end of Festac."

John was not sure that he could afford them or that he had anywhere with enough wall space to display them properly, but as he began to explain this to the girl he began to realise that he did very much want to continue the conversation with her, whether or not it revealed very much more about Ibrahim Kabeysi.

She turned round now, and was facing him, hands on hips, and with a slightly challenging expression on her face.

"Well, what does bring you here?"

John explained that he had come down from the Ikoyi club to deliver a message, and that having done so, he was just returning to his car when he saw what she was doing and wondered if he could help. She smiled sceptically, but he felt that as long as she continued to do that, then he might be able to go on helping to unpack the hangings, tablecloths, masks, or anything else. But for the meanwhile he just stood there, feeling awkward.

Fortunately, she was fully in charge of the situation.

"Oh, the club! Are you going back there? Could you give me a lift in a minute, and if you can wait that long, could you help me get the other tablecloth onto the trestle table?"

She was equally proficient at interrogation. Well before the second tablecloth was installed on its trestle table, she had learnt that he was Ibo, and that he worked for a publishing company in Ibadan and that they were

113

publishing the Festac book of Nigerian creative writing, which was associated with the festival, and that his boss was a club member. And yes, he would be going back to the club to pick him up after dinner. Rather curiously, he did not say that he was the chief's driver. He made it sound as if he was a sort of fixer, and she did not enquire further.

Every now and then she responded to some of his questions. Her name was Bimpe. She managed the flower shop at the hotel next to the club. She rented it from the same man who owned this festival shop. He had a franchise from the hotel, she explained, to run the retail outlets. Besides the flower shop there was a kiosk selling newspapers, sweets and tobacco, and a gift shop. Her employer was really interested in the gift shop, because his main work was as a dealer in traditional art and antiquities. And that's why, that smile again, we are standing here, she told John.

When they had finished the unpacking, John had walked her across the road to the car. She was plainly impressed by the big Peugeot. He showed her into the front passenger seat and closed the door behind her, and then, as they drove away, she asked,

"Why did you come and settle here in the west after the war, when you were a child?"

Fortunately, the road between First Avenue, and Seventh Avenue in the Festac Village was totally choked with traffic, and it took half an hour to get back onto the main highway again. John told her that he had been in the east during the war, and had been fortunate to find a new home in the west, and when he looked around and saw her huge, brown eyes looking sympathetically across at him, even the potholes into which he drove with a jarring effect on the chassis did not disturb his equanimity. All he noticed was the curve of her arm as she tightened her grip on the strap that hung from the roof above the door.

He was so busy concentrating on his driving that his next question - which part of the country did she came from? - he asked in Ibo.

She laughed, and he found that he could not be sure whether he'd said something funny, or whether she just found him funny. Either way he would rather like her to do it again. She then said something which he did not understand.

"What was that?" he enquired.

She laughed again. He realised that her voice was very slightly deeper than the voices of most of the women that he had known in his life, and that he really loved it. That, she told him, was Kanuri. While she understood Ibo, she could not reply in that language, so she had told him that in her own mother tongue.

"Oh, we Nigerians," she said. "We have all these languages, and we cannot speak to each other."

So for sometime in the traffic jam, they swapped language history. She came from Maiduguri and while she went to elementary school, speaking her mother tongue, she had to learn Hausa when she was nine, and then Ibo when she was twelve.

"In conversational terms, I was never very good at either of them, partly because I had to learn English when I went to teacher training college."

And here, at last, John's wits began to reassemble, and he found the courage to ask whether she spoke Hausa to her boss. He guessed that Ibrahim was a northerner, and he guessed right, but the question made Bimpe laugh her deep throated chuckle once again.

"No, we always speak English."

She went on to explain that they had never met before she applied for the job of running the flower shop, and that Ibrahim and the hotel manager had interviewed her in English.

"And how long ago was that?"

About three years, apparently, though much of her communication with him was on the telephone or in writing: he was a very busy man, and he often travelled abroad.

Only then, as they were drawing up outside the club, did John do something that left him wondering if he had not undermined all his good work down in the village. Perhaps it was because he just wanted to prolong the conversation, to keep her in the car for a few moments more. As he applied the handbrake, he looked across at the neat figure, which seemed so natural, so comfortable, so much in the right place in the passenger seat.

"I think my boss knows you. He often talks about a kind lady who helps him choose orchids for his wife. Chief Sam Mydogan?"

"Chief Sam? Oh, I love him. He is the nicest of people. Please give him my best wishes. And thank you so much for your help and the lift."

She opened the door and climbed out, leaving him paralysed in the driver's seat. Once on the pavement, she was about to slam the door shut, then paused, and pulled it back open. She rested a knee on the edge of the passenger seat leaned across and planted a kiss on the top of his cheekbone.

"And that's for your lovely chief!"

He heard the door slam, and he knew that she was

gone and despite the oppressive heat of Lagos, that had surged through the open door as she left, he shivered a little.

CHAPTER 7 PHILIP

OF COURSE, THE issues surrounding the death of Marcus dominated the whole evening. But even so, Philip thought, it would have been a memorable evening. For one thing, the chief had been on excellent form. The food, and especially the wine. was first rate, probably better than in the prestigious hotels that dotted the lagoon in Lagos, and certainly much better than anything you would get outside Lagos. Nigerians seemed to think that you could travel the world if only you had adequate supplies of pounded yam and Jollof rice. Philip remembered the war years, when you were lucky to get even those staples. So a sophisticated menu, like the one they were enjoying tonight, was something to be celebrated, even if the conversation never strayed from the issues surrounding Marcus and the mystery of his murder, only broken when he, or the chief, or Henry had suddenly recalled some personal memory.

"Do you remember the day, when Marcus said he had never eaten chocolate?"

Then, Philip recalled, we all fell silent for a moment, and it was in those moments, that, perhaps, each of us realised how very little we knew of Marcus.

The wine that Sam had ordered was called Cahors. He said it was not very fashionable in France and was grown down in the south west near the mountains. This, Philip guessed, was said to impress Henry. However, Henry's mind did not seem to be upon the wine. Philip was quite aware that even if the club could afford to buy great vintage wines from Bordeaux and Burgundy, he certainly could not afford to drink them.

But this wine was good, and it made the chief expansive. Philip thought that it exaggerated his real qualities. He was a caring man, and he wanted to soften the pain of loss for his subordinates. He was also a leader, in the best sense. Philip did not see Sam as an intellectual, but as a leader who identified where the group wanted to go, and then placed himself at its head. It was all the same if the cause was Universal Primary Education or finding out who murdered Marcus. Sam could energise, and Sam could vocalise and above all he could summon up confidence and enthusiasm in his followers.

Yet Philip found himself wondering just how well Sam had known Marcus. Whenever he spoke of the young man, it was about Marcus as his project, as his demonstration that tribalism was a thing of the past, of his insistence on social, caste and tribal mobility if they were to build a modern postwar Nigeria. Whenever they talked about Marcus, the chief reminded them that they were not going back to the bad old days when everybody stayed in their ghettos. Whenever he said this, he looked at Philip, as if he was saying that the Hausa ghetto in Ibadan was exactly like the Ibo ghetto in Kaduna, and both men knew what had happened to that. If, as he suspected, Sam did not know much about Marcus, then he wondered how much more Henry or even he himself knew. It seemed to Philip that they had each of them adopted Marcus, regardless of who the slim young man in the white robe and head cloth really was.

Henry, he thought, had found a brother, a companion who he had never had in his childhood, or someone even more shy, and less outgoing than he was himself. Whenever Henry said that Marcus was someone he could really talk to, Philip wondered whether he was also somebody that Henry could listen to, and that always brought him up sharply. Was he, Philip, guilty of not listening enough or understanding enough? He thought of himself as the boy's mentor, but did he really know enough about Marcus's actual life? He did not know, for example, how and when Marcus spoke to his parents, or to his siblings. Or to the imam. In truth, Marcus was a mystery. The three men sitting at this table, drinking this delicious wine after a splendid meal, could speculate forever about why Marcus did this or why Marcus went there, but at the end of the day, none of them knew enough about him even to make an informed guess. Philip found the thought dispiriting.

The chief noticed. He broke off from a monologue in which he was describing how he would restore courage and certainty to the police department.

He turned to Philip. "You are looking tired, my dear man. It is a long drive from the east, and now this as well. After these busy days, you must have some more restful ones, especially since we still have contracts coming in from the ministry. I think we have done all that we can for tonight. When we get back to the compound, I shall give you some of my wife's special pills. They guarantee restorative sleep and regular bowel movements."

Henry smiled sympathetically at Philip and Philip knew exactly what he was thinking. The chief's wife was a great believer in her homeopathic medicines, and a visit to the chief's house for dinner was a regular exercise in dodging the pillbox. While Sam went off to pay the bill, Henry teased him, and told him that he would soon be cured of everything he suffered from, and many things that he didn't. They sobered up when Sam returned, thanked him for dinner, and made their way to the club entrance.

Soon they were in John's car with a very excited young man who could not wait to tell them all about his evening in the festival village. If he held back from a full description of Bimpe it was only because he wanted to hold something back from the information about what happened on the night of the murder, and who Ibrahim Kabeysi really was.

He did tell the chairman that the manageress of the flower shop centre, sent her compliments to him.

"An excellent young woman, she comes from Bornu, I think," came the reply.

Philip had wanted to go to bed when he left the club, but the conversation in the car had re-energised them all, and so they sat down round the table in the compound dining room, and the gatekeeper, awoken from sleep, was sent to make a pot of coffee. It was satisfying to have solved one minor mystery and they were not, at least for a few moments, quite aware of the bigger mysteries that now stood revealed. Philip remembered from his childhood the accounts of men first climbing Mount Everest. Apparently you could only see the top once you had got onto a ridge halfway up. He recalled that it was the chief who celebrated getting onto the ridge:

"Well now at least we know why Marcus got into the car. This chap Ibrahim was taking him to see his brother. He knew he was safe."

Henry pointed out that knowing this only made the mystery even greater. "Why wasn't he safe with his brother? What happened up there in Mushin? What part did Ibrahim play in the events that led to his death?"

At this point, Philip felt that a more disciplined approach was needed. He told them that they should go round the table and for each of them to say what he really knew about Marcus and his family, in order to establish clearly what they did not know, and where they should next direct their enquiries.

The chief, naturally, went first. He had known Marcus's father for twenty years. He was the head man of the Hausa community, and very well respected. He had seen Marcus's mother but never spoken to her. and as it turns out, his connections with Marcus's father were fairly formal. They both served on the economic council for the municipal area of the town. For religious and dietary reasons they had never eaten together, or entertained each other's families in each other's homes. The chief had, however, visited the home where Marcus was brought up. He explained that the head man's house contained his extended family and was also a sort of community town hall, full of people seeing Marcus's father on administrative tasks. He had also met Marcus's younger siblings, but not his elder half brothers and sisters.

"You must understand that this family is an important family, not just in our town, but it is a junior branch of a very important political clan in the north. Their family home is in Kano. The elder children who are by a different wife were brought up there. I've always understood, and told you, that the family tradition is military, although I know that Marcus had a famous cousin who was an imam in Jos. I know as well that one, and maybe even two of the elder brothers went to Sandhurst. If I am right, one of them, and it must be the oldest one, is aide-de-camp to the Sultan of Sokoto. I could be wrong – maybe he has been moved – but this is what I remember."

Philip turned to Henry next. "Well, I'm not sure that I can add very much. We did talk quite a bit about our families. He told me that he hated the military. He did not want to be a soldier. He said to know what you want to do and then go off and do it would be really nice, and then never look back. But mostly he talked about his sisters and their worries and fears and uncertainty about who they would marry and what sort of lives they would have, and where they might live. We talked a lot, of course, about my family and how different things were in such different places on the globe. He told me that he envied me because I could go away and do something different. One of his brothers, and I'm afraid that I did not listen to the name, admired him for his certainty. We talked all the time about the differences between the ways of life in our home countries. He was profoundly grateful to the chief for the suggestion of accountancy and training, which he said had already changed his life."

Henry could not go on. The chief sighed a lot and shook his head. Philip turned to John, who swallowed hard, and said, "One day, he said to me that he saw that there were advantages to be gained from the horrors of war. The war for me, he thought, had wiped out all my background and all the expectations that people had of me as well as all of my family and traditions, and left me to do what I could, with the things that I had."

Marcus wanted to travel, he said. He was fascinated by a conversation that he had with the chief and his wife about the time they spent in London. The chief had told him about his year at SOAS, at the University of London, and at the City Business School, sponsored by the company of which he was now chairman.

"He guessed, chief, that this is why you sponsored his accountancy course, but the bit he loved in particular was what he called your love story, of how you met your wife, Enid, when you were buying yams in the West African market underneath the railway arches in Shepherd's Bush in London. He said it could never happen to him. Even his brothers, if they weren't on military training abroad, would have to come home to marry within the family definition of what was a good and proper wife. But he did so much want to see something of the world and make up his own mind."

"I did not realise that," Sam said, shaking his head. "I wonder if we were wise to awaken such thoughts in him, when these ambitions could not be satisfied in his family culture?"

"In my view," John responded quickly, "you were quite right, and you gave him great happiness. You must not blame yourself in any way. You must know that he really respected you."

Philip took up the conversation. "I think we have to be clear in our minds that what happened to Marcus is not connected to the various ways in which we all interacted with him. He loved that interaction. Chief, he told me many times how he respected the knowledge that you and your wife had acquired, and the kindness that you showed in extending it to him. He once said to me that if your wife had not studied pharmacology at Kingston College, then the health of your company would have suffered. In other words, he saw the company that you run as something like an extended family in which he lived, an organisation engineered to do good for its participants. We often discussed investment and profits, and of course his religious background, and sharia law gave him feelings about capital and labour, which were not always in line with some of the exploitative capitalistic practices that we see in Nigeria today. But he was fully convinced that he had something to contribute in the educational world, and no one in our company was more wrapped up in the whole idea of Universal Primary Education than he was, especially since he saw it as the legacy of the late president, a northerner like himself. Be under no illusions: Marcus knew that he had to live in traditional Nigeria and in modern Nigeria at the same time. But it was difficult."

Philip looked at his watch. No one wanted to leave the table without someone trying to wrap things up. So he looked at each of them in turn and told them that he felt it was true that they did not know nearly enough about Marcus, and it was now getting very hard to find out what they needed to know. They had to try. None of them would be able to rest until they found out why this murder had happened, but there was very little point in feeling guilty now for not having explored the life of their friend more fully.

"The fact is that we have two interesting lines of enquiry to pursue. We have to know which of Marcus's brothers was in Mushin that night, and we have to know everything we can find out about Ibrahim, his business and his connections. I suggest, chief, that you instruct us as follows: you and I will take the first question and Henry and John will take the second question. You have your connection to the family and can talk to Marcus's father and anybody else who knows more background than we do and is a member of your local council. Meanwhile, I have friends in the north, who may be able to help to give a little more background on the two brothers in the military. Henry and John can use Festac, where Ibrahim clearly has a connection, to try and ferret out more of his life, and the background.

Is this a plan that you can approve, chairman?"

"Without a doubt, Philip, you have echoed my thinking precisely, and summed up very well, if I may say so. Now, let me go and get one of my wife's little pills. She would never forgive me if I let you go to bed without one, and do not forget to tell her how well you felt afterwards."

As the chairman departed, Philip said that it would be good to keep the police inspector in the loop. Although his senior colleagues seemed to have blocked his work on the case, they would need police help at some point if, as a result of their enquiries, they found anything useful.

The chief reappeared with a pill and a glass of water, and stood over Philip until he swallowed it. "Open your mouth and show me."

He would be asked by his wife if he had done this, he explained. He did not believe that it was necessary to ask questions like this of his editorial director, but he knew that Philip would forgive him, while he wasn't sure that his wife would. Everybody smiled and thought it was time to be going to bed, and in a moment there was only Philip switching off the lights, and Henry waiting to accompany him across the compound to the bungalow that they were sharing.

There was a bright moon and Henry asked Philip whether Sam's wife and her love of homeopathy might not be worse than the sickness the pill was meant to cure. Philip said that he might have a touch of fever, or perhaps it was something he had eaten back home. He pointed out to Henry that in this climate everybody suffered from periodic fevers, from periods of lassitude and inability to cope, and often from depression. Add in the parasites that afflicted the human digestion, the massive amount of digestive ailments caused by infected water, and the national consumption of Lomotil and it always seemed to him a small wonder that the Nigerian economy worked at all.

He unlocked the door, waited for Henry and then locked it behind him. When he turned round, the younger man was standing in the centre of the room looking back at him. For a moment Phillip thought he was about to burst into tears. He looked suddenly and completely crushed. Philip, who had seen many complete mental breakdowns in the immediate postwar years, wondered if his young friend was about to have a breakdown himself. Henry asked him to sit down, and seating himself on the sofa, sat there for a moment with his head in his hands. Then he began to talk, and there was no opportunity to ask questions, since what he had to say just flowed out of him, almost incomprehensibly in places, in a great stream of words that he had been holding back for a long time.

He explained first of all that he had come to trust Philip's judgement. He said that he could never bring his problems to his own father, who would not understand him. But Philip, whom he had only known for a few months, was already, he felt, someone who knew him better than his own parents. He must have help, he said, and advice, but of far more importance was the effect of what he was about to say upon the investigation that they had spent the evening discussing.

"You see, Philip, I think I gave Marcus the information that sent him to his death. And you will know that I would never have done that deliberately, but at the moment when I told him I felt that I could not, as his friend, stop myself from telling him what I knew. But if I had thought that this knowledge would kill him ... I had no idea, dear Philip, you must believe me. Nigeria is not at all like England."

There was a brief silence in the room. Philip, recovering from his amazement, was struggling with which of the hundred questions in his mind should come first.

"I must begin by telling you what I'm doing here in Nigeria. The chairman knows and he was complicit in this arrangement, but he does not know what I'm going to tell you now. The arrangement is that I am on loan to the publishing company. It gives me a respectable cover story, but really I am employed by another organisation to do something else during Festac. Oh, Philip, my real fear is that you are going to hate me for this. I took a contract from the British and American governments to come to Nigeria to help them detect whether the country was being influenced by Russian or Chinese agents. I am no more than just another agent, a spy, and I feel so humiliated to have to tell you this. What can you possibly think of me? And then, in the course of my briefing by my spymasters, I heard something that I passed on to Marcus, and I live in fear that what I said to him with the best of intentions may have resulted in his death. It will come as no surprise to me if I am sent home in disgrace. Perhaps that would be a benefit. But most of all, losing the respect of you, and John, and Sam after my friendship with Marcus was so abruptly and terribly ended, would be a real disaster for me. I must try to explain myself, and make some amends, if I can."

Henry tailed off into silence, holding his head in his hands, his elbows on his knees, staring at the floor. Opposite him, framed by the moonlight coming through the window, Philip was also staring at the floor, equally pensive. But when he looked up there was a slight smile on his face. His first words made Henry sit up and seemingly struggle to get the drift of what he was saying.

"Well, in a way, that is a huge relief," Philip began, and as Henry looked incredulous, broke into a broader grin and said, "You see, when the chairman told me about your new role, I jumped to several different conclusions. We are always being told by our owners in London that we need to be more profitable and grow more quickly. Over the years, I know that Sam has protected us. On his trips to London for the meetings of the Group Holdings board, our owners, he defends us, but before Universal Primary Education was declared I was always worried that they would put someone in place to make us more efficient, reduce costs and increase the margins that we pass back to them. So when I heard that you were coming, I immediately thought of that. I imagined you were being put in place to learn the business and then become managing director under Sam, but still taking orders directly from London. When I met you, all those fears receded but they never quite went away. Until now!"

Philip looked across the room and saw the light returning into his friend's face. Henry was close to tears as well as being relieved and happy. He quickly said that he was not looking for forgiveness. He felt that he should earn that, and the only way to do it was to help his friends find out why Marcus died. Philip nodded and said that made a lot of sense. Henry should now tell him what he had learnt from the CIA and MI6 and what he had passed on to Marcus that he feared had made such a terrible difference.

So now Henry began to piece the story together. He told Philip about Cy and George and the regular briefings, and it turned out that Philip knew George Mainbrace, or had at least seen him at British Council meetings in his role as a cultural attaché. Henry said that it felt like the two separate and secret lives he had been living were coming together. Then he talked about the last meeting that he had attended, and about the intelligence fears of a new military coup based around a group of young northern officers, and how Baban's name had been linked to this.

Philip did not look in the least surprised. What had seemed to Henry like top-secret intelligence just made him smile and shrug.

"Walk into any bar in Lagos and you will hear somebody saying that a coup is just about to happen. Every reporter you meet, from the BBC foreign service to the Lagos Sun, has a story about the next military uprising. Many of these will tell you about their contacts in the Dodan barracks, about which regiments are stockpiling guns, or which officers have said they will be in the next military junta. Armed forces seizing the radio stations is no longer a surprise here. Didn't you tell me yourself that there were military vehicles surrounding the airport when you arrived because of such rumours? I am sure, dear Henry, that you did not tell Marcus something that he did not know already, or which was not part of the rumours he heard every day at home. In a family as well connected as his, such stories must have been commonplace."

Henry nodded and looked relieved. Now he thought about it, what Philip said was obvious. Yet there been something about the way that Marcus reacted that persuaded Henry that he was seriously concerned about what Henry had just told him. Henry searched his memory and tried to pull back as exactly as he could the things in the conversation which had alarmed Marcus, and things which he had said and done immediately afterwards. Henry had registered the sudden alert interest following the mention of the name of the Federal barracks and office of the head of state in Lagos, and then the mention of Baban in the same context as northern officers. He recalled Marcus rushing away from the canteen where they been sitting, saying that he had to get home to speak to his father. As he said it, Philip snapped his fingers.

"So that's it. He wasn't surprised by the stories of an imminent coup d'état. He had heard all that already at home. Maybe he suspected or knew that his brother was involved in the plotting. But he may not have known that Baban was said to be involved. That would introduce more danger, and he may have thought that if even the foreign intelligence services had heard about it. He needed to warn his brother of possible discovery. Or warn his father of his brother's danger. Don't you see, Henry, this explains the late night taxi journey, or at least is one possible explanation!"

Henry felt better. He was glad that he had found the moment to tell Philip everything and Philip felt pleased by his younger friend's evident relief.

"Marcus was killed by people we still don't know for reasons we still don't know. We have no evidence that what you told him put him at risk. In fact it seems probable that he went to warn others that what they thought were secrets were now common knowledge and even a visiting Brit had heard them. In the meanwhile, my friend, the thing you should be afraid of is life imprisonment when your fellow countrymen discover how com-

131

prehensively you have broken the UK official secrets act. And now you must break it even more comprehensively, since we must tell John and Sam exactly what we know so that they have the full picture."

As they went to their rooms the two men shook hands. Relief, secrets shared, and a bit more understanding around the death of Marcus. They felt they were making progress.

CHAPTER 8 CYRIL

CYRIL FAGUNWA THOUGHT a lot about interrogation. He had heard the woman screaming as he came down the stairs from his office, and as he put his head around the door of the interview room, he saw exactly what was happening. Felix, a sergeant on the drug squad, and the particular favourite of the chief superintendent and his Yoruba cronies, was "interviewing" a middle-aged woman. She was probably younger than she looked, and her clothes were old and worn. Her turban hair tie was coming adrift and there were dirty marks on her cheeks where she had been crying. Yet as he glanced at her, he could not help but notice her shiny bright blue leather shoes. Brand new shoes were something you did not associate with a woman of this sort, if indeed you associated any sort of shoes at all. Cyril supposed she worked in one of the old godowns in Apapa, one of the warehouses where all of the cheap clothing was manufactured. But she was not a problem for him, he realised, as he walked on past the door and down the next flight of steps to the front lobby.

Coming up the steps at the same time was the only fellow police inspector with whom Cyril had bonded since his arrival from Benin. Adegeyi ("call me Ade") was much less clannish than his colleagues, and had even invited Cyril home for dinner while he was settling in.

Ade was normally fairly expansive but now he was positively exuberant.

"Cyril, it's the baby, the baby is coming! I am going to be a dad! You see me rushing to the General Hospital. Kiara is there already. I am begging her to hold on so that I can see my son born. So excited, man."

He rushed towards the door of the interview room, but before he entered he stopped and turned around. "Cyril, do you have time to finish off this interrogation for me? Felix will beat this woman to death before she says anything useful. My notes and the case file are on the table and I will tell Felix you are taking over the case before I go. Please say yes! If you can do it then we may name the baby after you. That is of course if it is a boy!"

It was not a difficult decision.. "Go for it, Ade. And you will need a squad car to get through all that traffic. Name your boy after the chief superintendent, that will be much luckier than my name! But invite me to the naming party!"

These words were addressed to the departing back of the father-to-be. Cyril went into the interview room, explained the situation to Felix and advised him to go for lunch, while he sat at the table and reviewed the file and his friend's notes. It appeared that the woman had been arrested on drug charges, but this in itself would not have entailed a visit to police headquarters. The notes made it clear that the drug squad thought she had a close connection to the smugglers who brought in hard drugs, and charging her with possession of a small amount of ganja was simply intended to frighten some information out of her.

The plan had obviously failed. All of Ade's smart questions, and all of the shouting and face slapping that Felix had administered seemed to have got nowhere.

Cyril had her brought back out of the general holding cell – the "fish tank" – and placed at the table. In answer to the guard, he said, No, he did not want her to be handcuffed or shackled. She did not look up, however, and sat hunched in her chair.

"Hello, Mishika, do they call you that or do they call you Mishi? If I remember my school days, I think it means beloved of God in Yoruba? Is that right? And do please tell me about your beautiful shoes. You must love those shoes very much to keep them so unscratched and clean on our filthy streets."

Now she did look up.

She looked, Cyril thought, more like 50 than the 38 that her file claimed her to be, but when he caught her glance he did see that she was younger than he had first thought. She paused as if she was wondering whether she was really speaking to a policeman in Lagos.

"Mishi, my parents called me Mishi," she said. "If the gods loved me, I would surely not be living in Lagos."

"The shoes?" Cyril spoke softly to himself rather than to the prisoner. There was another short pause.

"They were a present. The lady who gave them to me knew how much I loved them. She was very kind and she did not believe bad things about me. Last year I worked in a proper shop. Not just a bench on the pavement or a shack at the street corner. Real important shop where I was properly paid and people came and bought expensive things. It was not an important job: I only unpacked things and put them on the display shelves, and when people came and bought them I put them in boxes and wrapped them up for them. But it paid enough. I could dress properly and eat properly."

In an expressive gesture, she blew through her cheeks and looked down at her clothes as if to say how much standards had fallen since then.

Cyril felt that having got her started he needed to keep the story moving. "So how did you lose this decent job of yours?"

"Simple. It is always men. The owner of the shop came into the stockroom. I sensed what he wanted from the very beginning, you see, I had a suspicion of this from him before. I went on working, but he came up behind me. He started to play with the back of my dress. I felt his hands all around me. Then his fingers are opening my bra strap. It was terrible but I know should not have reacted. This is what some bosses expect. They own you. But I had in my hand a small bronze figurine. Before I knew what I was doing I struck backwards. It hit him in the face, on the cheekbone, and as I turned around I saw some blood, I knew that I was fired. They said it was embezzlement. What does that mean? I never found out. Perhaps it means hitting people with souvenirs. But you asked about the shoes? The owner's girlfriend was always in and out of the shop, and she liked me. We always talk together. She is kind, she is educated, not like me. When she heard what happened she came to see me. I loved her style and especially her shoes. I told her so many times. So when I told her I was going, she rushed out, and then came back with the shoes in a box for me. She said I should wear them when I needed to feel strong, so I put them on when they came to arrest me. Otherwise I keep them in the box and walk barefoot like the rest of us poor people in the city."

Part of Cyril felt this was all taking too long. Another part remembered Mr Braithwaite, his course instructor. "Make them tell you everything. The clues lie under the inconsequential details. Just keep them talking."

Cyril quietly pushed on. "Tell me a bit more about

this shop of yours. Where is it situated? And what did it sell?"

Head down, Mishi's monotone answers continued. "The shop is in a big hotel – lots of tourists and business people. We sell tourist things, souvenirs, things which have no real use and which no one would want in their home anyway. Next door was the flower shop, and beyond that the kiosk for newspapers and cigarettes. My boss is boss of all of this. He called it his concession. But he is never there, always travelling, and then coming in suddenly and checking up. And, being the big man and doing what he did to me."

Cyril reflected for a moment. "I don't quite understand. You said that he had a girlfriend?"

She grunted, almost with impatience. "You don't know these men, inspector. When they call themselves businessman, have a big car, everyone is their slave. He has a girlfriend and she is lovely. Same time, he wants me to do things for him. Dirty things. Because he pays me to work, I cannot say "no" to anything he ask. Women have no rights in this city, inspector. If you are away from your village and your family, you are a slave to every man who has money. If you are asking if I told my friend, the one who gave me the shoes, what he tried to do to me, then the answer is yes. And she is so angry. She say she was going to leave him because she knew he slept around all over the place, but this was the last thing and it made up her mind. She say that after Festac is over then she going to leave."

She was now looking at him quite directly, Cyril found her gaze disconcerting, as if she now expected him to say something equally meaningful. It was true that he did have a question that could not wait.

"I would like to know your friend's name. Was it by any chance Bimpe? And did she run the flower shop at the Ikoyi hotel?"

Mishi did not speak, but she nodded emphatically and held her gaze. Cyril wrote out an order for the desk sergeant to bring her food and drink, and told the guard to watch her but not to put her back into the Fishtank.

Then he said to her: "Please be patient. I think I can help you but I need to go and make a phone call and I will be back in a few minutes. In the meanwhile I've arranged for you to have something to eat and drink."

As he left, he glanced down at the smart blue shoes and her eyes followed his glance. In the city of dust they were a small miracle of cleanliness.

As soon as he reached his office, Cyril tried to phone the publishing company's office number, and then its residential compound in Lagos. But as he was dialling, the power once again went down, as it so often did. How much better life would be, Cyril reflected, if you knew when these daily failures were going to happen. Not being able to predict either the time or the length of the interruption made life so much more difficult. How on earth was Festac going to manage? Only that morning the newspaper had a story that 60% of Lagos dwellings had now been rewired to circumvent the electricity meter. There was talk of military intervention to stop the blackouts, but judging by other military interventions, Cyril was sceptical that would be a success.

Instead, he wrote a note to John Williams, the smart driver who he felt would be his most secure intermediary with Henry and Philip and their rather intimidating chairman.

"John, I am at this moment talking to an arrested person who may be able to throw some light on the activities of Ibrahim Kabeysi. Please ask your people to check back with me as soon as they get this, since they will want to ask this person questions as well, and I cannot hold this individual for very much longer. Thanks, Fagunwa."

He read it back through, checking that he did not reveal the name or gender of his potential witness. Some things should only be spoken. He called up his sergeant and ordered him to deliver the note to the company compound.

"If John the driver is there, give it into his hands. If he is expected in the next day, give it to the gate man and leave him in no doubt about its urgency. If he does not know when he will next see John, then bring it back to me. And, my friend, keep this strictly between ourselves."

Maro smiled and nodded, and as he left Cyril went back downstairs to where Mishi was finishing a plate of pounded yam.

She looked up at him as he sat down opposite her. Cyril was gratified to get some real eye contact at last, but there was curiosity and suspicion in that glance as well.

"The thing is, Mishi, you can help me and some friends of mine to work out some things that we do not know about your old boss. If you help us, then I will try my best to get you out of here and into a safe place as soon as I can. I can see from the paperwork that you were arrested for having the ganja, not for dealing in it, and if you help me, I can pay your fine and release you. I will also try to stop my friends in the drug squad from coming after you again. But only if you promise to help me, to do what I say, to keep it secret, and to tell all that you know to my friends. Everything you know."

Cyril could read the fear and indecision that he had seen in a thousand interrogated faces. He knew the law of the Lagos slums: to say anything against anyone, especially anyone more powerful than yourself, usually resulted in a visit from a man with a machete.

Then they were interrupted by Felix returning from his lunch.

"If you are finished now, inspector, I am ready to take over the interrogation again. Did she say anything useful to you? if not, I will remember to bring down my little enforcer."

The crack of his rubber truncheon against the edge of the table made both Cyril and Mishi jump. It also had a critical effect on decision-making. Mishi immediately nodded her assent, and continue to look gratefully at Cyril as he assured Felix that everything was under control, and that he would decide the next steps in the investigation conjunction with the sergeant's superior officers. When Felix had gone, he took Mishi over to the desk sergeant, paid the possession fine, and had her discharged before he led her upstairs to his office.

Finding a place where he could put her safely was not difficult. Finding a place where the drug squad would not find her again easily was much more difficult. He thought about sending her to the Sisters of Mercy refuge right around the corner from where he lived. They were always full, but he knew he had done enough favours for them for them to stretch a point for him. But this was just the sort of place where the drug squad might look first. Then he remembered that his landlady had several houses, and might know of a free room, but at this point his sergeant came back into the room.

John was apparently in Lagos, driving his chairman to a meeting at the Education Ministry. The sergeant had left a message with the gate man.

Then the lights came back on and immediately the phone began to ring. It was Philip. Cyril was able to explain in more detail what he had gathered from Mishi, and his problem of finding a safe place for her to stay. Philip was immediately helpful.

"Please feel free to bring her here. She can stay in our staff accommodation. The compound is as secure as anywhere, and she will have the gate man's wife for company."

Cyril agreed, but pointed out that he was off the murder case, so any questioning of Mishi could only be undertaken by Henry and Philip. Philip understood this and they arranged for Mishi to come to the compound immediately with Cyril's sergeant.

"There is a Festac organisers reception at the National Theatre this evening. Please tell her that she will be safe and welcome and we look forward to talking to her in the morning."

Next morning was a "trying to rain" morning. Or at least this is how Cyril thought about coastal weather in the west. He remembered the breezes off the Bight of Benin in his childhood. Or was that just a fantasy? Perhaps the truth was that the weather was pretty oppressive right around the coast. But on these "trying to rain" days in Lagos, with dark clouds overhead and very high humidity, it was as if the world was sweating profusely as the clouds struggled to produce a raindrop. Walking was more like swimming, Cyril thought as he struggled up the flight of steps led to the door of police headquarters.

Hearing a voice behind him calling his name he turned and saw Ade crossing the pavement.

"Hey Cyril! I am a father now! It is so wonderful and, guess what, it is a girl!"

"So I miss out on her being called after me?"

"Well, I don't think we can call her Cinderella! But she is so beautiful, man, you would fall in love with her if you saw her."

"I am sure I would and I really want to see her. But, Ade, I must also tell you that I had to release your prisoner. I just fined her for possession. Thing is, you need to make sure your career is safe and secure. That woman, she has protection. Not just a drug gangs, Ade, but also in the military. Goes all the way into the big barracks. Very important that you do not upset anybody at the moment, what with all your extra responsibilities, leave alone the cost of having a baby! So I am very glad I was around to help."

Ade stood still for a moment, as if taking the whole question into consideration. Then he said, "Thanks for having my back, Cyril. I owe you for this. I guess we know where to find her if we ever want her again. Thanks so much for your help."

He clapped his arm around Cyril's shoulder as they went together into the building. It was almost as hot inside as outside, despite the noisy efforts of the roof fans in the lobby. Waiting there, eyeing the incoming crowds, was his sergeant.

"I have the car here in the yard ready for you, sir. We have to go quick!"

Cyril guessed what the emergency might be about as the two of them hurried back out of the building and into the squad car. He wound the window down and luxuriated in the breeze of travel.

Cyril noticed that there were several cars in the

company compound when the gate man let them through. One was the chairman's Peugeot, normally driven by John, and there was John on the veranda of the main bungalow. As the police car drove up he came down and greeted them. Cyril was anxious to see if Mishi had been talking to him.

"Did you know that this woman used to work for Ibrahim at the hotel? She won't say much to me, but when I asked her if she knew the manageress of the flower shop there, she said this woman was her good friend."

John looked up bashfully at the police inspector. "My good friend too."

That was something Cyril didn't know. As he followed John into the bungalow, he wondered if this made any difference. There was no time now to think it through, because in the sitting room he found Henry, Philip and the chairman sorting out papers and stuffing them into his briefcase.

"Can't stop now, inspector, I have breakfast with the minister of education and then a meeting of the curriculum board. Come along, John. Do we have the right number plates on? We will have to find a quick way onto the island today or we shall be late."

With this the chairman bustled out of the room, closely followed by John, who returned a moment later to collect a set of car registration number plates from the side table. He winked and left again.

In the pause that followed, Philip said "Are you guys keeping a strict check on vehicles only going into Lagos on alternate days? You are certainly building a new industry creating false number plates to allow us to go in every day."

Cyril smiled. "Thank God I am not traffic police.

I hear that less than half of the force signed into work every day, so I imagine the checks are a bit sporadic, but they say that army units are going to do spot checks. Prepare for heavy dash!"

Henry cleared his throat. "Really good to know that you are still thinking about us, inspector. Thanks for sending us Mishi last night. While we were out, John chatted with her and got a bit of background, but when we started talking to her this morning she just clammed up. She thinks that her life is in danger if she says anything to us, and we were afraid that asking more questions would just make her more scared than she is already."

Cyril explained how he had come to meet her the previous day and what she had told him. He felt that she probably knew a great deal about Ibrahim and his life as a trader, and she may have overheard things in the shop that would be very valuable if they could get her to talk about them. Her police record said nothing about a husband or children, and she had not mentioned any attachments or dependents. She did seem very scared of Ibrahim, more than you might think she would be scared of just some ordinary hotel shopkeeper. Talking of which, had he inferred correctly from something that John had said that John had a soft spot for the woman who ran the flower shop in the hotel?

Philip and Henry smiled to each other.

"Yes," Philip said. "One glance from an attractive woman and his mental age drops back to 15 all over again! Apparently he met her when he went down to the Festac Village to follow up on your investigations amongst the taxi drivers and the porters. He hasn't stopped talking about her ever since. Frankly it's getting a bit wearing."

"I'm not quite sure how all this fits together, gentlemen," Cyril said, looking thoughtful. "If we need the complete story on Ibrahim Kabeysi, and I suspect that we do, then these two women could be vital to us. if we can get Mishi to trust us, then she, together with John's obvious attraction - presuming that she has warm feelings for him too - could be the means to get Bimpe to tell her story as well. She may have met other members of Ibrahim's circle, including the brother who was so important to Marcus."

Both Philip and Henry nodded in agreement. "We are still left with the problem that we do not know how to start, given that she feels, not unnaturally, totally insecure, as frightened of us as she is of Ibrahim, her drug dealers, and the Lagos police. Poor woman, she must believe she cannot say or do anything without instant retribution."

Cyril had two thoughts about how they might tackle the problem. The first was that he would speak to her now, before he left, and tell her, that if she had no ties here in Lagos, he would ask them to move her to another town, find her accommodation and a job, and give every guarantee of security that they possibly could. She might change her name or even her appearance.

"A witness protection scheme is what my old UK teacher would have called it. Except we don't have such a thing here unless it is funded privately."

"We can certainly get her accommodation in Ibadan, if that is far enough away," Henry said.

Philip agreed that they could find her a suitable job of some sort, adding brightly, "If she speaks Kanuri then she can certainly be an editor."

Cyril's second recommendation followed on from

this. "In the early stages, while she learns to trust you, have only John speak with her. He speaks in the multi-lingual street slang of Lagos. He has already got something out of her, and he is certainly less threatening than you two. If this is all decided then I will take my leave before my presence here becomes an issue. You two must back me up, that I dropped by to pay my respects to your chief and to ask if he was happy to have the murder investigation left as it stands, closed at this point. I will write a report saying that as a result of this visit, you have all said that you acknowledge that nothing further could be done. I hope that this will stop my chief, the DCI, the chief super and the commissioner himself from taking any further interest in what I am doing."

Philip and Henry did not look at all happy about this, but, as Henry put it, if Cyril doing this was his only way to keep an interest in this case, and that his continued involvement must be kept secret, they were sure that the chief would agree. It was hard to know what Marcus's family might think, since there had been no communication with them since the funeral. Presumably they wanted to know why he had died, but if his brother was implicated in some plot, maybe they would not want to know, or maybe they knew or feared that something terrible was happening?

Cyril shrugged. "The great families and the military high-ups are so full of secrets that it would take a lifetime to untangle them. I am just a simple policeman from Benin trying to solve a complicated crime in the chaos that we call Lagos. I cannot worry too much about what they think. My police duty is clear. I have to get to the bottom of this, with the family's help or without it, and with police headquarters' help or without it. So far, we three, with your chief and John, are the only people who really want to know what happened. I must admit that I got more interested after I was told that I should not be interested at all!"

Cyril now laid out what he thought they must do. Henry and Philip should go next door into the dining room, where they could listen but not be seen. The gate-keeper or his wife should be asked to bring Mishi to see Cyril. He would then tell her that he had negotiated her safety in return for her cooperation.

"You must make sure that she cannot see you and me together at any point. I can explain why I came here, and I can explain why I sent her here, but I cannot explain her being in the same room as us three in a shared conversation. We have to protect ourselves in case a subsequent enquiry makes it look as if we were acting in some sort of conspiracy."

With that he got up and started to take some papers from his briefcase, as if he was embarking upon official police business. Philip went to ask for Mishi to be brought round while Henry stepped next door. Then the door opened and the woman herself came in.

"Good morning, Mishi. Come in and sit down," the policeman began. "Would you like some coffee – I'm sure these people have plenty if we ask."

"No thanks, inspector. They are kind and generous people. I have had a good breakfast."

"And did you sleep well?"

"Better than in my previous place, in fact better than for a long time."

He looked up at her and indeed her face did seem more relaxed. "I am so pleased by that and I think it was the right thing for you to come here. I want you to understand that these kind people are really interested in anything they can learn about your boss, or former boss, Ibrahim. They think that he helped somebody do a dreadful crime. They need to find out if you know things about Ibrahim that might be useful to them in helping to solve this crime. If you will talk until you have said all that you know, they are happy to move you to a different town, find you somewhere to live and get you a job that enables you to pay your rent and live property. They have asked me to find out if there is any reason – husband, boyfriend, parents, children – that means that you have to stay in Lagos. And they have said that I can only make the offer to you if I am absolutely sure that you are going to be honest and helpful to them."

During this speech Mishi nodded several times, her eyes firmly fixed on Cyril's face. But now she was looking down, thoughtfully, causing Cyril to ask whether this proposal gave her problems. When she looked up he could see she was crying and having a little difficulty in responding to him. He told her to take her time.

A few moments later she began: "I am crying because the young man who spoke to me last night and welcomed me, said that the people he worked for were some of the kindest people he had ever met, and I wondered why you had chosen to put me amongst them? If I can help, then I must, and I will do so by searching my memory honestly for everything that I can find that you need to know. And as to leaving Lagos? My parents died in a ferry accident on the river Benue. My husband was a rifleman in the federal army, killed in Biafra. I had a child before the war, when I was thirteen, but she died at birth. They say I can have no more babies. I am alone in the world, which is why Ibrahim and people like him can use me for what they want, and I cannot resist without putting myself into even more trouble."

She looked down again and Cyril could see that her shoulders were heaving slightly. He felt that he had got as far as he could. He was useless at comforting the distressed and rendered powerless by a woman's tears. This was the time to go.

"I shall tell them that they can trust you completely. You must trust them as well. Please speak to the young man who greeted you last night. He will soon come back. He will be the person to whom you must talk. Meanwhile, please see that this is the beginning of something new, and better."

Cyril gave her shoulders a little squeeze as he passed her chair, walked rapidly to the door, and breathed a huge sigh of relief as he walked out into the compound. As he did so, he raised his arm in the air to indicate to the watchers in the dining room window that he had had a successful conversation.

CHAPTER 9 JOHN

THERE WAS A big gap, John recognised, between imagining oneself in a conversation with someone you really wanted to know, and actually making that take place. Ever since he had met Bimpe and helped her in the tourist shop in the Festac Village, he had wanted to meet her again. Yet the chances of that happening seemed remote. The chief, Philip, and Henry had all seemed very interested in the information that he had given them, but nobody had sent him back there with further questions to ask. What is more, the chief had said that he himself might stroll over to the flower shop in the hotel and, using the need to buy orchids for his wife as an excuse, might get into conversation with her on matters related to Ibrahim. Fortunately the others had deflected him from this course of action, but for a moment John had felt a pang of jealousy. Jealous of the chief? Or his own boss, a man thirty years older older than himself, or of the woman in question? He felt embarrassed that the thought had occurred to him. Yet it had. He needed to be back in the company of that woman, whatever the pretext.

When he drove back into the compound after taking his chairman to and from the Ministry of Education, his sole thought was a despairing one. He had no pretext. He could think of no excuse. When Henry asked him to join him and Philip in the dining room while the chief wrote up his notes and phoned some instructions through to Ibadan, he welcomed the distraction. When they briefed him on the conversation with Mishi, he was happy to help. When they said that they suspected that Bimpe was far less attached to Ibrahim than any of them had first thought, his heart sang. and when they suggested that he might be the right person to win Mishi's confidence, and that her relationship with the flower shop manageress might be vital in getting behind the facade and discovering what Ibrahim was really doing, his heart began to beat a good bit faster. He was impatient to get on with his new assignment. He was glad when they left him in peace. As he poured a cup of coffee and waited for Mishi to appear, he concentrated on what he was going to say.

When she looked timidly around the dining room door, he was calm and smiling. He beckoned her in.

"I'm just having some coffee. Would you like some too?"

When she nodded, he pulled out a chair for her and offered her condensed milk and sugar. Her fingers pulled nervously on the tab that opened the tiny container of milk, and he reached over and gently took it out of her hands. He opened it and poured it into her mug and she smiled gratefully.

"We have this English guy working with us here and he has the same problem opening the milk. He can't understand why we don't have fresh milk and cows in Nigeria, so I had to explain to him that we had no fields and grass, and the aircon for cows would cost more than the milk! I mean, he is a really nice guy and everything, but he just couldn't see why we didn't have cows."

Mishi smiled back at him. It wasn't that she fully understood the joke about the milk, but she saw that it was a joke and that he was trying to be nice. And the coffee was good.

John went on. "They say you will be with us for a bit and that you need to get out of Lagos. My name is John – I am the driver and I will be taking you up to our place in Ibadan I don't blame you wanting to be out of Lagos. In Ibadan we are on a hill, and there is some breeze. You will really like it."

She took the outstretched hand and smiled timidly again. John felt the rough hand of a manual worker and knew, from his experience as a boy, that he was dealing with someone who had endured a hard and difficult life. The first task now was reassurance, not questioning.

"Listen, I do not know why I am driving you out of Lagos. I know nothing about your life. I do not need to know and I do not want to know. But I do know about the people that you are with now. They are good people, they are kind and they want to help. If you have any questions about them, please ask me. Whatever language we use, you will get it the honest truth."

At this, she smiled again. "I speak some Hausa and a little Efik, and like everyone some pidgin, but I have no Ibo. I guess that you are an Ibo man. Not so?"

When he nodded she smiled once more and said, "Speaking English is good for both of us?" She paused again before asking, "Do you know why these good people of yours are being good to me?"

He shook his head. "All I heard was that they were doing it at the request of the police inspector. He is a friend of theirs and he asked them to help. I think it is simply that."

There was another, longer pause. John sensed that she wanted to say something else, but she sat staring into the depths of an empty coffee cup. Then, with a sudden determination, the question came out.

"If they help me, what will they want from me? Or will they want to sleep with me? In Lagos, everybody wants something. I have no money. I am no longer young. I have nothing to give except that."

John now leant across the table. He put one hand on top of hers. "The inspector brought you here because he knew you would be safe. Nothing like that will happen to you here. or in Ibadan. I can promise you that."

When John reported back on this first conversation, his colleagues agreed that he should drive Mishi back up to the office on his own. It was often easier to talk in the car. Once John had introduced her to the chief's wife and settled her in a hotel room, he would come back the following day to pick up the chief. In the meantime, the chief was insistent that listening to a high-life band was an essential part of Henry's education. Philip should take him to dance to the music of Ebenezer Obey and his All Reformers band. This was an important Festac preliminary. The ballroom of the Lebanese hotel would be crowded but Philip had to make sure Henry learnt to dance, high-life style.

As he left the room, John put a friendly arm round Henry's shoulder.

"Look, Philip can teach you nothing about dancing. He is like a camel from Kaduna on the dance floor. But at the entrance to the hotel you will find girls who will dance with you for an hour for 10 naira. Do it. And, please, leave it at that! These young women will show you all the moves on the dance floor."

Then he headed off to get petrol for the car. Here he had a stroke of luck. The long queues at the pumps that he had noticed earlier in the day were now reasonably short. A few hours later, he was back and picking up Mishi. As he opened the car boot he asked if she had any bags. When she looked as if she was about to cry, he kicked himself for not realising how much adrift she was in the world. She possessed nothing. He opened the rear door of the Peugeot for her to get in, and this too made her feel embarrassed. So he put her in the front passenger seat. He noticed with approval that when he blew his horn to get the sleepy gatekeeper to open the barrier and let them out onto the main road, she smiled at the man as they passed him.

John eased the car into the horn-blowing cacophony of the main road and headed for the slipway to the bypass. As they slowed into the crawling traffic jam, he said, "I have never really got used to this. The driving is much easier in the east because we do not have so many cars, but then again our roads have not been repaired since the war. I drove Philip to Abba and I swear that there are still shell holes in the road. Someone said that when the rainy season comes crocodiles come to live in them."

She giggled before she remembered to suppress it. He felt however that it was a sign that she was more relaxed and thought he would try a different tack.

"So, which part of this Nigerian world do you come from?"

Once again, there was a long pause before a reply came, as if she was resolving some conflict in her own mind.

"Oh John, I am a long way from home. If you really want to know, my father's people were Mango, and I was born in Plateau state. We are really mixed up there. Our village was Mango but there were forty different tribes in the state and the Mango people were not powerful. They were not the ones in charge. My dad worked in the mines before the war, but during the fighting everything closed down where we were and we were forced to move. You know what they say about things that are loose in Nigeria? They all roll down into Lagos eventually!"

John breathed a sigh of relief. Maybe this was not going to be so very difficult after all. By the time they got onto the main road out of town to the north, the conversation was flowing easily. When she told him about the tragic death of her parents, he thought that he could remember the headlines about the ferry tragedy on the river. Maybe not, though: deaths from ferry accidents were fairly frequent on the great river. She talked about various boyfriends and was very categorical in her judgements about Nigerian men.

"Never trust a Yoruba man who likes to drink. When a Hausa man gets serious religion, he will beat you to make you better!"

How much of this was a street talk and how much of it was a reflection of experience was hard for John to tell, but it made him brave enough to push on with another question.

"So, Mishi, in ten years down here you never found a worthwhile man, as a boss or a boyfriend?"

This one hit gold, like a seam in a Jos mine.

"Well, yes, I thought I had a fairly decent boss. I worked for him for four years in the hotel on the lagoon where he had a shop selling antiquities. I worked in the storeroom, packing and unpacking. You know, I really hoped that one day I could be a shop assistant. I tried to listen and learn. I had a friend who helped me to learn all the labels. In English, you know. It was difficult."

" I can imagine that. But you say this boss was good to you?"

"Well, yes, he was at first. I was lucky to have that job. It paid well. And regularly. Sometimes with shops they stop paying if times are hard and you just have to wait till things get better. Money was not a problem with this man. He was a bit flirty you know, but then they all are. You have to put up with these things. It was a good place to work, in a big hotel. The air con kept going in the blackouts because they had their own generator. There were some problems but I loved it there."

" Problems?"

"Yes, not serious ones at first, but eventually it got bad, and I had to go."

"This is what made you unhappy?"

"Yes, I was really sorry. But I should've seen it coming. Even right at the beginning he looked at me like some of these men look at you. I think you are not so much like this, Mr Ibo driver!" Here she giggled at her effrontery. "In my experience, all Nigerian men when they look at you, well they look you over with their eyes and their eyes say that they expect you to fall on your knees and beg them to take you into their bed.

He could tell she was looking at him enquiringly, though he concentrated on the traffic and used his driving as an excuse for not looking away from the road. He knew that he needed to say something reassuring to make her confident about moving on.

"I am so very sorry, Mishi. It sounds as if you have met some very bad people. We are not all like that, and it is really sad that you trusted this man and were disappointed."

"Yes, John, you're right. I was disappointed. I ignored the fact that he looked at me like that, and that every now and then he made some suggestions. I thought it was just his way. I knew that his girlfriend worked there in the hotel, so I thought nothing would happen there. You see, I really did like the job. And then something did happen."

When she described the incident that she had already recounted to Cyril, and blamed her reaction as much on surprise as anything else, and Ibrahim's on as much a loss of dignity as anything else, John found himself warming to Mishi immensely. As he knew, if you fell outside family, village, clan and had no education or money, Nigeria could be a very tough place in which to survive. In the circumstances he admired her, yet he knew that thinking the best of people could be very dangerous if you were on your own. He gripped the wheel in gratitude for having Philip as a surrogate father and the chief as his boss.

Concentrating his mind again, he went back to the question of knowing more about Mishi and her boss.

"So did you have to fight off this boss of yours every day?" he asked.

"No, not at all. In fact the reverse. He was more often away than in the shop. For a start he was a member of the club next door and he was very often there entertaining people. Clients, I imagine. He sometimes brought his guests into the shop to show them things. Then he was often travelling. Sometimes up the country and he would talk about going to the north. Sometimes he flew out of the country, often to Europe and would tell us about places he had been when he came back. I think I learnt more about what he was doing from his girlfriend than I did from him. She ran the flower shop next door, and on her breaks she would come and sit in the storeroom with me and we would chat. She is a lovely person, much younger than me but full of confidence, which I do not have, and with a good education. Then I think I made things bad for her."

"Why on earth do you say that?"

John's question was not contrived, but direct, urgent and from the heart. When he glanced across at his passenger he saw that she was crying quietly, and he did not think that his question was the reason for the tears.

"You see, when he did what he did to me and I lashed out and cut his face, she asked me what had happened. I am her friend and I know that I must tell the truth. When I did she was angry and went to see him, and they had a row. She came back to tell me that while she had to go on working for him, because he owns the flower shop as well as the other shop in the hotel, she could no longer be his girlfriend. She said, well, she said…"

All eyes in the front seat were now looking through the windscreen fixedly at the road.

"What did she say?" John asked gently. He felt that in the long silence that followed the person sitting next to him was searching for for the right words to use in the chief's official car.

"She said that he had replied that women like me were made for Nigerian men to wipe their manhood on."

When the words came out they were said with a certain deliberate vehemence. John was silent for long time. When the conversation resumed, it was Mishi herself who asked the question.

"When I first met Ibrahim, I thought he was just a Nigerian man. Like them all. Wanting to be in charge and all that. Wanting you to give everything to him the moment he feels he want it. But now everyone seems to

158

want to ask questions about it. Do you think he is a bad man, Mr John?"

"Well, for a start, please do not call me Mr John. I am John, and today I am your driver. I do not really know the answer to your question. I recognise that here in the west men seem to dominate. But women are very strong in family matters, and you know that in the east, where I come from, women are the traders and managers, and the decision-makers in village councils. If I was at home, I would be a worker in the yam garden, and my wife, if I had one, would be selling the yams on her market stall.

He was about to launch into a description of Philip's fearsome mother, and the way he both loved and feared her, but he sensed that Mishi was about to reply and above everything else he wanted her to talk.

"Yes, I know this," she said, "but somehow Lagos is different. All of our peoples are mixed up together. Everyone is only after the money. Nobody respects anybody. And yet if you have been here for years, you realise that you have no home to go to in the villages anymore. The villages I knew before my parents died would not recognise me now. They would call me unclean because I had been living on my own outside family protection."

This was not where John wanted the conversation to go so he tried to direct it back to Ibrahim.

"Do you think that this is why Ibrahim tried to take advantage of you – because he saw that you were unprotected and vulnerable?"

"Yes, I think so. For a start, he is a town boy from the north. He told me so. He is from Zaria. His father was a pepper merchant, and until he died they were prosperous. Then his uncle took over the business, and wanted it for his own sons, and Ibrahim was sent into the army. He went to the military training school in Kaduna. That's where he met his army friends. There were three of them. I saw them when they came into the shop. They used to walk into the shop and ask where Ibrahim was. Sometimes they left messages for him to come over to the club, or to join them in the hotel bar. Sometimes they asked for Bimpe, his girlfriend, to leave a message with her. I can remember times when I could smell that they had been drinking. After my years down here I am quite used to drinking and drunken people. His army boys, they were brought up like me. Our religion said no drinking, but I thought, they were only young, even Ibrahim is only young, and maybe they would grow out of it."

They came into a small village and John stopped the car beside a stall. He wound down the window and bought two bottles of water. He checked the seals to see that they still had the factory caps on them, and offered her one. She smiled gratefully and took it.

"Are you hungry?" He indicated the small crowd of stall keepers who had left their positions and were pressing forward with plates and trays of street food. She shook her head. He decided to press on and make sure she had a good meal when they reached the hotel. He had to concentrate to weave through the cluster of vehicles, animals and people in the centre of the village, but soon they were picking up speed on the main road. He wanted to get back to the subject of Ibrahim as soon as possible.

"Sounds as if Ibrahim had a very good time and didn't do much work."

"No, that would be wrong. We used to think he worked very hard. The army men were often in the shop because they were stationed in the Dodan. Ibrahim was very proud of them, because he had been with them in officer training and they had all been a group together before he left the army. He told me he missed the army. If he had stayed he was sure that he would have been promoted, just like they were. One of them, he claimed, was on the president's staff. He really loved talking about them. I do not know what they did. Like the rest of the army I expect, riding around in jeeps and shouting at people. But I do know that two of them were brothers, because I had to find identical birthday presents for them. I know that these brothers came from a big clan in the north. Ibrahim said even I would know the name."

"Still, it sounds as if you and the shop assistants did all the work, and Ibrahim went drinking with his friends."

"When he was in Lagos he was always in and out of the shop. especially at times when we had special packages to be made up for people in Europe. And this happened most months. There is a driver who comes down from Jos. He brings little bits of pottery which have to be packed up very carefully. This man and I have many jokes. He is a Jukan fellow and you remind me a bit of him. He is based near Jos and he always says he knows my village, but I wonder. Anyway, I have a few words of Jukan and he learnt some Mango at school and I like to pretend that we are speaking together as we would at home. But then we both speak in Hausa, mostly, because this includes Ibrahim. It is our shared language in the north. I always say to him that I do not know why people collect these broken bits of pots, we put them carefully into the bottom of the packing cases in special containers so they won't get even more broken. Then we fill up the packing cases with the things from the shop.

We have lovely brass heads which are made specially for us by a factory down in Benin, and wonderful big masks from Ife. And then we seal the packing cases and I help my friend, whose name is Sabo, by the way, to load them onto a van to take them to the airport. This will show you how hard Ibrahim works. He always drives out to the airport to make sure that everything is okay with the customs and that the cases get onto the right plane."

All of this seemed perfectly normal to John. He wanted to get back to the soldiers. His ears pricked up when it seemed as if not one but two of the Diello brothers had been involved with Ibrahim. They were nearing Ibadan and just passing an army truck. He gestured toward it.

"Many of us, since the war, are really scared of the soldiers. Doesn't sound like they had that effect on you?"

"No, not at all. They mostly ignored me. I was only ever scared of soldiers in the shop once and that was only because Ibrahim wasn't there."

"What happened?"

"Well, this sergeant came in, dressed in military fatigues and holding a machine gun, and said he was from the military HQ. You know the sort – you can see them every day on the streets of Lagos. These boys, they expect to be obeyed instantly, and I had not come up so close to one before. I swear, John, I could smell him. He asked for Ibrahim and I said that the manager was not there, and he said I was to fetch him immediately. Well, the shop assistants are gone home since it was after closing time. Bimpe was not in her shop across the corridor or I would have sent him over to her. What was I to do? I told the man that I could not help. Then he shouted at me. He put his hand round my neck and with his face inches away from my face he shouted that there was something that I could do. I could find Ibrahim and send him to military intelligence where his boss needed to see him straight away. And if I could not do this, it would be the worse for me and then he brought his gun up and put the barrel onto my cheek. I was so scared, John, I almost wet myself. I was also so angry, so I shouted back at him, louder than I thought I could. 'Tell me who wants him and I will tell him as soon as I see him.' You know, this big man with his shiny shaved head and his gun, he just stopped and said, 'General Baban.' He told me not to keep him waiting and then he left. I have never heard of this fellow. When Bimpe came in, I told her. She said he was very famous and and we must find Ibrahim very quickly for him."

They were in the outskirts of Ibadan now and soon he was drawing up outside of the hotel. He spoke to the manager and gave him the Chief's message, found her room in the accommodation block, and pointed out that he was close to her in the same building if she needed help. The manager gave her a ticket to eat in the dining room. John asked her if there was anything else he need-ed to do to make her comfortable? She shook her head but then stopped and put a hand on his arm.

"There is just one thing. My friend Bimpe, she has been trying to find me another job. We arranged to meet this afternoon. I know she will be worried. When you are next there, perhaps taking your chief to his club, please could you go to the flower shop and tell her I am okay? And, John, please give her my thanks and my love and..."

John's heart bounded. He had a real gold-plated ex-cuse to go back and see Bimpe once again. He almost skipped back to his own room, found some hotel note paper and started to write down everything he had learnt during the drive. He knew that Philip and Henry would want to weigh the significance of everything that Mishi had said, and he wanted to be sure that he had captured every element before it faded from his memory.

CHAPTER 10 HENRY

THE TIME FOR guilt and introspection was over. I looked across at the three faces around the compound dining room table and I knew that I had to bury my worries, my fears, my guilt, my history, my background, my inadequacy and just about everything else. The three other faces were concentrated, intent. As Philip put it, we were going to solve an African crime in an African way. My job, as I began to recognise, was to bring a view from outside the culture, asking questions which perhaps might otherwise not be asked, and to use my sources in external intelligence agencies to add anything that they could reveal to the events now emerging. As I looked across at those faces, I realised that I wanted to do my best for them. The chief's troubled, jowly features made him look like a worried bloodhound, anxious to get back on the scent. John's face was all expectation, awaiting the command to rush out to the car and drive furiously away on some impossible mission. Philip, counsellor to chiefs and father figure John and me, was silent, thoughtful.

Sam opened another bottle of Star beer, topped up the four glasses.

"Well, I find it all most confusing, and so, Philip, I am going to hand it over to you to use that big editorial brain of yours to summarise what we have, where we are and where we are going. I could not be with better people. I know we will catch the men who killed our dear Marcus and bring them to justice."

We all nodded and raised our glasses. We put aside Philip's often stated conviction that justice was a commodity only obtainable if you were a military governor or one of the super rich, and we discounted John's suggestion, made to me in the kitchen a few moments earlier as we prepared some sandwiches, that the only justice that the killers of Marcus deserved was a knife between the ribs, and he was prepared to be the instrument of such justice. I had reflected that justice sounded a bit abstract given the descriptions that Cyril had provided of the unwillingness of the police to investigate this case, but I too bought into the idea that even if we did not bring the culprits to a court of law, we wanted to be able to explain to ourselves and to Marcus's family exactly why he was murdered.

When Philip cleared his throat and began to speak, we were suddenly members of his class in his days as the young headmaster of a small primary school somewhere in the bush beyond Umuahia. It wasn't just that he spoke with authority. It reminded me of how important certain features were to the country that I was learning about. In Nigeria, it often seemed to me, people wore their education in a way that I had never experienced before. In England, I knew the class distinctions of education inside out. Tell me where someone went to school and I could tell you a great deal about them. But my assumption was that everybody had some form of institutionalised educational experience.

In Nigeria the situation was totally different. Not only did you meet people every day who had no formal education, or who were entirely self educated, but people educated to the age of eleven whose attitude to their education was totally different to my British experience. They venerated their teachers as the people who had changed their lives. Teachers occupied the front row at weddings, naming ceremonies, and funerals. Teachers spoke publicly on behalf of their former pupils in company celebrations and anniversaries. Your teacher was part of your pedigree, and being taught by a well-known teacher could be like going to a famous public school in England. I had seen men come to the reception desk at our office in Ibadan just to shake the hand of "Mr Philip," despite the fact that he had not sat in the classroom for fifteen years.

Now he cleared his throat like the great teacher that he once was.

"First of all, I want to say how much I support the chief and how confident I am that we will get to the bottom of this dreadful affair if we only concentrate, investigate and, above all, listen. We have very good places in which we should be listening very carefully. It is a huge advantage to us that the chief has so many good friends at the highest levels in the army, in the civil service and in the police. Henry too has valuable listening posts in the US Embassy and at the High Commission. And we seem to have made a good friend of a frustrated investigating detective, Inspector Cyril Fagunwa. I feel that he is an honest man trying to do his job, and I do not think that he will stop investigating just because the formal investigation has been closed down by his senior officers. So where are we now and what exactly do we need to know next?"

Phillip's voice became more definite and his small class stiffened to attention.

"Let's begin with Marcus and his movements. We know now that he left the compound late in the evening in a taxi bound for Mushin. In the taxi was a man called Ibrahim Kabeysi. We do not know whether he had met this man before, but we are now sure that the man introduced himself as a friend of Marcus's brother, and we are fairly sure that it was Marcus's brother who greeted the taxi when it arrived in Mushin. We do not know what happened next. Did either of these two men murder Marcus? Or was it somebody else? We can be sure that it happened that night sometime between 10 pm and midnight, and that Marcus did not go into the mosque. We do not know whether Marcus was murdered where he was found the following morning, or whether that happened somewhere else and his body was dragged there.

"Then let's come to Mr Kabeysi, or Ibrahim as everybody seems to call him. We know that he was once in the army, and he's obviously well-connected there. We know that he worked in military intelligence and is close to Baban, its chief, and we know that this head of military intelligence keeps coming in and out of the story in a very disturbing way. We also know, thanks to you, chief, that Ibrahim is a member of the most exclusive club in Lagos, and runs a gift shop and other shopping concessions in the hotel next door. We presume that this is his source of income. John, who is not only our fearless driver, but a fearless interrogator of suspicious people, has learnt from his former employee some fascinating details about how the shop worked and who visited it. This positions both brothers of Marcus as friends of Ibrahim, and brings Baban once more into the picture.

"It also throws an interesting light on how Ibrahim actually earns his money. Mishi was employed to pack parcels containing tourist trinkets to go to addresses in Europe. Before they go, a packet of broken crockery, as Mishi describes it, is put into a secure area in the base of the parcel. This suggests to me the smuggling of antiquities.

"We must bear in mind where Ibrahim comes from. After the war, in this decade, archaeology has recommenced on the plateau at a greater level than ever before. The discovery of a Neolithic culture with advanced terracotta artefacts has excited the archaeological world. Named as the Nok culture, it became an iron-using, crop-growing civilisation some 2500 years ago. It was an inconvenient fact for the imperialists, who claim to be bringing light to the dark continent, and the slave traders, but it is now clear, from the beautiful, grotesque and fascinating terracottas and other recovered artefacts, that this was a civilisation capable of creating great works of art. All accomplished," and here the schoolmaster looked directly at me, "while your ancestors were cowering in caves in the Welsh hills!"

No sooner were the words out of his mouth than Philip began apologising. He was sorry that he had got a bit carried away. In particular, he was sorry for lumping the entire historical crime of slavery and imperialism on my shoulders. For me, however, it was a point very well made. While I did not feel exactly responsible, I did feel that if I had been an Englishman walking around in Nigeria without a recognition of the dreadful things which my ancestors had done in that country, then I would have been very insensitive and irresponsible. Philip, perhaps to hide his embarrassment at his sudden outburst, was anxious to push on.

"I think that each of us can push this inquiry further during these opening days of Festac. Henry, can you please ask your British and American contacts about antiquities smuggling as well as further information about coups and plots. If one of the reasons for the murder of Marcus was his discovery of his brothers' involvement in one such plot, which he may have discovered by putting two and two together after your conversation with him, we need to know more about the plotters and how far the Diello family is involved. Equally, John, we need to know more about those packages and where they went. Bimpe may be able to help as she may know much more about Ibrahim's associates. Since she has obviously put some distance between herself and her former boyfriend, she may be willing to tell some of this to you, John, if you give her space to speak between telling her how beautiful she is."

John covered his face with his hands at this point, but I could see his eyes glinting between his fingers as he tried to guess our reaction to Philip's jibe. When he saw that we were all smiling, he took his hands away.

"John, please keep up your conversations with Cyril," Philip continued. "None of us can do this since if we are seen with him the senior people at police headquarters will think that he's pressing on with a inquiry from which he has been withdrawn. With you, they are more likely to think that he is asking you to wash your dusty car."

More smiles. "And, chief, I imagine that you will not be able to help very much, what with the company, and the official events of Festac."

The chief sighed and his shoulders dropped. "Well, I shall do what I can, and I certainly take the point about listening. I shall be an intelligence gathering machine. I should be here all the time from now until the end of the festival. Henry and I will go to the regatta in Kaduna at the end of the festival. Whether we shall bring the culprits to justice in this world or the next I do not know, but I owe it to my friend the Hausa head man, Marcus's father, to let him know what happened and whether there is a rotten apple on the wonderful Diello tree."

We got up to go in our different directions. I asked John to get me a taxi into the centre of town. As I passed the chief, I asked him if his absence from the office in Ibadan would not be noticed.

He shook his head. "No no, not at all. My wife is going to sit in my office." He must have seen my slight look of surprise. "Not to do any executive duties, you understand, but simply to sit there. She is, very rightly, widely feared, and while she is sitting there the office will run like clockwork, you may be assured of that."

Soon after that exchange, I was on my way to the US embassy. I realised as we ground through the heavy city centre traffic and over onto the island, that my attitude towards my paymasters had changed entirely. Whatever respect that I had felt during our earlier meetings in London and here in Lagos, had dissipated entirely. I imagined them providing bland reassurance to their masters in Washington and London that all was well in happy Africa, and while the inhabitants sang and danced in their traditional ways, the oil would continue to flow uninterruptedly.

I was now cynical enough to accept that my own appointment been a part of the reassurance: "We had a chap out here listening but he heard nothing untoward. The great thing was that he didn't know what he was listening to, so his intelligence was entirely unpolluted."

George Mainbrace was on his own in the meeting room in the US embassy. He greeted me in the heartily enthusiastic but emotion-free terms normally adopted by two middle-class Englishmen.

"I say, old chap, wonderful to see you again and looking so chipper."

I nodded and looked at him before saying, "But you look a little down ,George. Anything the matter?"

"Well, funny you should ask, dear boy. I suppose I can tell you, since you have nobody here to tell. Truth is, old chap, London is on my neck good and proper. I'm getting it from Curzon Street and I'm getting it from the Foreign Office and today, for my sins, I am even getting it from the director of the British Museum. It's all about some ivory mask, except of course it isn't. Actually it's all about everybody getting on the wrong side of everything and then blaming the man on the ground. Me, in other words."

At this point the poor man looked quite distressed, and in a curious way my heart went out to him. His reason for being here was probably to escape stress, competition in business life, or even domestic disharmony. I had not a clue, and certainly did not seek enlightenment, but residual guilt, perhaps derived from breaking the Official Secrets Act or perhaps from my change in the view of my duty towards my employers, pushed me towards a sympathetic response.

"I am so sorry to hear this, and I'm sure that I cannot do anything about it, but since we have a moment, please tell me what happened. An extra pair of ears often adds something."

He looked at me gratefully. "Dear boy, that is so kind. And you did, after all, read philosophy? I am, as you know, the cultural attaché, but my reading is all geared up on things military. I tend to duck when things cultural come my way and send people across to the British Council offices. I did so when the federal government asked if they could use, as the symbol of Festac, the image of some old mask or other and I just said yes. Well, wouldn't anybody? I mean it's not as if they wanted to use a picture of our Queen, who, because of the Commonwealth is of course the Queen here as well. Why should I object if they wanted to use some old ivory mask from Benin? Then, of course, I did not know at that time that the mask in question was, in fact, in the British Museum.

"The thing is, dear boy, I had not quite understood the question. Not only did they want to use the old girl's image as the logo for the event, but they wanted to bring the ivory mask itself back here for the duration as a centrepiece for their cultural olympiad celebrations. Whizzo, I probably said. I'll ask the museum to put it in a plastic bag and send it over in the diplomatic pouch. That was when I got a bollocking from the British Museum. Apparently Queen Motherly Oba Idia of Benin was not in a fit state to travel, and they did not trust people who could not keep the air-conditioning on continuously to look after her in an appropriate manner. Fairly rough, I call it. After all, we did nick it off them in the great Benin raid of 1897, by which time they had already looked after it for some hundreds of years. Anyway, the BM was pretty sniffy, and made a complaint to the Foreign Office, and they sent me a real zinger. Told me that if there was any more of this then I would have to take my pants down in public and get six of the best. Recall home to Blighty and reassignment as cultural attaché to Ascension Island."

"George, this sounds awful. How did you get out of it?"

"By living on my wits, as ever, dear boy. Got an appointment with the Federal Minister of Culture and went off to do my diplomatic best to explain and apologise. It was a real punishment."

"So he wasn't keen to take the truth as you presented it?"

"No, not at all, and even worse, he had brought along the vice chancellor of the University of Lagos, who is apparently a great expert in all these things. This man read me a lecture. 50 minutes no less. Explained in great and glorious detail how the Brits came up the river and sacked Benin in '97. And how they ransacked the royal treasure house and took the mask away as hostage to future good behaviour, but the officers and men raided private dwellings and took away all the bronzes and images that they found. The professor claimed we made off with 40,000 items. Most of them went into private hands and keep turning up in the sale rooms. The federal government paid £200,000 last year to get two bronzes out of a New York sale room."

"Did they let you go after you'd heard the professor out?"

"No, not immediately. As soon as he ran dry Van, the minister, opened up. He was a lieutenant colonel from the midwest and said that if I wanted to do anything by way of an apology, then I should do something to help stop the continual loss of antiquities from the country today. He pointed out that he had piloted through a law in 1974 to make exporting antiquities illegal, but it still went on and apparently there is a roaring trade in Europe in things like the Nok terracottas. You won't know about this, but these apparently are as old as the hills and keep coming out of the ground in the plateau regions. He said that they are doing a book about this stuff for publication after Festac so I promised that the High Commission would sponsor it. You better bid for it, George, and get it done as cheaply as you can, my boy, or we shall be completely out of budget and I will have to live on pounded yam for the rest of the year."

As he spoke these words, the door opened and Cy came in, in a rush as usual and grabbing hold of the last sentence of a conversation that had not involved him.

"As a result of which you'll get much thinner, George!"

I looked at them both. If George looked harassed and depressed, then Cy looked as if Foggy Bottom had been giving him electric shock treatment.

"Has he been telling you about his problems, Henry? In my book, a few old artworks are not a problem. My problem is guns, and all sorts of people are asking me awkward questions about guns. So let me ask you this, young man, where would you go if you wanted to buy 1000 or so powerful submachine guns, with no questions asked?"

"Not a clue," I responded, with an inner feeling of happiness about my total ignorance.

"Well now, as it happens, you are a very privileged young man and I can tell you the answer. Neither my people nor the Brits will sell you those guns and neither will the French nor the Germans for that matter. But in East Germany or Czechoslovakia you can pick them up kinda easy. No problemo. Darn commmie bastards don't much care who shoots whoever out here. They just need the foreign exchange. And guess who I'm learning all of this from, Henry? Your friend that you met in the airport! Do you remember Baban? I get towed down to the Dodan barracks last week, and I am told that consignments of Czech munitions have recently been tracked into the country by his men, and that they hear that more are on the way. I'm informed it's my job to stop this trade, and if I cannot do that, I can at least tell Baban and his colleagues where they are going and who is involved. So of course you know what I say. We are not involved. We don't meddle in people's internal affairs etcetera, etcetera. He raises one eyebrow and says that meddling in other peoples affairs was exactly what he thought I did. But if we want oil concessions and mineral rights this was an affair which we should start meddling in right away."

Cy paused for a moment and looked at me very intently. I thought that he was about to ask me whether I had discovered anything relating to the enquiries that I was meant to be pursuing. Yet neither now, nor later, did either man ever ask me to report on my work, which was indeed fortunate because I didn't have anything to report. Both men were far too full of these pressing issues.

Cy soon resumed. "I think, Henry, we are going to have to alter your brief a bit. I can at least tell you about my conversation with Baban. He told me that the federal government was worried and perplexed by rumours of an imminent coup. Well, we have discussed that here before. There are always rumours of a coup and it's always about to happen tomorrow. He said that he could vouch for the fact that it was not the senior officers who were disloyal. He had them covered. The junior officers were much harder. In any case the senior officers did not need guns: they commanded regiments, and they had armoured cars and defensible barracks. The generation of soldiers who won the war had now been sitting on the government for a decade. It was a junior officers who joined the army after the war who now felt that the older generation should move on."

"Did he mention any names, Cy?" asked George.

Cy laughed in a nervous, high-pitched cackle that seemed to include the questioner as well as the question.

"Now has he ever mentioned any names? The man is discretion personified. All he said was that he wanted to find out where those guns had gone and who had them, and that he wanted real evidence that he could put in front of a military tribunal."

I thought it might be time for me to ask something. Almost without thinking, I said, "Last time I was here, in your very interesting briefing, you mentioned Baban and showed us a picture of a close associate of his, whose name if I recall correctly was Ibrahim Kabi. He was a younger man with army connections. Might he be a good person to talk to?"

"Actually, his name is Kabeysi," said Cy. "Henry, your instincts are quite right and your memory very good. Last time I checked he had sunk out of sight but we know where to find him. I certainly think that he is the sort of person who might pick up useful rumours and gossip. I'll make sure we follow that up. Right now, however, there is a guy in northern Virginia waiting to hear from me. Thanks for coming in, you two. I will be in touch shortly to set up the next meeting."

I walked with George out in the building and into into the intensity of the late afternoon sun. His car and driver were waiting. He kindly offered me a lift to wherever I was going, but I declined. I said I would walk over to the nearby hotel, have a drink and get a taxi there. In truth I had had enough of my two strange bosses, and wanted to be back in the company of Philip and John and our own doughty chairman. But no sooner had I began to cross the yard in front of the embassy building than the chairman's car swept into view, with John hanging out of the driver's window and the grin which split his face, telling me that he had had a successful mission and was full of information that he was dying to divulge. I climbed into the passenger seat and the cool interior of the car with great gratitude.

CHAPTER 11 PHILIP

WAS IT ENOUGH? Philip questioned himself as the meeting broke up. Henry was rushing off to the US embassy, John was heading for the hotel to see the flower girl, his chairman was already on the phone to the Alaafin of Oyo, paramount chief of his branch of the Yoruba, tracking down coup rumours. He liked to feel that he was a mentor in different ways to all three of them, and that he'd been useful in the meeting by pulling all the strings of the narrative together. Yet he was still left wondering whether this was quite enough.

It was a familiar feeling. The frustration of the war years, when he could not get back inside the enclave and could only speculate about what was happening to his wife, his children and his friends, told him everything that he felt anybody needed to know about feelings of frustration and inadequacy. In his powerlessness, he had quite consciously decided that he had to accept that the very worst had happened, that the life that he had led as a schoolmaster was now over, that it was unlikely that he would ever again see his wife and children and return to his previous state of life. He had wondered for a decade about the paradox that this implied for him. So many people had told him that you could only go on if you had hope in your heart. Yet he never shared with anyone his own conviction that he could only go on by abandoning all hope and fully accepting that he was the sole survivor of the life that he had once known, and begin to build an altered existence.

He felt that he had been right in his choices. He

had soon learned the dreadful truth about his immediate family. In the months after the enclave was starved into submission, there was a daily drip feed of news listing the death toll. The only person about whom information was scarce was his mother. A few people had seen her but said that she had disappeared as they were being surrounded. No one knew anything for sure and so she joined Philip's private list of the lost, the dead.

He remembered that he was rebuilding the house, ruined by shelling, when he heard a real commotion at the other end of the village. He consciously did not want to be involved. His mind was playing a mantra: "Finish the house, then leave for the west and find a job." He smiled at the thought when people asked him why he was rebuilding the house if he was not going to stay. He said it was so that his ancestors would have somewhere to live. No one questioned that. No one knew that the war had entirely separated him from any of his earlier beliefs in his ancestors, in the guardians of forest and river, or in the austere Christianity that Father Campion had tried to instil in him at the mission school. Philip felt that he had looked at the limping war wounded begging at the kerbside in every town and village in the state and thought of himself as a sort of moral amputee, shorn of a sense of duty and direction, of right and wrong, of leaving things just a little better than he found them which motivates the lives of many people.

In his mind's eye, repairing his old home that day, he saw himself turning away from the wooden steps that he was hammering into place. He recalled the shock when he realised what the commotion was all about. There, surrounded by the remaining villagers, shouting, laughing and cheering for the first time since the war had ended, stood his mother. She was not smiling. She looked at him with a look of unbearable intensity, until they collapsed into each other's arms. As she did so, he realised that she was carrying a baby on her back, and that there was another toddler clinging to her right hand.

He remembered in the following weeks, as they restored their home together, he regularly tried to pry out of her the story of her survival. She was revealing nothing. Mostly she would refer to it as the time when "I slipped away." Of course, he and everybody else assumed that she had hidden in the forest, but how she had kept alive all that time remained a mystery. Even the children she brought with her were a mystery. However, they were the foundation of what became an orphanage in the house.

Philip postponed his plans and worked to get the yam garden planted again. Soon this resolute woman – Philip guessed that she must be about sixty in age – was resuming her market stall, one of the first as the Enugu market reopened. As time went on the weight and shape of the mother he remembered gradually returned, and something returned to him as well. When he said how much he admired her work with the orphans, she had shrugged.

"Well, they are there, and we must do for them everything which is humanly possible. It is not a choice."

He had felt that she was right, and that he had no choice other than to help her. Now, he knew why he was going to the west. That was where the jobs were, the jobs were that would pay the surplus that he could send home to support the orphanage. That was why he was needed. As this began to sink in, some of his anger about the war, its devastation, and his own losses began to retreat.

His mother gave him back a renewed certainty, and simplicity, of purpose. He too would do what was humanly possible.

All of this made him wonder about that meeting in the compound dining room. Back in the village, immediately after the war, he could not bond with anybody. Yet here he was now, ten years later, with a friend like Sam, who, if he had been a fighting man, would have been on the opposite side, and they were both of them really dedicated to getting this Universal Primary Education thing right, ensuring the resources reached the hard pressed schools and helping to compensate for the lack of classrooms and teachers by getting a book into every child's hand. This was a wonderful relationship, Philip knew, but not the most wonderful thing that had happened during his time with the publishing company.

First , of course, there was John. Again, he owed so much to his mother. She had taken the boy in when, he guessed, the orphan was around ten or twelve. He had attached himself to Philip, who had found him looking at an old car manual and used it as a way of teaching him to read. Every time Philip went back to the west, the boy begged to be allowed to go with him. His loving and generous nature made that an easy wish to grant, and when some years later the chief had needed a driver, Philip made a recommendation. He grinned at the memory of the risk they had taken. No one knew how old John was, whether he really could drive as he boasted, and it was certainly true that he'd missed most of his education because of the war. But Sam wanted to help. Philip was delighted at the way in which things had worked out, and he relied upon John's companionship as his lodger.

Then along came Marcus, another bright young man caught between religion, a conservative society, family expectations, and a deep desire to explore the world around him. And then, most unlikely of all, came Henry, a young Englishman, the product of a traditional middle-class upbringing, but with the same desire as Marcus to explore the world around him. Each of these people, Philip thought, had a variety of reasons to suffer from guilt and anxiety. Is this, he knew, they were just like himself, only his guilt began when he wondered why he was alive in a world inhabited by the ghosts of the Biafran dead.

Philip had realised, too, that each of them craved something he could offer: a listening ear. Like his mother with her orphans, he decided, he would be the person to whom they could tell anything and everything. He would be non-judgmental. He was not beyond asking a few gentle questions, but he was very careful never, in any circumstances, to advise people what to do. He thought that, once they had discussed it, these three people would always know what to do. Yet, as he thought about it, he realised that he now had a family once again. Nothing could replace the one that he had lost. But the one he had gained included an "elder brother," who was apt to act in haste and then repent, an old mother who would never ask for anything for herself, and three "sons," with one of them crudely struck down at the very moment when his adult life was just beginning. Bringing clarity and understanding, important elements of justice, to that dreadful event, came into Philip's definition of what he should be doing as he struggled to do what was "humanly possible."

When he had a real problem, Philip found, thinking about something else often meant that when he returned to the problem again, it would seem to have solved itself. He felt he needed to make a practical contribution to the detective work, and the answer was staring him in the face. The scene of the crime. We are all rushing around trying to gain new information. Yet we cannot be sure that we have gleaned all that we can from the crime scene up in Mushin. My best contribution is to speak to that nice Inspector Cyril whatever his name was and then go up and look for myself. We are trying to be amateur detectives, but if the police have given up on this then we must try to be a little more professional ourselves.

Philip then did something which even he, in retrospect, admitted was fairly crazy. Having glanced out of the window and seen that all the compound cars were absent, he picked up the telephone, dialled police headquarters from the card which Cyril had given him, asked for the inspector and actually got through to him. He was so shocked by all this working in the way that Lagos never worked that he almost forgot why he had made the call. But not for long.

Soon he was asking Cyril whether in the circumstances, it would be alright for him to go up and look at the crime scene, especially as the police were no longer interested. Cyril was happy.

Then he added: "If of course it was the crime scene. I can't recall if I've told you this, but the only thing in the file for this case is the forensic report, and the only thing that they found which would interest anybody is that there was probably not enough blood underneath the body for him to have bled out there."

"So what does that mean?"

"Well, it could mean that he was murdered somewhere else. The forensics people, strange to say, do have a certain logic. They argue that if the body was dissected in the way that we saw at the scene of the crime, all of the blood would have poured out of the body. In fact there was some under the body but not enough to satisfy them that the killing and the dissection took place there."

"Am I looking for a large pool of blood somewhere else?" Philip was thinking aloud, but Cyril answered the question.

"Probably won't be there now – covered in dust or eaten by dogs. Unless, of course, the murder took place indoors. But you can hardly do house-to-house searches in Mushin, looking for blood on the floor!"

Nevertherless, Philip found himself in a taxi going up to Mushin. He half regretted it. What did he really expect to find? Something that nobody else had seen? Had he made the wrong choice? Would he have helped more if he had gone to the National museum and investigated antiquities smuggling? He had friends there who would help.

He was at the point of telling the taxi driver to turn round when he realised that they were coming into the square in front of the Baptist church. The taxi driver stopped beside the railway track that ran across the open space. He had also pressed the automatic door-opening lever, causing the passenger door to swing open suddenly. Besides almost knocking a tiny schoolgirl off the pavement, this invited Philip to get out, which he did. As he paid the driver, he wondered, as he had many times before in his life as a schoolteacher, how it was that these little children, in immaculate uniforms and starched white shirts with braided hair appeared for school in the biggest cities and in the smallest villages, despite the poverty, the filth, lack of mains water, and the scarcity of bathrooms . The sacrifices of their parents said it all. The little girl was skipping away laughing with her friends, all equally immaculate despite the coating of dust settling on them all from the departing vehicle.

Philip walked slowly in the heat, across the square, past the front of the mosque, and into the narrow lane where the body of Marcus had been found. It took more of an effort than he thought to get to the turn in the track. Of course, the forensic team tent had gone – he had half expected it would still be there. He gazed at the pavement, and the weeds and the dust where there was nothing to remind him of what he had once seen. Remembering the cursory police search of the area, and the fact that the briefcase that they had given to Marcus was still missing, he walked down to the end of the lane, and then came back up, carefully looking over fences onto the flat roofs of shacks and huts. But this, he thought, was stupid. Surely, a black attaché case from a smart London store would stand out here so obviously that either the police would have seen it or someone else would have stolen it. He had wasted his time. He strolled back up the lane, and into the square, trying to work out where would be the best spot to find an empty taxi. Probably on the other side of the church. He picked his way over the railway lines and was scanning the traffic on the other side, choking with dust and diesel fumes, when he was surprised by a voice behind him.

"Hey, Mr Philip, you come to Mushin and not visiting me?"

He turned to see the local bookseller, Ola Oladipo, and realised that he had just passed the man's shop. He knew Oladipo well. He was one of the main school book contractors for Lagos state. Without thinking where he was, he had been standing outside of the man's retail premises, where it said, on the side of the building "Oladipo Books, stationery and school supplies. Since 1950."

Philip turned to the bookseller. "I think I must be going blind. Of course, I am outside your beautiful building, and I am reminded that last year we came to your 25th anniversary."

"Yes, and you were one of my sponsors for my dinner, out there in the square. Your chief spoke, and so did my school teacher. It was a grand night. We certainly drank some beer, and you look as if you could do with one now."

Philip's response was immediate. "How welcome a cold beer would be!"

The two men stepped across the pavement and reached the door of the shop just as all the lights inside it died.

"Feel your way through to my back room. Now we will have to have several beers, since there will be no customers during the power outage, and the beers will get warm if we don't drink them."

"Excellent reasoning," said Philip, feeling his way to a chair at the little table in the back room. Oladipo produced the beers and they sat for a moment in a contemplative silence, as the cold beer washed a layer of Lagos dust off lips and tongues and throats.

"I had not realised that you had so much space here," Philip began. "I always thought the shop itself was impressively big, but I did not know you had rooms behind as well."

"Well, yes," came the reply. "You know that I used to live here when I started? Then I got married." He smiled." You will know that marriage changes everything! She wanted a bigger house, and both of us did not want to live together all day as well as all night. Then came children."

"You could've built more rooms at the back or on top – that's what everybody in Nigeria does."

"You forget, this is Mushin. We are all crowded together here. No space for anything. And in any case, up on top of me in the shop was the gymnasium, where they trained the boxers. Then I rented my space here from the state government."

"I thought the Boxing Federation had brand-new headquarters down by the city bus station - and yes, thanks, I will," he said in response to the offer of a second beer.

They clinked bottles and Oladipo sought to clarify. "Yes, they do. But when they moved I saw my chance. With the military government in charge things are always easier, although let me tell you, the cost of buying a policeman these days is quite incredible. But the expectations of the staff of a military governor – that's something else, man."

"But you came out alright?"

"Oh yes, I bought, but in order to do so I had to rent a warehouse that just happened to belong to the brother of the man I was dealing with here. This is Nigeria."

"How ridiculous! So you have to rent a warehouse somewhere else when up above in the old gymnasium you have enough space to do your warehousing!"

Oladipo nodded somewhat sheepishly. "It's true, but what can I do? They said that I could get a good rent for my upstairs room, but it has always, until recently, proved really difficult. This is a place where 20 people live in a room of half of that size."

"You have found a tenant now by the sound of things?"

"Yes, I have been lucky. A guy came in here and asked if they could have the room for a reading group. They are all young guys, and they say that as they are a reading group it is very good to meet in a bookshop. They choose a Nigerian novel and say they read to each other. They meet in the evenings, so I do not know since I am not here, but to judge by the bottles this reading is thirsty work."

Philip was impressed. "Even if they drink, what we want is young Nigerian men to read Nigerian writing. Surely this is so, Ola?"

"Of course, of course. I quite agree. And they are nice people. Pay rent on time. Buy the books from me downstairs. Multiple copies. I find nothing wrong with this and even if I joke, I am grateful. The only odd thing about them is that they say they want nobody else to use the room, so that only if they meet a few times each month, they pay the rent as if they were there every day. But again, I cannot complain."

Philip's mind was elsewhere.

"What I want to know is what they read?"

"Nothing too surprising. Chinua Achebe. Cyprian Ekwensi. Recently some TM Alamo."

Philip considered this carefully. Two prewar Ibo writers: that seems slightly unusual, although the Yoruba family sagas and village stories of Alamo would be quite natural. Oladipo broke into his thoughts.

"The guy who took the room seemed well educated

to me. Of course I have not met the rest. He said they were mostly like him, ex-army. He said that he is now in the tourist business with gift shops."

But Philip was still pursuing his previous train of thought. "Perhaps, Ola, I should send you some of our new African writers series for them to try. They really do need to move on to the postwar generation."

As he said those words the lights came back on, flickering and hesitating and then brightening the whole room.

"Only an hour," said Oladipo. "We were lucky this time."

"We were," Philip confirmed, "but now you will have customers and I must get on my way. I imagine you are bidding for the Universal Primary Education state contracts? We shall look forward to working with you on that, especially since our addition of "Forest of 1000 Daemons" is on the book list in the Yoruba language section."

"You bet," said the bookseller, ushering Philip towards the door, and almost bumping into him as Philip stopped dead in the doorway.

There it was. Or its exact copy. Standing next to the door alongside a box of empty bottles, a black attaché case. Philip was stunned and struggled to ask an innocent question. "Where did you get that very fashionable briefcase? I would like to buy one too!"

"Oh, that's not mine!" came the reply. "The cleaner found it upstairs and I'm holding onto it until I see my tenant again. And there you see," he pointed to a box, "What I mean about empty bottles!"

A customer had come into the shop and was standing by the till. Philip took in the initials MB on the handle of the attaché case.

"You need to look after your business, Ola," he said, "but I wonder if, before I go, I could have a look at the room upstairs. If ever your reading group departed it might be a good place to do some teacher training sessions, especially with the new maths curriculum coming on. Promise I won't disturb anything."

"That's quite okay, no readers here until the evening, help yourself. Here is the key and the stairs are just to the right on the other side of the window."

As he told it afterwards, Philip climbed the stairs very slowly. The key opened the door easily and he found himself in a large and surprisingly light room, lit by two skylights. All the same, he flicked the light switch and four wall lights added more detail. In the centre, on a large mat ,was a table and nine chairs. Philip imagined the boxing ring being there. There were benches around the walls, and on one of them were several piles of books, all of which seemed to be copies of titles by the authors that Oladipo had mentioned. So they don't take the books home to read outside of this room. He walked to the centre of the room and rested his hands on the table. What had happened here? What really had happened in this room?

He straightened up, and as he did so his eye caught something at the edge of the mat, extruding from beneath its edge. It looked like a shadow, was his first thought. No, not a shadow, a stain, a yellowish, brown stain. He bent and pulled the carpet to one side and saw an extensive and much scrubbed mark beneath the matting.

He knew, without a shadow of a doubt, that he was standing at the very place where Marcus had died. He had to get Inspector Cyril Fagunwa and his forensics friends into Oladipo's bookshop as soon as possible. But right now he had to get out of there himself without letting anybody know of his suspicions, or indeed his certainty about what had happened in the former gymnasium.

He pulled the mat carefully back into place. Then he put out the lights and locked the door behind him as hurried down the stairs, and put the key alongside the till, where Oladipo was serving another customer.

"I'll be off now, Ola, but the room is perfect and if ever they don't want it, then we certainly will."

And with that he was out of the door, searching the traffic for an empty taxi. He was lucky, and soon he was heading down to the company compound. As he sat there, the two problems that he now faced seemed overwhelming. On the one hand he had to get Cyril into the murder scene without alerting Oladipo, and through him the people whom he presumed to be the murderers.

On the other hand he felt strongly that they needed to find out what was happening in that room. Whatever was being discussed there obviously had wider implications. The murder itself, however dreadful, was part of something larger. Yet no one was going to find out about what was really happening unless the plotters continued their work without being aware that they were being watched.

It would have been less difficult, Philip thought, if he could simply take the issue to the "authorities". But it was the police commissioner and the detective chief superintendent who had called Cyril off the case. Even the chief might not know who to trust in the military government. Everyone that they were likely to speak to about this created fresh risks of being stopped from continuing the investigation, risks of warning the murderers that someone was on their trail. This was a problem that Philip had to reveal at the compound dining room table, and see what the four of them came up with as a group.

CHAPTER 12 JOHN

JOHN COULD HARDLY contain himself by the time he reached the hotel. The traffic had been so slow. They were checking registration plates again on the bridges, so he was glad that he had remembered to put the right ones on before he set out. The roads around the lagoon were crammed as usual, and he kept on thinking that he should use the time to work out a strategy for questioning Bimpe. But what if she wasn't there? She had been angry with Ibrahim when he last saw her. Was she still running the flower shop and was she still employed by him? He recalled that his excuse for a visit was to report on Mishi and her state of health, but how did he turn the conversation to Ibrahim and the need for more intelligence about that mysterious man and his business activities? How did he convey to her, beyond what he had said already in the Festac Village, that if she was short of companionship then he knew of a company chauffeur, with use of a car some evenings, who could provide it. Fela was performing at the festival. So was Stevie Wonder. Despite their conversation last time he really had no idea of her tastes in music or indeed in anything else.

Elated and worried, anxious and happy, burdened and eager, he at last guided the car with difficulty into the hotel car park, got out and locked it. Then, as he edged through the hotel doors, he was disconcerted to see her coming across the lobby, carrying a large bouquet of flowers.

"Oh John, how very convenient. Please hold these

while I get a taxi to deliver them. Then I will fetch your chairman's orchids. His wife will love these. They come from the Cameroons, although I think they are sometimes seen in your part of the world. Won't be a minute!"

This was not how it was meant to have started. "Have you got a spare minute?" Or: "Can I buy you a coffee in your break?" Or even: "Are you free for dinner?" The chairman had given him a 50 naira note that morning "pending expenses," and it was burning a hole in his pocket. That was what he had rehearsed during the drive. Nothing had prepared him for standing in the centre of the lobby amongst the smartest people in Lagos, carrying a large bunch of flowers. But nobody seemed to notice anything out of the ordinary, and Bimpe quickly returned, smiled, took the flowers and left him again. Then a few moments later she was back and in charge.

"Well, John, it is really good to see you again. You were so helpful last time we met and I was so grateful. I now hear you are helping again. Come over to the shop and let's have a chat."

He did what he did best, and obeyed. Soon he was telling her all about Mishi, about her new job and her accommodation, and her pleasure at being out of Lagos.

Then, it seemed to John, a miracle took place. She took his hand and pressed it and said that he must be her messenger and send her love to Mishi. Then she pressed it again and said how grateful she was to the chairman and John himself for making sure that all of this happened, and that she thought often of her duty to help the poor woman, a victim of attitudes to powerless women that were so common amongst Nigerian men, including the dreadful Ibrahim. She of course could look after herself much better than Mishi. She could walk away, whereas poverty and lack of education made it much harder for Mishi.

This gave John his chance. "Well, my chief is not like that, and we do not like those attitudes in our company. But I am surprised that you are still here at your shop and working for Ibrahim?"

"Well, that's the funny thing. Ibrahim seems to have disappeared. I have not seen him, well, since the day after you and I last met at the festival village. He told me that he was selling his franchises at the hotel to somebody else, and that it would be their decision whether to continue to employ me to run the flower shop. Two days later the man who delivers parcels came in and said the gift shop was closed and would I sign for the parcel. So I did! Then the hotel manager came in and said that Ibrahim was nowhere to be found. He had checked out, and the porter said that he had mentioned that he was going up north. But when I was over at the club doing the flower arrangements there, the secretary said that Ibrahim had gone to Europe on one of his trips. So I do not really know where he is. The hotel manager said that the flower shop must go on working, and that he would pay me to look after it and the souvenir shop and the kiosk until Ibrahim came back. Suits me! One job and three salaries! We put a spare bell from the reception on the desk in here and then people can press it if they want flowers when I am next door selling postcards."

She leaned back and stretched out her long, curved and beautiful arm to ring the bell on the counter behind her, stretching her blouse over her chest in a a way that made John feel distinctly uncomfortable. It was a relief when she noticed a customer in the gift shop and got up to cross the corridor and serve them. Yet it seemed that in only a few moments she was back, and this time she was carrying a parcel.

"This is the parcel that was delivered earlier. It might be that I should be doing something with the contents – putting them on display or something – but I'm a bit reluctant to open it without a witness. Will you be my witness, John? I certainly don't want Ibrahim to come back and accuse me of stealing something!"

John was certain that he too wanted to see inside the parcel, but decided that too much enthusiasm would be out of place.

"Of course, I'll help if you really want me to. Why don't we get a piece of paper and write down on it everything that we find in the parcel, and both sign it afterwards. If anything is broken in the box then we should note that as well. We should also note down any indications on the outside of who sent it, and attach any delivery notes or enclosures that we find inside."

There was a short silence. John could see in her eyes that she was considering his caution and wondering if he was protecting himself against her as well as against Ibrahim. Then she seemed to come to a decision. She broke into a slow, teasing grin and responded.

"We business people certainly must be methodical. I admire that. You see I had no proper training. Everything I know I've learnt from doing the job. My dad worked in the docks but he was killed in a container accident four or five years ago. Mum was Efik, she went back to her people, a village near Bonny. She's better off there. I couldn't look after her here. And if I couldn't, my brothers certainly couldn't. So I think I've really been very lucky."

There was a pause, and then she said, "Why am I going on like this to you, John? You are so quiet and easy to talk to, I suppose, but you must tell me if you don't want to hear all this rubbish. Tell me to get on and open this parcel."

John smiled and looked directly at her as she fiddled with the string on the package. Once again she had made him a little compliment. Did it mean, as he hoped against hope, that she was at least a little interested in him? It was so hard to tell, especially as she seemed now totally concentrated on undoing the string.

"Surely a flower shop has a pair of scissors?"

His words made her look up, and she pointed to the sideboard. He was there in a moment, found the scissors on the shelf, and handed them back to her.

"Is there any name on the outside to indicate the sender?" he asked.

"No" , she replied, "only the details of the carrier company in Jos."

She was inside now, unfurling the brown paper and exposing the cardboard box. The scissors got her quickly inside that, and her fingers went down into the straw inside. Her fingers emerged with a small terracotta figurine, about 4 inches tall. She held it up and turned it round, and they gazed at the face of what seemed to be a clown. Its eyes protruded, its tongue poked out over a jutting lower lip, and its ears seemed to be bent forward, as if listening.

Bimpe spoke to the terracotta directly. "You are a really ugly little fellow, but if, as Ibrahim says, these were some of the first models of people made in Africa. over 2000 years ago, he claimed, then maybe everyone was ugly then. Pity we don't have the originals, not just these reproductions. Then we would be rich."

She had now finished unpacking the box, and was refilling it with the straw. Between them, on the table, were six pieces of terracotta. Four were complete, and two fragments. One of the other complete ones, of a woman whom John presumed must be a goddess, had a huge nose and long ear lobes that came down as far as her chin line. They fascinated him.

"Does the shop get a parcel like this at regular intervals? And do you sell them from the shop?"

"No, they come about once a month, and then Mishi has the job of packing them into boxes which go with a selection of our other tourist stuff to Europe."

She leant forward in her chair and peered at the shop across the corridor, and then pointed.

"You see there, on the middle shelf? We send some of those replica Benin bronzes, for example, and some of those small masks, which are actually made, Ibrahim said, in a factory in Dahomey."

John knew that he now had to keep this conversation going at all costs. He could no longer tell whether continuing to listen to this deep, resonant and musical voice, or the cause of his detective work was uppermost in his mind, but he knew that he had to keep her talking.

"Now let's write down the details of each of these little fellows."

He proceeded to do so, trying to note some distinctive features of each one until they were happy that they would be recognisable from their descriptions.

"I bet people laugh at them a bit when they come out of the box in Europe. Where do they go to, anyway?"

"Oh, only to two addresses, I think Ibrahim said one was in Czechoslovakia and one was in East Germany."

"Do you want my help to do Mishi's job, since I was responsible for helping her to escape?"

Bimpe smiled. "Remember, I wanted her to escape and you gave her a better chance than she would have had in this Lagos human dungheap!"

The last words were said with vehemence, but John wanted to keep things on track.

"Well, if you need it," he said. "I am sure I can be trained as a packer. However, I don't suppose we even know exactly where they have to be sent."

"Oh yes we do."

This was said in a tone of triumph and Bimpe got up, strode across the corridor and into the packing room behind the gift shop. She was back in a moment.

"Here it is, the packing instructions. They always are hung on a peg behind Mishi's packing table." He took the clipboard from her and looked at the two sheets attached to it. Each one had a list of objects to be included. At the bottom of each list was the single word "Nok." Below the lists, on each sheet, was a different address.

He concentrated hard. This was where you needed a photographic memory. He could make it simpler if he just focused on the companies and the towns in the address, rather than the names of the people, since this would give most information to those who were awaiting him back in the company compound. But even this was very difficult.. The one that had East Germany at the bottom of the address was going to something termed "Wiesa-Kamanz" in a place called "Saxony". The address with Czechoslovakia at the bottom was going to something called " CZ" at "UHERSKY BROD".

It made no sense to him, but Philip and the chairman were clever, and Henry had good contacts, and he was sure that they could sort it all out. He had to re-member it all and to do that he felt he had to go and go quickly. He had to escape from the distracting and beguiling influence of this splendid young woman, or he would forget everything, even his own name.

Yet leaving was the last thing he wanted to do. It was a real wrench to get up and say, "Bimpe, I really have enjoyed our talk and I really do want to come back and help some more if I can, but right now I have some jobs to do for the chairman and I must go and do them!"

She looked at him with what he thought was a mo-mentary sadness. Then she said, "Of course, of course, you have your job to do. But, John, I have so enjoyed your company. Do come back when you can. I will ask the manager what I should do about packing things up for these addresses. I have the chairman's phone number but do you have a number for your Lagos compound where I could reach you?"

He wrote it down for her, and then picked up the notes that they had made on the terracotta objects.

"I am going to sign this and put the date on it, and perhaps you should do the same?"

She nodded and added a scrawl that could've been anything. It seemed just possible, John imagined, that she could be one of the millions in Lagos who could not write, though he had seen that she could read.

He grinned cheerfully. "Keep it in a safe place," he said as he left.

He had not yet reached the lobby before he heard her call his name. He turned to see her standing there with the chairman's orchids.

"Oh, thanks, I almost forgot. And, well, I wonder if it's possible… You may like to go to Stevie Wonder, or

Fela, I am sure we could get tickets … Through the company I mean… We are always being sent tickets, complimentary ones I mean, and the chairman never uses them, so I could ask… If you were interested."

She ended his misery. "Of course, John, I would love to. I like everything, anything you can get. Let me know."

John fled to the car park and drove out into the Lagos rush-hour, almost indistinguishable from any other hour. He sat in traffic repeating the names of the European towns and companies in his head while simultaneously trying to build a mental archive of every word uttered and every movement made during the afternoon.

He entered the compound with the barely controlled propulsion of a space vehicle returning to earth. The guard scarcely had a moment to raise the barrier. He abandoned the vehicle in front of the bungalow steps, the driver's door swinging open as he bounded into the building. Finding Henry in the living room, he seized a piece of paper and a pencil and demanded that Henry should start writing things down.

They had a forceful argument about whether the first letter in "Czechoslovakia" was a "T" or a "C", with John insisting on what he had seen and Henry insisting upon what he had been taught. The visual record won. Then both of them realised that they were competing because they were excited, so they sat down on the sofa and stared at the piece of paper.

"This means something, Henry, and it means something important."

"Yes, I know, but what exactly what does it mean?"

Then Philip ambled in, a shambling, bear-like figure foraging for food.

"Are you two hungry or is it just me?"

"John is back," Henry said, "and look what he has brought us! Just what we asked for."

Philip leaned over the back of the sofa and read what was on the piece of paper. "These are the firms to which the parcels are going? Well done, John. This is terrific, especially when you have had other things on your mind."

John did not respond. Philip tried again: "Yes, Henry, I was aware of the return of our investigator, and no doubt the chief was as well. He's probably out there now checking to see if he has any rubber left on his tyres."

Normally this gentle teasing produced a strong rebuttal from John, who gave as good as he got. All it got now was a slow smile, and putting a hand in his pocket, he passed the slender figurine of the laughing man up to his tormentor.

"All these jokes at my expense, and after I brought you a present from the souvenir shop."

Philip took the terracotta in one hand while passing the paper back to Henry with the other. He gave it a cursory glance, and then stepped past the sofa and threw himself into an armchair. He held the object close to his right eye for what seemed an age, and then said,

"John, I take it all back. This is a real breakthrough. This is no souvenir. I am as sure as an amateur can be that this is a Nok figure. We will have to get that confirmed by the National museum, but you, John, my brilliant friend, have given us our first clear indication of what Ibrahim is all about: he is a smuggler of antiquities, whatever else he might be!"

The three of them looked at each other. Their thoughts came out in a jumble. John was wondering aloud whether Marcus was killed because he had discovered this secret, while Henry was trying to add up the value of a shipment using the figures quoted by his paymasters at his last meeting with them. Philip, as was becoming his way, gathered up all the strands and tried to summarise.

"Okay, let's imagine that each of these little objects" – he held the figure in the light – "has a price for collectors or the museums between 30 and 50,000 naira. Mishi worked for Ibrahim for about two years. We do not know the frequency of the parcels – some of that will have depended upon illegal digging up in Benue or Plateau – but if a parcel went to one or other of these addresses every month over this time period, we could be talking of a robbery worth 5 to 6 million. But I really wonder if Marcus and his brother and other army officers were involved in a plain, straightforward theft. Surely there must be more to it than that? I think, John, that you have successfully got us to the beginning, but certainly not to the end!"

The three looked at each other, and then up at the chief as he came in to the room.

"Philip, good news from the Ministry of education. They are extending the Kanuri language contract in Bornu. Just imagine it. Typesetting a language for the first time in history! I find that so inspiring."

Then he looked around and realised that the minds of his colleagues were running on a different track. Once they had briefed him on the findings from Oladipo's bookshop and then John's conversations with Bimpe, he looked closely at the precious terracotta figure and then nodded at Philip.

"Philip is right. Our big issue now is timing, as much as all the other things that we still do not know.

And I agree with the thought that these army men were probably not just criminals: they had something else in mind as well. So we have to go about things quietly and carefully, or else everybody will run to the bush and cover their tracks. I am going to go and see the police commissioner. I need to find out who stopped further investigation into the death of Marcus, and why he thinks that happened. I may have to pull hard on our boyhood days in Abeokuta, but there is kinship for those of us born in the shadow of the Lion Rock and I intend to lean on him very hard! And I am anxious to hear, Philip, what the rest of you are going to do."

"For my own part I think I have privately and quietly to verify that the little fellow is genuine. To do this I may have to pose as an illegal reseller, but it must be done. John, I know you will want to be seeing your friend the inspector. Tell him from me that if he can get someone into the upper room at the bookshop, there may be blood remaining between the cracks in the floorboards and this could provide a sample. A police raid would create the sorts of problems that the chief has alluded to, so he will have to think of a clever way of getting in there. And Henry, you really do need to get back to your contacts and ask them about these addresses in Europe: see if they mean anything to them. If at the same time they know any more about our friend Ibrahim, then that could be pretty useful too."

Everyone nodded, and the chief stood up, still holding the terracotta. Philip gently eased it out of his hand and said, "Sorry, I need this little fella with me! But I do share your fascination. We were doing this 2000 years before the British empire, then itself only 200 years old, invaded and "discovered" us! This is the story you should be telling back home in Shropshire, Henry!"

Henry shrugged. "They would not believe me any-way. No one knows any history, no one knows very much about the world outside England. World history? Not a chance. It would never get onto the curriculum. Now, if you guys could arrange a breakthrough in the artificial insemination of buffalo that we could apply to cows then it would be talked about from Oswestry to Much Wen-lock, and even beyond!"

John thought, as they left the room, that these sessions usually ended with jokes that he did not fully understand. It was also true that, once it was decided what they were all doing, he ended up driving the car. This time he had the chief in the back and was heading for police headquarters once again. The chief was going to have "cocktails" with the police commissioner and while this was going on he would try to have a covert few minutes with Cyril to brief him on what they had been doing.

They were driving in the opposite direction to rush-hour, so he had to change his registration plates again, but the journey was quicker and there were no police checks on the bridges. Soon the chief was making his way up the main steps, all swishing robes and chiefly importance, while John slipped up the side staircase and knocked timidly on the inspector's office door. Cyril was delighted to see him, put the engaged sign on his out-side door and sat silently while John gave a full account of been happening. Cyril made notes and asked a few questions.

When John's briefing was over, Cyril promised that he would find a way into the upstairs room above the bookshop in Mushin, and then, as if he had had a sudden thought, he rummaged in his in-tray and held up a piece of paper with a photograph of a thin faced European man with a note attached.

"This man is wanted by Interpol for drug smuggling, arms dealing and stealing artworks and antiquities. Can this possibly be a coincidence? The circular came to all of us in the detective squad because he is said to be in Nigeria at the moment. His name is Holgar Pipek. You and your friends should keep your eyes open for him – he sounds a very dangerous character, although I know nothing as yet to connect him with Ibrahim, who, by the way, seems to have disappeared or is anyway lying low. We checked the hotel and they have not seen him, and if he went out through the airport he certainly used a false name on the passport. We will keep looking. Give Philip and Henry my best."

John reached the car again just in time to see the chief sweeping majestically back down the steps. He threw himself into the back seat and rubbed his hands vigorously together.

"Well, John, I've put the heat on that old fellow properly this time, and, as we detectives say, he came clean! All the same I am not sure that this takes us very much further forward. In fact, it was Baban and military intelligence who were putting the pressure on him. Even before the body was found and identified, he had a message that a high-ranking Hausa family member would be found murdered in the city and that he should put his most incompetent investigator on the job. With typical Yoruba prejudice, though, I say it myself, they gave the job to the one officer who wasn't like them. Wrong choice, I would say. Fagunwa may not be the smartest investigator in Africa, but he was smarter than they were.

"They soon got worried that he was finding out too much and going too quickly, so back came Baban and his people with the demand that all investigations cease. So why was that? Well, the police commissioner says he does not know, and I believe him. For a start, anyone who told him would have to kill him immediately afterwards. That man is such a blabbermouth! He was like that aged eight, and nothing has changed. Incontinent with the truth! How he ever came to be a senior policeman, only his family bank account and his relatives in the military government can tell us.

"But even if we do not know why military intelligence acted like this, then it would be an un-Nigerian activity not to use our ignorance to speculate wildly. And do you know what, John, we both concluded? This whole thing has something to do with the rumours of a coup. Did this murder take place during the plotting of a coup d'état? Baban has form in this sort of race. No wonder, if this is true, that the police ran away from the problem. We have seen so many governments overthrown that nobody wants to be implicated in the knowledge before it happens. If it doesn't happen, that can be as fatal as being on the wrong side when it does. We come back, John, to the simple questions. Why was Marcus there and what did he know? And how was his brother implicated?"

John glanced at the rear view mirror. The chief in this mood was better than having the car radio on playing Sunny Ade. Then he would fall asleep, fully fortified by the police commissioner's cocktails.

CHAPTER 13 CYRIL

CYRIL SAT AT his desk for a long time after John's departure. He realised that he had a real liking for the young Ibo driver. He had a sort of openness and directness that the policeman, dealing daily with the lies, deceit and complicity of the criminal classes of Lagos, found hugely refreshing. For a moment he almost fancied that in the east people were more direct. Was it a function of huge cities, or a characteristic of Yoruba officialdom? Or perhaps for the teeming mixtures of people from all over who found themselves in Lagos, keeping yourself to yourself became a form of survival. Lagos was so big. He had seen a UN estimate that the population was over 10 million and would rise to 25 million in the next 50 years. The newspapers said that it was the biggest city in Africa. He wondered about all these estimates. Who knew where Lagos began or ended? Who could measure the flow of people coming in looking for work, and the flow returning to their homelands? He felt sure of only one thing: it was always bigger than the last estimate.

Something bugged him about this murder investigation. It had taken an amateur and an accident to find the murder scene. He and his men, banging on doors and looking over area walls, had signally failed to do that. They had to do better with this next stage.

When he and his sergeant drove into the square in Mushin, he told Maro to park beside and not in front of the bookshop building. He got out and walked round to the front door. There were two or three customers in the shop, and a man was sitting behind the counter, reading a newspaper.

Cyril walked over and leant on the counter. "Mr Ola Oladipo?"

The man looked up at the policeman. Something in his expression told Cyril that like every other citizen of Mushin, this man could identify a plain clothes policeman at 500 paces. No point then in trying to hide the truth. He produced his police ID and showed it to the bookseller.

"I am here on private business. I am chairman of our school's Parent Teacher Association. Our kids, my eldest included, have to learn Hausa for their second language. But, man, the books are so poor. I have a little Hausa myself and I think I probably have more than whoever wrote that book! Has one of the big publishers done a better course? Longman, or perhaps Oxford? When I saw your shop, with such a huge stock here, I knew that I had to come in and investigate. If you have something, then perhaps I can buy some samples to take back. If our teachers like them, then maybe we could order class sets from here?"

If Cyril was hoping that an appeal to the bookseller's cupidity would overcome his suspicions of a policeman, then he was quite correct. A class set was thirty-five copies, a language course was a book a year for three years. Oladipo could already hear his till ringing through 105 books, despite the fact that Cyril's children down in Benin were in fact thumbing their way through Nelson's Ibo Mbu Book 1 at this very moment.

Cyril recognised his moment and took it. "We had a nice guy in from one of the publishers to speak to our parents and teachers the other day about the importance

of making the right choices. He said that they were setting up some teacher in-service training sessions to help
teachers get the most out of their resources. We promised
to send some of our staff to try it out, and when I asked
where it was taking place, he said they were considering
holding it here, above your bookshop. He certainly spoke
highly of you, Mr Oladipo."

The bookseller looked slightly flustered. He evidently was not used to praise, and flattery from a policeman was both disconcerting and slightly suspicious.

"He is one mighty fine man, many of these publisher guys are. He said you were renting out your upstairs
room, Mr Oladipo. That put me in mind of my other
problem. I am in charge of the police gymnastics. We
are competing next week against Ogun state. You know
how it is, Mr Oladipo. Some of my colleagues have a
tendency to get slow and fat. Sit on their backside in
an office or a squad car. Chew too much Kola. Smoke
too much ganja. Drink too much beer. Have you tried
this new one? The one that is meant to reach parts of
Nigerian bodies that other beers do not reach? It has
suddenly reached parts of our division. Secretly, between
the two of us, I am sweating on the line here. When we
lose to Ogun and the police commissioner is saying to
me, 'Fagunwa, you are in charge of training. Our gymnastics squad could not catch a criminal in a wheelchair,'
how am I going to explain this to the people of Lagos?"

Oladipo saw the point. The idea of policeman doing gymnastics was new to him, but he certainly caught
the drift. Indeed, he often joked to his friends that the
reason why policeman walked so slowly was the great
weight of naira notes folded into their wallets in their
back pockets.

"I see that you have a real problem there, inspector. It must be very hard to make a policeman perspire. But buying some books for them is not going to help them, surely?"

"No, no, I am telling you my problem, Mr Oladipo, but I am not sure that you can help me. Real issue is this: these men hate to train in police headquarters, because the other policeman laugh at them. Such heartless people! They laugh at good men who are trying to improve themselves. So I always need a quiet place to train my men. And when this publisher guy said he was renting your room, I thought, surely he won't need it all the time, so I wondered if I could rent it too. beginning very soon, if it is free. We only have a few weeks until the competition, and my needs are urgent."

Oladipo believed in the power of networking, but this was ridiculous. Two people trying to use his upstairs room in two days! Yet he saw that it all happened quite naturally. He had not seen Mr Ibrahim since his reading group had held their last meeting. After a meeting, Ibrahim normally checked in with him and paid the rent. This time, no visit and no rent. Was the reading group still in existence? Had it broken up? Linda had said the room was left in a dreadful mess. Maybe it would be wise to take rent from whoever offered it. Bird in the hand, as people said, although he had never had a bird in his hand. Stupid English saying. At the same time, could be good to have friends at police headquarters. His only "friends" at the local police station were the ones who came in and took protection money off him every month. Maybe he could pay them out of rent paid by the police: now, that would feel good.

"Well now, inspector, it all depends. When is you

wanting it? How much is you paying? And can we fit you into the schedule?"

Cyril reflected on the ease with which deals could be made in Nigeria once the ground was cleared. A few simple checks in diaries and a pretence at paperwork, the seamless passage, so fast as to be almost invisible, of a 50 naira note from one side of the counter to the other, and soon both men were making expressions of great satisfaction.

The rental offered by the police was just right. Amazingly, the room could be ready this evening for the first practice session of the gymnasts from police headquarters. No, they did not need to have it cleaned again since they were quite sure it would be perfect. The two men shook hands, and Cyril was about to move away from the counter when his eye caught an object in the doorway leading to the bookseller's private office.

"I did not realise that you sold attaché cases as well, Mr Oladipo."

The bookseller turned round in confusion until he followed the inspectors gaze.

"Oh that, that's just something that got lost, some folks left it here, it's not mine, and I don't sell those things. It would be some kid in Mushin going to school with something like that."

The inspector was still considering the case closely. "It's just like one that we gave the old detective chief superintendent before he retired. We had to order that one from London. You know what? I really envied him that case. Anyway, do you know who lost this one? I expect you are waiting for him to come in and collect it."

Ola was now confused. What did the inspector want him to say? Did he expect to be given the attaché case? Was this part of the deal? He squirmed slightly and played for time.

"I really don't know, inspector. The cleaner, she found it. She didn't know where it came from either. It's just lost property."

"Aha," said Cyril, with obvious satisfaction, "this is really good, Mr Oladipo. You have helped me out no end today by being so flexible and in particular letting my gymnasts use your room this evening. And now I am able to do you a good turn. I am on my way back to police HQ and I can drop this off at the lost property office on our ground floor. Save you a trip into town. Gives me real pleasure to be able to help in some small way."

Oladipo was about to urge the policeman not to bother, but before he could speak the man was across the room and had grabbed the case.

"Good day, Mr Oladipo," Cyril said as he left with the case under his arm. "Look after my boys when they come this evening."

Moments later he was climbing back inside his car. The sergeant was asleep and there was a faint smell of ganja. Cyril was too excited to ask questions. He placed the attaché case carefully on the backseat and issued his orders.

"Now, Maro, I want you to get that case finger-printed carefully, and especially around the handle and clasps. Then I want it opened and an inventory made of everything inside it. Then go and see the forensics boys. I have briefed them already. They need to be wearing their sports clothes, by which I mean tracksuits and trainers." He paused for a moment, reflecting that this was what they normally wore anyway, before continuing, "And you should go with them, dressed the same. You are a sports team at a training session. Make sure they are very thorough. If blood was spilt in that room we must find it. and no one must know that we were there looking, especially your fellow police officers."

Waiting made Cyril restless. He spent the next few hours wandering around HQ asking his colleagues if anyone had seen Ibrahim recently. No one had. Cyril was surprised to find that they all knew him, or knew of him. Many of them, when you mentioned the name, often said something like. "Oh, you mean the army man?" One even called him "that spy from the Dodan in civilian clothes" and a very senior inspector called him "Baban's agent covering the club and the hotel."

Cyril had asked why he said this, and his colleague replied that they had always assumed Ibrahim's businesses were a front, and that he was placed in the strategic meeting places on the lagoon to check on visitors and pass on messages for his master in military intelligence. Nobody seemed to know much about Ibrahim's associates, or his family background. Everyone said that he seemed to have come from Abuja, a small town in the centre of Nigeria. It was a complete mystery to Cyril, he had heard of it but knew nothing about it. No one had seen Ibrahim for two weeks or so, though someone said, "I expect he's gone to Europe on shopping missions for his masters – they tell me in Customs that he does this all the time, and he never has to pay any duty on anything."

This was all gossip, Cyril acknowledged to himself, but he found it interesting all the same. He was building a picture of Mr Ibrahim Kabeysi, this genial, party-loving man who had left a bright career in the army to run some retail concessions in a major hotel. A man who entertained lavishly at the club next door to the hotel, whose circle of friends seemed to include many of his former contemporaries in the army, and who seemed close, if rumour was to be believed, to some influential people at the very top of the military high command. This man was a dealer in antiques and seemed to have regular trading connections in central Europe. But his profile seemed in some ways empty. Cyril could not explain it to himself, but he was worried that he did not know Ibrahim's mother tongue. As well as his native language, he did not know his travel background or his religion. Given where he came from, he could be anything. His first name sounded vaguely northern, and at first hearing it Cyril thought he might be Muslim. But his second name could have come from anywhere in the west. Ibrahim was a puzzle, and Cyril knew that his purpose in life, or certainly his purpose in Lagos police headquarters, was to solve puzzles.

The afternoon power outage, and the rising heat in his office, slowed every thought process down until sleep came to the rescue. He was eventually awakened by his young sergeant breezing into the office. He liked the young man, and he thought that he would go far, but he did sometimes wish he was not quite so aggressively noisy in his movements. Most Nigerians were born in huts, Cyril thought sourly, and only came to a world with doors later on in life. The convention of knocking on a door, or opening or closing it quietly had to be acquired, and in these skills his young protegé was definitely deficient.

"What is it?"

The young man was excited and unabashed. "I got three clear dabs from around the clasp on the attaché case, boss, and they match the body in the mortuary. Did you notice? The case has his initials on it just like Mr Henry said it had. No other prints that I can find. Maybe he just brought it into that room, put it down and, well, didn't take it away because then he was dead."

Cyril looked at his sergeant thoughtfully. "Mr Henry also said that he was worried that the boy was killed for robbery, for someone to get the attaché case."

"No sir, I do not think that this is the way it went." The sergeant was on a roll now, and had more to give. "The attaché case was locked. There is no robber in all of Lagos who steals something and does not open it, or who steals it, closes it afterwards, and locks it up again. Besides, the locks were not broken and the case was not forced. These are combination locks. Did the dead man handover the combination? No, sir, it is my belief that robbery was not the motive here."

Cyril's duty as a mentor compelled him to put a spoke in these confident wheels.

"Now we will have to open the attaché case and see if its contents are disturbed, or there are blood stains inside, or anything else that would indicate a robbery."

"I have done this. I have picked the lock." (Cyril wondered for a moment about skills unsuspected – and how they had been acquired). "I have examined the contents. They are undisturbed. There are no blood stains."

Cyril was impressed and annoyed, though for reasons he was unsure about.

"Okay, Maro, very good. Now go and make me a list of the contents."

"Yes sir, the contents are as follows." The confident young sergeant held up a list that he had been holding all the time and began to read. "Two pencils, one rubber, 28 paperclips in plastic box, seven rubber bands."

Cyril sighed: he was being punished.

"One pencil sharpener, one stapler, one clear plastic ruler, metric on one side and inches on the other, three documents. The first document is a prioritised list of duties for the warehouse management and for checking and auditing of consignments of books being brought into and out of the warehouse. It is three pages long and it is signed by the chairman of the company. The second document, which is 29 pages long, is a plan for bringing in containers full of books from printers in Hong Kong by way of the docks and the airport and distributing them to schools across the country. It is signed by the dead man and by Mr Henry Kettering. The third document is a letter, handwritten and in Hausa. It is one page long."

Cyril smiled. "You have done very well and I am very pleased. Now all we have to do is to get the letter translated and we should've done a good day's work."

"I think your Hausa is probably as good as mine, sir, so I went to a sergeant in traffic division who I know comes from Zaria, and he was pleased to help us. The letter is from the dead man's father. In it he tells the dead man to do his duty and to abide by his faith. He says that he is confident that the man will do well, that he and his mother have faith in him, and that he must work loyally for the chairman of the company who has given him this opportunity. He says that his son will always be his son and must come back and visit often and that his house will always be his son's house forever. It is a very touching letter, sir."

The two men were silent for a moment or two, until Cyril said, "Well, I would have been proud if my father had written me a letter like that, only he could not write his name, let alone a letter. Now, my most excellent sergeant, do you have anything else to report?"

"Yes sir, as instructed I went with the forensics team. It would have amused you, sir, to see those clowns pretending to be gymnasts. But I took the precaution when Mr Oladipo let us into the room to lock the door on the inside so that he could not see what we were doing. I do not think, sir, that he had suspicions. We searched the room carefully and our colleagues took away three good samples of congealed blood from between the floorboards, which would explain why the cleaner did not sweep it up. I also found this."

He held up, for Cyril to see, a brass pin, about 3/4 of an inch long. On its head was a tiny shield, with a dark blue background, and in silver letters the initials 'CZ.'

"Do you know what this is, sir? I have never seen anything like it. I'm sure that no Nigerian ever brought this into that room!"

Cyril took the pin into his fingers and turned it round ruminatively. "I think this is what Europeans and Americans call a lapel pin. They wear them to identify themselves in some way or another."

"So this could be a man's initials, sir?"

"No, I think it identifies the wearer with some form of club or college or religion or political group or something like that. I will ask Mr Kettering what he makes of it."

At that moment, power returned to the grid and the aircon began again with a great shudder. Combined with a knock on the door it made both men start slightly. The two forensics men were there, now looking more professional in aprons.

"I knew I was right," said the younger one. "He

could not have been killed on the pavement, there simply was not enough blood."

The older one was like the straight man in a comedy duo, trying to hush his companion while getting the story out in a logical fashion.

"What he means, inspector, is that we came back and did the blood test immediately. Our samples from the room we visited this afternoon match exactly the blood type and make up of the victim's blood. We are now sure that the victim was murdered in the room above the bookshop, and it is all here in our report."

He put the document down on the table and Cyril leafed through it.

"A very thorough job, gentlemen. I am grateful that you were able to play along with my little trick, and that you were able to be so thorough and get your results to me so quickly. This is excellent work and the Lagos force should be proud of you."

The two men smiled and the younger one said, "Well, sir, we like working for you. Interesting work and you are always so appreciative."

The older, taller one nudged him into silence. "What he means, inspector," he said, "is that you are the only one who uses us. The others think that they are too clever to need us, and that it is easier to beat up a suspect than to use some science."

"Or get paid for walking away," chimed in the other, before his companion made excuses for both of them, said the inspector would need time to read the report and pushed his workmate back out through the door and closed it behind him.

"Well, sergeant," began Cyril, "we now have the place where the murder took place, and we have eliminated robbery as the reason for the crime. What do we need next?"

"The murder weapon, sir, the motive, and the murderer."

"Yes indeed, sergeant, these are all things that we must now concentrate on, but what are our next steps?"

"Sir, our objectives must be clear. We must detain and question Mr Ibrahim and the dead man's brother: both of them are possible witnesses even if they did not commit the crime themselves. Then we should ask our new friends in forensics to describe the murder weapon that we are looking for. And then, sir, we must think, and you have all the knowledge here, about ritual murder and why this looks to us like a ritual murder."

"You are really getting the hang of this, sergeant. Your priorities are quite right. But remember, we've been taken off the case, so anything we do must be cleverly disguised. If we are able to locate Ibrahim and the dead man's brother, our amateur friends must do the questioning. I wish it were otherwise, but we are not officially doing anything to solve this case. I should be telling you not to work on it."

"I will work on it just the same, sir. This is the first real police work that I have done since I joined this force, and it makes sense of the training I did for my sergeant's exams and which I have not used for two years. I suggest that we get to the bottom of this, using all the help we can get from the victim's friends, but doing all we can here without the detective chief superintendent getting suspicious."

He grinned in a way that made Cyril aware of how real his enjoyment of the work had become. The inspector leaned forward over his desk and gazed at the tiny lapel pin. When he spoke, his voice was full of conviction.

"You know, sergeant, this case is not about ritual murder. That is part of an effort to distract us, and we will not be distracted. I am more and more convinced that young Marcus was there by accident, that he gained knowledge which was dangerous to somebody, and that he was killed to secure his absolute silence. In the morning, please get the photos that forensics took at the scene where we found the body and put them on my desk. Let us have a long hard think about ritual murder."

CHAPTER 14 HENRY

NOW THAT I was down in Lagos almost all the time, the heat became a major factor in every day life. I had found Ibadan, away from the coast, and catching the breezes if there were any on its hill, far more comfortable. In the compound, by contrast, I woke up perspiring, felt tired by lunchtime, and collapsed onto a hot, sweaty bed with real gratitude and as soon as I could politely do so after dinner. I knew now that everyone felt the same, whether you were born here or had only arrived a few months previously. People spoke of "acclimatisation" but for most it was a joke. Many had debilitating fevers like malaria that came and went in regular, often monthly, cycles. When I thought about it, I did not know how the great festering city got through each day. The dense humid air laden heavily with dust, smoke and petrol fumes made me feel as if I was carrying a backpack full of bricks.

Yet, looking out of the window of the taxi on the way to the US Embassy for my regular meeting, the streets were alive with activity. Everyone in the city had a business, and many had several. Every time I walked down the pavement or crossed the street, someone pressed a business card into my hand. Not content with trying to buy the M&S shirt off my back – "it has resale value, man" – people wanted you to have your car washed, use their gardening service, patronise their laundry, repair your barbecue, and lay tarmac on your drive. No one was content with buying a billboard, handing out leaflets or taking an advertisement in the newspaper. They all told me, with unbelievably loud conviction, that the services they offered were the cheapest, the best, and the most valued anywhere between Morocco and Cape Town. At first I had found them slightly intimidating. I wanted to be polite and refuse these offers in a kindly way. Now, like the dust laden air, they were just an impediment to walking.

Entrepreneurial Nigeria was hard at work on the steps of the US Embassy, which seemed right. I pushed past a man cooking strange-looking snacks on a brazier, avoided a large lady with a brightly coloured turban who wanted to interest me in children's glove puppets, and reached the swing doors with the relief that I had sometimes felt when climbing out of the sea after a tiring and energetic swim amongst the breakers. It was cooler inside.

The desk clerk recognised me and directed me to Cy's meeting room. George Mainbrace was there, kicking his heels as usual, and we both stood looking out of the big plate glass windows over the gently waving palm trees in the lagoon. It must have been one of the coolest rooms in Lagos. As English men did then when they were embarrassed by an inability to talk in a way that may lead to a personal revelation or, worse, an opinion, we let the talk turn to cricket. Both of us were fearing humbling defeat at the hands of the West Indies, but I saw hope in a new young player, a real allrounder, called Ian Botham.

George disagreed. "Flashy fellow, always playing to the gallery." His stated preference was for Geoffrey Boycott of Yorkshire. "Now, here's what cricket is all about. A man who can come out to open in the morning and still be there at end of play in the evening. No matter if we score ten runs – cricket is not about spectacle, it's about defending your wicket."

Further discussion was fortunately curtailed by the arrival of our host.

"Cricket! It's the ageing process delivered as a sport! I went once to Lord's cricket ground with George's boss. Said I wouldn't go again unless I was anaesthetised! Now, Henry, the festival has been on for almost a week. Do you have anything to report?"

I confess that at this point I felt a new sense of importance. I had never had anything to report to my employers before. Now I did have something, I was not quite sure how to present it. The main thought in my mind was to tell them as little as possible about how I had come by the information that I was going to discuss. I would start where they had last left off.

"You remember when I was here last time, you showed me a picture of a man called Ibrahim Kabeysi?"

George did not look as if he remembered anything, but Cy said impatiently, "Yes, yes, of course, but you do realise that he is not really very important, and we only showed his picture because he is a known associate of Baban?"

"That's what you said last time," I replied. "But I did notice that he has opened a shop in the festival village selling the same sorts of souvenirs and trinkets that he sells in his hotel shop. I was able to come across the addresses that he uses in Europe when he sends parcels of these things to his dealer network there - "

"I don't see how that interests us at all," Cy broke in.

" - in East Germany and Czechoslovakia, behind the Iron Curtain."

As I finished my sentence, I saw Cy and George exchange glances.

"Do you, by any chance, have a copy of those addresses about your person?" George asked, in a deliberately unexcited sort of voice.

"Yes, indeed I do."

I reached into my pocket and took out the piece of paper upon which I had written the information which John had delivered. I was passing it to George when Cy snatched it. The American scanned it quickly, gave a low whistle and handed it on to George. Then he dashed across the room, took a fat reference book from the shelf and started flicking the pages furiously.

I watched with amused pleasure. I had never made any impact on either man before this moment. Cy dashed out of the room, came back carrying a folder, took a piece of paper out of the folder and handed it to George, who read it, nodding all the time.

This was turning into a performance. I felt that I was being left out of the loop. "Are those addresses significant or somehow important?"

The question I floated lay in the air for a moment as the two men looked at each other and the paper that Cy had brought into the room.

"Well, Henry, there are things here which we cannot discuss because you don't have the necessary security clearance. But I want to say to you that this is really significant, and to my mind it fully justifies our experiment in taking you on in the first place. Well done, young man."

The American flashed a brief smile, and George leaned forward and offered a hand. After giving me a vigorous shake with his meaty paw, he said, "Well, Henry, I can go a little further than our colleague here, since you are a British citizen and you have signed the Official Secrets act."

I must have blanched slightly at the very mention of the act that I had so blatantly broken when I had briefed Marcus. The palms of my hands were suddenly wet with sweat despite the air conditioning.

"CZ is the Czechoslovak national armoury. It's specialises in the manufacture of high power assault rifles. The export of these is a major source of foreign exchange in that country. They made over one million rifles last year, and we have found them in the hands of terrorists fighting the British in Cyprus, Malaysia and elsewhere. The East German address has less history but no less interest. It is also a military armoury. Last year it designed and created a new assault rifle and was proudly awarded with a supply contract for parts of the Russian army. In other words, they produce a gun that they think is as good as the AK-47. Yes, Mr Kettering, the two addresses that you have shown us do have real significance."

I heard what they said but my brain was whirring. Why would Ibrahim be sending tourist souvenirs to arms factories? I was not quite quick enough to get this into the conversation as a question. George had more things to say to his part-time spy.

"The really odd thing here is the fact that we are in Nigeria. These addresses, individually and together, have cropped up elsewhere in Africa in the last three months. A steamer hit a tug in Mombasa harbour and before it sank its cargo was salvaged. Kenyan customs found two crates from CZ marked to await collection from the freight forwarders office, but nobody ever came to pick them up."

"There was a similar consignment from East Germany that South African police reported in East London," Cy said. "They caught it in a routine check on its way up to Butterworth in the Transkei.

"Some of our people assigned to help security forces on the border between Namibia and Angola found a broken-down Land Rover with two cases of these guns in it, apparently abandoned. So we are very interested in people who may be running guns into African countries, yes sirree, as my friend on the other side of the room would undoubtedly say."

I had never seen the two men looking so animated. Cy kept waving my piece of paper in his hand. "I've got to get a cable off to DC, and there is a guy in Foggy Bottom who will want to run analysis on this!"

"Steady, my dear old fellow, let's first think this through. All the other instances we have are of guns being sent from what we may call the sources to peaceful African states. Now you would look at that and think to yourself one thing: destabilisation. Stands to reason. That's what these chaps do. Send in some guns, start a war, and get us in the west all upset and involved, free trade threatened, sources of raw materials at peril, et cetera et cetera. What we have not had, and this is clear from your file note, Cy, and I think my own notes would confirm this if I were in my own office, what we have not had, I repeat, is an instance of anyone sending anything to these addresses. I do not think that we even know the route the money takes to pay the manufacturers for their services. Indeed, I do not think we know even where the money comes from that makes those payments. But I think I can say with confidence that these people are paid. These arms consignments are not a charitable gesture. This is not Oxfam, or even the Red Cross."

The portentous weight of this blinding glimpse of the obvious silenced us all. It was the silence that I felt that I should break, however timidly.

"Look, I am not a professional in these matters, and you may laugh at me for saying this, but have we really explored the significance of what Ibrahim is sending to these addresses? Surely it is not likely that these rifle manufacturers are overjoyed to receive parcels of African tourist tat. Fake masks and imitation Benin bronzes. And can it be true that they run a wholesale dealership in such objects from behind the Iron Curtain? So might it be true that something else is going on here which we haven't quite grasped? I remember, George, that you told me that Baban had called you in and forced you to listen to a lecture by some professor or other?"

Cy was there first this time. "Okay, okay, I get your drift. George was subjected to a lecture on antiquities theft, and how these things are getting very valuable, and how the federal government is having to buy them back. Very expensive. And you seem to be suggesting that our man Ibrahim is not just sending over a few trinkets to amuse the gunmakers' children. You are saying that in those packages may be some high value artworks which these boys can turn into hard-currency and recompense themselves for their gun exporting efforts? Is that about the size of things?"

I nodded, and I heard pennies, cents and possibly even naira dropping all around me.

All of a sudden the whole subject of what I was doing in this room, the spying, the subterfuge, even the breaking of my undertakings regarding the Official Secrets act, felt deeply distasteful to me, wrapped up as they were in guilt and some less than worthy motives. Confusingly, I also felt a little satisfaction at this moment. I thought that I had made a contribution to the meeting, and so, plainly, did my colleagues. I had failed to spot "commies and chinks" wandering around Festac, but I had produced some intelligence worthy of the name, and even if that happened entirely by accident, I had confirmed the shady business which Ibrahim was conducting. Beyond that it did not take me much further down the track of finding who had murdered Marcus. I had to press a little further.

"Of course," I said, casting a fly over the tranquil waters of British and American intelligence, "this does not tell us who is behind Ibrahim. I doubt very much if he's working on his own. Are his backers planning a coup here in Nigeria as someone is in the other places you mentioned?"

"Holy moly! That is one hell of a thought, young man." The American raked his hand vigorously up-and-down his cropped crewcut hair as if he were trying to make electricity. "George, the boy's question poses us with one hell of a dilemma! Where does Baban stand in all of this? Is he pointing us towards a fire that he wants us to put out, or is he the guy with the matches, lighting the blue touch paper?"

"Well, we are probably fucked either way," said his British partner in crime. "If we tell him what we know, and he is eating Caspian caviar and drinking vodka with the comrades, then our tour of duty ends and we get to go home early. On the other hand, if he is pointing us towards something that he wants stopped, and we failed to see it, then we are off his Christmas card list and there will be no more snippets of insider info on which we depend to persuade London and Washington that we are actually doing some sort of a job without getting out of our armchairs to do it."

All of this suddenly made Cy more thoughtful. He

was no longer hovering, waiting for a fresh titbit to drop into the open maw of his pelican government.

"Jeez, George, we have to steer clear of Mr Baban for a little while until we know a bit more about exactly what is going on here. First of all, we need to put a watch on this Ibrahim character. We know where he hangs out, and those are the sort of places where our people do not look out of place. Check out his known associates, they pay some heavy dash. Money talks, people talk, we will soon get to the bottom of this."

I did not mention that it appeared that Ibrahim had gone missing. Some things are much better tackled by professional intelligence operatives.

Now the meeting broke up. Cy was quite effusive in his thanks. George accompanied me down the corridor and into the lift.

As we crossed the lobby he leaned over and whispered confidentially, "You know that this was all my idea, don't you? I mean setting up this job and employing you?"

When we got outside we found, to my relief, that we were going in different directions. He was bound for the club ("Who knows, Ibrahim might be in the bar"), while I was going back to the compound.

Just before he got into his taxi I received another whispered confidence.

"This could be really big you know. Could get me a NATO posting. Come to think of it, there could be an OBE in it for you – I know people who have access to the diplomatic list! And I know of people who have got a gong for much less."

As my taxi chugged its way through the melee that results when three lanes of traffic try to drive on one lane of highway, I wondered if the meeting might have been less successful than I had initially thought. I was sure that I had started something but I could not be sure where it would lead. I could see that I was now in their confidence and regarded as an important intelligence asset, but how far and how quickly was this getting me towards finding the murderers of Marcus? I was working myself into a degree of gloom by the time we reached the compound.

Philip saw me arrive and came to the door, exuding enthusiasm and clearly anxious to tell me something. I let him go first.

"You will never guess, Henry, where I have been this morning."

I saw that he was carrying a bag from the National Museum of Nigeria, so I said, "National Museum."

"How did you know?" Looking down, he smiled and said, "I see, the master detective at work! Listen to this. I went to see Bernard Fagg's assistant. I know him, you see. I coached his son in maths before the war so that he could pass the university qualifying exam. And the father is still grateful after all these years. Anyway, he looked at the figurine and agreed with us that it could be valuable, but actually the professor was there, in the building, visiting the festival. So we went in to see him, and when he saw the figurine, he said it was worth the interruption. He identified it as an early piece in the time period 200 to 400 BC. It came from Kaduna state, from one of three villages. He would have to check with the University of Frankfurt who did the original dig at the village, but he thinks might be the source. He had no doubt that it was original, he added.

When I asked him what its the value would be on

the open market he said, "£50–£60,000. What do you think of that?"

I was impressed. Getting the world authority to validate our little figurine was really important.

"He's going to provide us with a written opinion which we can show to the police," Philip continued. "I asked him to keep the little fellow himself in the museum and give us a receipt, which he did. I suggested that if everything turned out okay we might donate the terracotta to the museum. They were delighted at the thought."

"Even though we don't actually own it, Philip!" I broke in.

He smiled sheepishly. "I know, but if we catch the murderer and break up the smuggling ring, I bet we can wangle something from the museum. Wouldn't it be great to make a donation in the memory of Marcus?"

Oh yes it would, I agreed. It would be great but anything else that I might of been about to say was drowned out by the arrival of the chairman, driven by John. We went out to greet them in the yard, and I brought in the chief's overflowing briefcase full of books and papers and contracts, while John brought in a cardboard box full of food made by the chief's wife for our kitchen. He staggered under its weight. She obviously thought that the chief was being starved to death. Once we were inside Philip and I recounted the events of the day as we saw them, and it was then that I noticed how worn and worried the chief was looking, and how solicitous and comforting John was being.

"I am so glad," the chief said, in a very weary voice. "I wish I could say the same for myself. I no sooner reach the office when I had a message from Marcus's father.

"This is rare so I knew it was a real issue. John drove me down there, and we listened to a quite dreadful story. It appears that their oldest son, who, as you know, was the aide-de-camp to the Sultan of Sokoto, has been shot. They think that he has been murdered, but there were reports when I got back to the office that he might have killed himself. With a shotgun. And if this is the case, then this is awful for the family and their faith. Perhaps just as bad is that their middle son, their last remaining son, the elder brother of Marcus and his youthful companion, well, this man is nowhere to be found. The barracks at Kaduna have not seen him for weeks. Disaster is raining upon the heads of this fine couple. I do not know what to say or do to comfort them. John and I said what we could, and my wife will go down later to sit with Marcus's mother. But what is happening to this good old family? In all my years, I have not seen its like, and I do not understand it!"

We saw that we had a task in hand in reviving the spirits of our good old chairman. We set about it with goodwill, quickly getting a meal, sending our security man for fresh palm wine and engaging in conversation on anything else but the dreadful misfortunes of the Diello family. In time, the wine did its good work, and when the conversation touched upon Festac, something triggered the chairman's memory.

He reached deep into some secret pocket in the folds of the great agbada that swathed his body, and produced two tickets. Waving them in the air, he shouted, "Stevie Wonder, and I of course cannot go! But John, you can go and represent me!"

John looked at his boss in amazement. "Who is going with me? I am not used to these social occasions — I'm going to get it all wrong and make mistakes!"

The chief laughed. "This is not a social occasion, all you need for a concert is your ears. But I agree, you do need a chaperone to look after you. So, when I phoned up the nice lady at the flower shop at the hotel to thank her for my wife's orchids, I asked her if she would kindly undertake this task if I paid for dinner. This is one gracious lady. She kindly accepted the mission. So, are you now happy to go? And if you go, my boy, please, take a taxi."

He waved a bundle of banknotes in the air. "I am not having you drive my car on such an outing. I have to sit in the back, and who knows what things might have happened there if I loan the vehicle to you for this evening!"

The sentence ended on a guffaw of laughter from the chief. He enjoyed the moment, just as he enjoyed John's discomfiture and John's pleasure.

I glanced across at Philip and I saw that he was enjoying the chief's return to his normal buoyant spirits as well. We parted laughing, although, in retrospect, I am sure that each of us in the cell of himself was trying to come to grips with the latest twist in the Diello family saga.

CHAPTER 15 CYRIL

IT WAS RAINING quite hard by the time that Cyril reached his car, and the sergeant obligingly leant over from the driver's seat and opened the passenger side door. Cyril climbed in and looked through the windscreen at the dark grey clouds that covered the lagoon.

"Do we have this all day?" he asked.

The sergeant nodded. He needed to find a time to ask Cyril about the next stage of his sergeant's exams, but you had to catch the moment just right when you were dealing with Cyril.

Cyril was still gazing at the sky, reflecting that the rain was warmer on the streets in Lagos than the shower in his digs, and that even a real storm, not just steady rain like this, did little to dampen the dust or overcome the stench of open sewers, dead animals and discarded food that made the city so hard on the nose.

"Where are we going now, boss?" The sergeant had the engine running and was playing with the gear lever.

"Let's go down to the hotel again. I think we can both do a little more to see if we can find out where that man Ibrahim has got to. Even here, no one disappears completely. What do you say, sergeant?"

The sergeant grunted. "If you want a nice smell, sir, don't go anywhere near the lagoon waterfront, is what I say."

"I do not know where I would go to find a good smell in this place. Even Ma Rooney's massage parlour smells like a wet dog that has been rolling in bullock droppings."

"I don't know, sir. I never got to go there, on a sergeant's pay."

Cyril intervened quickly. "I didn't go as a paying customer, only in the course of a police raid. We were after a money laundering set up, but the raid was all hushed up in the end."

The sergeant judged that this was not a good time to talk about examinations and increases in the sergeant's pay. It was better to be a diplomatic listener.

"So you didn't find what you were looking for?"

"Oh, yes, we did! And we could have proved our case if we had not also found a military governor from the far north lying on his back and anticipating a happy ending momentarily. Military intelligence came down on the police commissioner like a ton of bricks and we were told that we had never been there at all."

The sergeant concluded that the rain had got into Cyril's sense of humour, and drove on in silence. When they got to the hotel, Cyril bounded out of the vehicle, and then leaned back through the open window to speak to his man.

"Park the car and then walk over to the club and talk to the staff and anyone else you can find. They should be used to answering questions by now. Have they seen Ibrahim? When was he last around? Then do the same up here at the hotel. Very casual, mind you. You are just curious, interested, not pursuing enquiries exactly but it would be nice to have a chat with him. Meanwhile, I am going to see the manager of the hotel."

Cyril went through the swing doors and found the lobby deserted. Just what he wanted. He went up to the reception desk and asked the clerk if Ibrahim was around. He did not want to disturb him if he was in his room, but had he been seen in the public areas of the hotel?

The clerk was just about to answer when the door behind him opened and the manager came out of the office. "I heard that. You are the police officer, aren't you? You've been here before asking questions about Ibrahim. You and everyone else! I am fed up with all of you asking questions I cannot answer. What I want to know is, why everybody is asking? Since he's not here I am having to do his work and arrange for his shops to be run and his concessions to be kept open. It is intolerable!"

Cyril smiled sweetly. "I thought that I was the only one who was looking. I am so sorry about your troubles. But, please, tell me who else was asking?"

"Well, for a start, we had a guest checking in here two or three days ago and he did nothing but ask for Ibrahim. Now he has gone as well - and without paying his bill. You are a policeman? You should be investigating that! Then we had military policemen here. Twice. Always asking for Ibrahim. I am really upset and so is the woman who runs the flower shop. She could not work yesterday afternoon, and she is not much better this morning. Those guys are rough, and according to her they wanted to see Ibrahim as well. What on earth has this man done?"

"I haven't a clue," lied Cyril proficiently. "I am just sent down from police headquarters to ask some questions. I will certainly chase up this guy who ran out without settling your bill. We do not approve of that. Let me have his name and address."

"His address won't help you very much – from memory I think he came from Czechoslovakia. I doubt if police expenses will allow you to go and collect it there!

His name, for what it is worth, was… boy, look in the register and give the man that guest's name. We gave him room 202, one of the best we have."

The clerk, who had been transfixed by the conversation, suddenly leapt into action. He flipped through a few pages of the register and then looked up and said, "Bruno Teitelbaum."

"Means nothing to me," Cyril said. "I can't recollect it from any of the wanted lists that get sent to us, but I will check carefully when I get back to the office. In the meanwhile, any idea where Ibrahim maybe?"

The manager shrugged. "I tell everyone, and I'm sure I have told you already, he comes from Abuja which, in case this news never reached you guys down in the Delta, is a little town in the middle of nowhere where nothing happens. Then again, he was always getting on aeroplanes and going to Europe, so maybe he just did that and forgot to tell any of us."

Cyril sensed that the prospect of further reasonable conversation with the manager was diminishing. He had heard all he needed about dumb people from the Delta. So he thanked the man, told him he would be back in touch in due course, and asked politely if the flower shop manageress was still on the premises. Could he have a quick word before he left?

The manager's face clearly indicated that he could speak to anybody he wanted to as long as he got out of the foyer quickly. He left and went down the corridor and into the flower shop. Bimpe had her back to him and he thought he noticed that she was shaking slightly. She turned as he came into the room and he saw that she had been crying.

He raised his hands and showed his palms and said,

"Goodness, my poor dear girl, you have had a rough time, I can see that. I am not here to cause you any difficulties, and I won't come in if you do not want me in this space."

She gave a faint smile. "Oh no, inspector, you are welcome. My friend John says you are a good man and that you try to help people. I'm just at a really bad moment. Can you or anyone help me to get away from here? I have just begun to realise that it is not safe for me here any longer. At least my friend Mishi is in a safe place, and I was just about to see if I could find John to ask him to help me in the same way. But you know, inspector, he is always driving a car and never near a telephone, and every time I try to phone his company the telephones are not working – power cut, line down, line busy – you know what it is, inspector."

She looked down despairingly and Cyril desperately wanted to see that broad smile and those laughing eyes once again.

"My sergeant will be back in a minute. As soon as he's here I am going to get him to drive you down to the company compound. I know that John and his boss are there all week, and so are their friends. I know that you will be in safe hands and that they will look after you."

She looked up at Cyril with pleasure and relief creeping back into her face. "Oh, I would be so grateful. I have a bag in my quarters. It will only take a few moments to collect it. I was going to go back to my people, but it is a long journey and I do not know whether they would welcome me."

Cyril gestured toward the chairs at her little table and they both sat down. "Before you go, just tell me, if you can manage it, what has been happening to you that has made you so upset?"

She paused for a moment, seeming to look past his head at the displays of tropical flowers in the window. "Well, this week began brilliantly. John took me to the Stevie Wonder performance at the festival. I have never seen anything like it, inspector. It was brilliant and I was so happy when I got back here. One of the waitresses from the restaurant had looked after things in the evening and I wanted to check if she had locked up and, perhaps, if there were any messages from Ibrahim. I was shocked when I walked in here. The door was open, and there was a man in here. He grabbed my wrist, before I could scream put his hand over my mouth. It was terrifying!"

Cyril clucked sympathetically and put a hand out as if to stop her from going too fast. "Please go slowly, and give me every detail you can remember. These details could be valuable if we are to catch this man and stop him."

"Yes, I see that. Well, at first I thought he was English, but when he spoke the words came out in a funny way like a Yoruba speaking Ibo. He was not used to speaking English. And he smelt. Tobacco and some sort of hair cream. The craziest thing was, he was wearing a jacket and a tie. And big black shoes."

"Sounds like someone who has never been in Nigeria before."

"Yes, that was what I thought, but I only had a moment to think because he bent my wrist behind my back, up towards my shoulders, until I was screaming at him to let go."

"While he was hurting you, did he ask you anything?"

"Yes, time and time again. He kept asking where

Ibrahim was. He said Ibrahim owed him money, and if Ibrahim and the money were not available he would take me as a hostage."

"This was very frightening. And you, poor girl, you must've been terrified."

"Oh yes, I was. I could hardly breathe because of his hand over my mouth and nose. At last he could see that I could not answer his questions and he relaxed his grip a bit and I was able to tell him that Ibrahim had left, and that I would not be a good hostage because Ibrahim would not want me back. I said he could have any of the money which was in the till here, or in the gift shop. But it would only be the float, you see, because the hotel manager would have cashed up the tills at the end of the evening and put the day's takings into the hotel safe. Then he said something, not in English, but from the way he said it you could tell it was something rude. Then he said he would kill me if I ever spoke about his visit. Then he left."

Cyril considered the story for a moment, before saying gently, "You must've been shattered. So what did you do after that?"

"Well, I sat here for a good while. I thought that if this man really was a client of Ibrahim, will I get into trouble when Ibrahim comes back? If I tell the hotel manager about this will I also get into trouble? I wanted to tell Mishi but she was not here. I wanted to tell John but we were in a power outage. So I went back to the staff quarters and went to bed, and got up early and packed my bag in case I needed to leave quickly during the day. Then I came back here first thing in the morning."

"Was that when you started telling people about this man's awful behaviour?"

"No inspector, it was not. I opened the gift shop first, because people like to come in and buy a newspaper. The papers were in a big pile by the door and I started to carry them in and sort them out, when all of a sudden two soldiers came in. They were northerners, for sure, inspector. I recognised the dialect of Fulani. It was all so sudden. One of them grabbed me and pushed me down on my knees. He held my hands behind me. The other slapped my face. Ibrahim, Ibrahim they were shouting. Where is he? Tell us where he is hiding! I was screaming and they were shouting, and guests were looking through the glass side of the shop from the corridor, and the manager came running in and told them that I did not know where Ibrahim was. He said I was just a shop assistant. He didn't know either."

"So they let you go?"

"Yes, inspector, they did and everyone could see that I was a mess. My nose was bleeding onto my tunic. Look inspector you can see the bruises are still on my arms where they held me."

She pulled up the short sleeve of her dress and Cyril could indeed see the deep indentations of strong fingers from the day before. But she had not finished.

"Then, inspector, the hotel manager told me not to tell anybody about what had happened. He said making complaints about these people would lead to trouble for the hotel, and if the complaint was traced to me then I would be sacked. I need this job, inspector."

"So you have not said a word to anyone about the hotel guest, and only the hotel manager knows about the army people?"

"That's right, inspector, I was very scared, and, even more scared this morning when I came in and there was an army man waiting outside of the door of the flower shop. More senior than the other guys, better spoken, a more educated man. He asked politely if I had heard any more news of where Ibrahim was since yesterday. I said no and I began to cry. And he came over to me and he stood very close and said, not loudly but in a very determined strong voice, 'Baban wants to know this. What Baban wants to know he finds out, whoever gets hurt on the way. Do not speak to anyone who asks about Ibrahim: just speak to us.'"

Cyril now found that he had put his hand on top of hers and was patting it in what he imagined was a fatherly sort of way.

"Don't worry, we will get you to John and his friends as soon as we can. But after all those dreadful warnings - what gave you the courage to tell me?"

"My experience of policeman in Lagos has not been a good one, but something about you gave me confidence. Maybe the fact that you don't sound like someone from Lagos. John said he liked you and that gave me courage to tell you what I know. I thought, what sort of country can I be living in if I cannot tell these things to a police inspector?"

It is a good question, thought Cyril, and the answer is "the sort of country where the army can push the police around any time they like." But he did not say this to Bimpe. Instead he said, "Now you go and collect your things from your room and I will locate my sergeant and we will get you on your way. And by the way, while I'm thinking of it, you did great things by showing John what was in the parcel, you know. The little terracotta statues that were sent here for the gift shop. I would like to take the box with the rest of the things with me back to police headquarters. I will give you a receipt for them. Are they around here somewhere?"

"Yes, John said they were useful and I was so pleased. I have the box here with the rest of the items, and would it be useful to have this as well?" She held up another box, the same size and shape is the first one, but this time unopened.

"This one arrived today and I've not yet opened it. I was a bit upset, not working as I usually do, you see?"

Cyril did indeed see, and as he took the two boxes from her, his sergeant came into the room.

"Just when you're needed" said his superior officer. "Please put these two boxes into the boot of the car, and then drive this young lady safely down to the company compound of chief Samuel. Please make sure you leave her in the safe custody of the chief, or his driver, John. Then bring the boxes back to me at police headquarters."

Cyril wrote out a receipt which Bimpe placed in the gift shop till. He said goodbye and watched as she and the sergeant crossed the foyer and went out into the car park. As she went through the doors she turned her head and smiled back at him. In a moment he felt a surge of relief that he was bringing her to a place of safety, and a dim echo of the sensations that she aroused in John. "Lucky young devil, that boy John."

He found a taxi and began the journey back to his office. Once there, he reviewed the day. It felt productive, but for the life of him he did not know what it meant. He now had a ton of evidence for lots of different people wanting Ibrahim, and he could only presume that this was to do with a deal or deals that had gone sour, but what deals and where still evaded him. And who was this mysterious stranger who spoke English with an accent and had terrified poor Bimpe? He did not find it hard to believe the girl: she would have to have been an extraordinary actress to have carried that off. He felt also that the business of people being blackmailed not to say anything rang true – it came up daily in almost every police interrogation that he conducted. Power over employment in a country which had no safety net - losing your job could mean eviction, homelessness and starvation – was a force that could silence even the most resilient.

Before he settled down to routine work on the case files (this usually meant reading reports from patrolmen or traffic police and deciding not to do anything else about them), he thought he would just check if they had anything on the guest list who had neglected to pay his hotel bill. The "wanted" file had just three items in it. One was a note from the Portuguese police about Joao Olivares who had committed a murder in Lisbon .He was thought to be a crew man on a ship coming south down the west African coast. The second was a note about a Lebanese merchant who was accused of smuggling Mercedes cars for the use of army chiefs in various west African states (they will never find him, thought Cyril). And the third was something already seen: the Interpol notice on the wanted criminal Holgar Pipek. So nothing new there, thought Cyril as his eyes lightly drifted down the closely typed Interpol information page.

'Known aliases and false passports,' he read softly to himself. 'Shlomo Hayek (Israel), Klaus Guderian (Federal Republic of Germany), Bruno Teitelbaum (German Democratic Republic).'

Cyril tipped his seat back, put his hands behind his head and whistled at the ceiling. He sensed this was a breakthrough. While he could not yet put all the pieces into one place, he now had enough to speculate about the shape that they made. Was this man the recipient of the smuggled artworks? Had he quarrelled with the Nigerian smugglers, of whom Ibrahim was undoubtably one, if not the leader? Did Marcus, and Ibrahim, and Marcus's brother make the journey to Mushin that night to meet this man? And then the elation of speculation slowly subsided. Where was this man, this Holgar Pipek? And where was Ibrahim, for that matter? And why was Baban on the trail of both of them, or at least of Ibrahim?

For the next few minutes Cyril busied himself with creating a new case file. The assault of a female shopkeeper and a guest who absconded without paying. Both relatively small crimes in the general Lagos scheme of things, he thought, but tourism had been made a key priority in policing, with the festival in mind. He felt fully justified in opening this investigation. More valuable, in a personal sense, it gave him wiggle room in avoiding the police commissioner's ban on further investigation of Marcus's murder. He finished the folder, typed a brief report of his interrogations at the hotel, added his copy of the receipt that he had given to Bimpe and placed it carefully on the top of his in-tray. He contemplated the job with satisfaction and was still turning over the new knowledge about the case he had acquired that day, when the phone rang and he jumped with surprise. The phone seldom rang, and its ring was so unfamiliar that it always gave him a shock. He grabbed it, knowing that the line might well go down before he discovered who was on the end of it.

When he reached and lifted the bakelite handset he half expected the voice of John, or his sergeant, reporting on the safe delivery and arrival of Bimpe. He was all ready to greet the news with enthusiasm when he heard a rasping voice.

"Inspector!" It sounded strange and familiar at the same time. "I am calling you from military intelligence. You do not know me. My name is Baban. Some while ago I told your superiors that my department would handle the case of the murder of Marcus Diello. It appears that communications in your department are ineffective. I understand that you are still interfering. This will cease immediately. You will hand over to me all files, evidence and reports pertaining to this case. You will then not bother your stupid head about these matters again. Failure to obey this order will result in your return immediately to Benin City and the only antiquities that you will be contemplating in future will be the backside of the ancient bullock pulling the cart that you will be driving. Do I make myself clear?"

The phone went down at that point, either because the connection failed or because Baban did not feel that his communication required assent or an answer from its recipient. The elated detective of a few minutes before now sat with his head in his hands. In all the detective fiction that he had read, nothing but good came of defying your bosses in the police force. When you finally solve the case they are forced to admit that you were right all along.

He was not sure that the same was true of the most powerful military officer in the country, who was rumoured to be able to make or break presidents. Surely squashing flat a policeman from Benin, who was not highly regarded in Lagos, would be as simple squashing one of the many mosquitoes on Cyril's window pane.

Whatever he was doing, or thought he was doing, with this case, it seemed to Cyril that this telephone call altered it.

He began to clear his desk in an automatic way. It then occurred to him that one last duty remained in terms of the Marcus Diello case. He would have to get down to the compound to see his friends, tell them what he knew, and reluctantly release himself from any further involvement. It seemed a sad anticlimax with which to end a day when he had felt that he was really getting somewhere.

CHAPTER 16 HENRY

I HEARD THE argument raging as I crossed the compound to the dining room for breakfast. Once I was on the decking, I could work out that it was John and the chairman who were shouting at each other. I had never heard any of my colleagues having an outright row before, and certainly not a cross word between these two. John had always been so respectful of his boss, and the chairman had been such a fatherly figure to the young driver. The dining room door was open and I slipped in and stood listening for a moment.

Neither of the combatants seemed to notice that I was there, although Bimpe, seated on the other side of the table gave me a quick smile of recognition. At the end of the table the two men were standing, almost nose to nose, hurling verbal brickbats at each other and what is more, to my amazed fascination, they seemed to be arguing about a pop singer.

"All I am saying, chief, is that Bimpe will be as safe with me at the Fela concert at the Empire hotel as she would be here in the compound. We do not exactly have huge security resources. One steward and one very arthritic gate man. More likely it seems to me that the crowd would protect her and me from a European attacker, and the army are less likely to try to seize her there, surely? I think, chief, that you just don't like Fela!"

"I am only thinking of your safety, John. Of course I cannot give you orders about what you do in your spare time. But if you will take the advice of an older man who tries to look out for you and be your friend, then you certainly will not go. I agree, I think this popstar is a bad influence, and he attracts bad people to hear his music. I'm not sure that it is music, or whether it is African music. I do not like his politics one little bit. Fancy calling an album 'Zombie' and referring to all the federal troops who fought in the civil war as zombies. This man is outrageous. He is asking for trouble. More likely the army will come and arrest you all!"

"But, chief," John's voice was moving from anger to pleading. "All the young people in this country love Fela Kuti. Your music maybe highlife, and I admit to also loving Sunny Ade and Ebenezer Obey, who we play in the car all the time. But Fela has been in the US, and there is jazz and rhythm and blues in his music. That's why he calls it Afrobeat. I wish I could really understand your objection, and even more I wish I could explain what this music means to our generation."

The temperature in the room was falling from boiling to very hot, so I thought I might venture a comment.

"Am I listening to an argument about what music appeals to different generations? My father said that Lonnie Donegan should be permanently handcuffed and Elvis needed a haircut, while are my mother thought the Beatles should've had elocution lessons."

If I thought that I was putting sand on the fire, I was much mistaken.

"It's not about that at all, Henry," said the chief testily. "The fact is this man, Fela, is a political renegade. He has declared that his compound is no longer part of Nigeria, but some sort of republic on its own. He rejects civil government entirely. This will end in tears, I predict, and I do not want tears on the night when these two young people go to listen to his excruciating music!"

"But, chief, don't you see how important this is to young people like us two?"

John's glance took in Bimpe but I thought excluded me. I thought this was unfair because if you actually knew what his age was then he was probably much the same as me, and certainly not younger. But he was now in full flow again.

"I thought, chief, that you would be a supporter. After all, Fela was born in your hometown, and went to Abeokuta grammar school just as you did. Many would say that he was in the great Yoruba tradition of artists and poets and singers. And when was it a crime not to like the government?"

"Oh my goodness! We wanted to make you a confident young man and now you are becoming a stubborn young man. He can say what he likes about the government, but if you are under military rule, a wise man says this in his own compound and not outside of it. Yes, I knew both his mother and his father. Chief Israel was a great man, a great headmaster and I think I am right in saying the first leader of the Teachers Association of Nigeria. We should honour him. But, you know, his mother and all of that Ransome clan that she came from, there is certainly a streak of madness there from time to time. His mother was crazy for women's rights. I remember my mother telling me that she was the first African woman to drive a car in Nigeria. She shocked my parents and her son shocks me."

John would still not let go. "Your great friend, Wole, is a first cousin of Fela, and he hates the government who have put him in prison more than once."

The chief sighed. "Sadly this is true, very true. What a lot you have learnt, John, from sitting in the front of my car! But I would say to anybody that I think that Wole Soyinka is a truly great playwright and a real man of literature. Yes, you are right, he did come from Abeokuta, and he did go to the grammar school and he is part of the same clan as your crazy musician. And he has always opposed military government and ministerial corruption. They shut him up for twenty-two months during the civil war in solitary confinement, so we asked him to translate a new version of 'Forest of 1000 Daemons', which is, I would say, the Yoruba oral poetry equivalent of the Odyssey of Homer. He did a magnificent job. I was proud to publish it. I do get some snide remarks from high-ranking military men but I am very proud of him. Do you know that he is published in London? Only Achebe before him has been recognised in that way."

The chief fell silent, and while my other two companions were clearly wondering why it might be important to be published in London if you were no longer part of the British Empire, Philip came into the room.

Taking a seat at the table, he asked what the discussion had been all about, and since nobody else volunteered I offered a two sentence summary.

Philip, pouring coffee and reaching for the toast, supplied the solution.

"Well, chief, if that is all that you are worried about, then Henry and I will accompany these young people and fight off any intruders. The army will not arrest us during the festival because we have a British citizen with us and they will not want a diplomatic incident. This unpleasant European will see that Bimpe has a Praetorian guard surrounding her. Or perhaps we are the knights of the Round Table protecting Queen Guinevere."

These references, I felt, were largely lost on the rest of the room. Even the chairman looked slightly confused, but he grasped the chance to get out of the discussion at this point.

"Well, be it on your own heads. I agree that the four of you should be safe enough, but, Philip, you are in charge and I look to you to bring the rest of these valuable people back home in one piece. Now, I really do have work that I must be getting on with."

The agbada swept against the door frame as he made a spirited exit, followed shortly after by both John and his young friend, who made feeble excuses about domestic chores which needed to be accomplished. Philip and I continued to eat breakfast. When he had satisfied his immediate hunger, and taken a long swig of hot coffee, he looked at me steadily across the table.

"Are we losing our grip on this investigation, Henry? I am beginning to get worried."

I hastened to reassure him, but as I did so it did seem to me that we had suddenly become very dependent upon other people. The inspector was looking for this mysterious Czech fellow, who might be either the antiquities smuggler or an arms dealer. So were my spymasters. No one seemed to be on the trail of the other two Diello brothers. What had happened to the older one seemed to be a mystery, while the younger one, who definitely seemed to have been with Marcus on the fatal night, had totally disappeared. Who was investigating them? And since my paymasters had undoubtedly shared what they knew with military intelligence, what were they doing, or planning to do, about any of it?

"I know exactly what you mean," I said to Philip. "We seem to be paused, waiting for news from elsewhere. I thought for awhile that we were really getting somewhere, but now I wonder."

"My feelings exactly," came the reply from the other side of the breakfast table. "I was thinking about it in the night. I know that we have to wait, but there are aspects of this case that we really have not investigated very fully. I keep on thinking that the ritual murder aspect just does not fit, and I know that this concerns the inspector as well. He promised that he would do something about this, but I imagine that he has not had much time. So I decided to do something myself."

"Yourself?"

As far as I was concerned we had been together for most of the time that we had been in the compound. Philip's smile told me that he enjoyed having something over me.

"Yes, with a little help from John. You see I remembered that I had an old friend from back east who is now a doctor at the General Hospital in Ikeja. That is hardly a separate town these days, more like a suburb of Lagos. So I got John up at dawn and we went over there. With the traffic lighter at that time, it only took about half an hour, and I caught Doctor Iyke before he went on shift. He is a really good guy, and I remember how he helped one of my pupils before the war. Like so many of us he had to come west to find a job afterwards. As he said, there was no shortage of people needing treatment for nervous diseases in Iboland after the war, just no hospitals or jobs for doctors to treat them. So he ended up here."

I took another slice of toast and asked if the man was a specialist in ritual killing.

"No, not exactly. But the boy he helped me with

back in Enugu had been blinded by body part hunters. And Iyke had gone into all of the background and many of the reasons why these crimes take place. I remember being horrified at the time."

He seemed to be dwelling upon a memory, but I wanted him to go on so I asked, "Are there various types of ritual killing?"

"Oh, yes, and there are people who kill for ritual or other reasons, and people who kill to provide other people with body parts."

I realised that I had not quite thought it through in this way

"So, in your discussion with the doctor, were you able to work out whether Marcus was dismembered by somebody sourcing organs for a ritual, or somebody performing a ritual?."

Philip nodded. "Exactly the issue. As Iyke said, this probably was not the work of someone performing a ritual. Those do not happen by accident or where interruption is possible. They are usually done, if they are the works of organised religious believers, in temples or religious sites. It was more likely to be the work of someone foraging organs to sell to others for ritual purposes. They usually work in gangs, and at the dead of night in a narrow lane in a very quiet part of the Lagos suburbs they would not have been disturbed. Therefore the fact that they left the organs behind in a row is a problem. And when I described things to him in detail, he was even more decided that this was not people gathering organs for resale. He pointed out that the eyes, tongue and lips were intact, and not all of the other organs had been removed."

I must admit that I shuddered at the direction this

conversation was taking, but I readily saw its importance.

"When I try to reconstruct what we saw in that little tent on the pavement, Philip, I do not think that we saw anything that told me about rush or hurry or disturbance. The way things were arranged in such an orderly way spoke more of things being done meticulously."

"Yes, indeed," he responded. "That's my impression too, and indeed you used the very words that the forensics people said in the report, which Cyril shared with us. So we are left with the idea that somebody did this for their own purposes."

I gulped. For a moment I could not imagine any reason why someone would try to harvest body parts from somebody else. However, I tried as hard as I could to keep to the logic of the discussion that Philip was reporting upon.

"Hold on a minute. I thought that we had dismissed the idea of a ritual being performed there in the lane, just as we had dismissed the idea of it being the work of a gang of professional organ hunters."

"Well, Henry, there is an answer to that," came the reply. "At least in some rituals, and the gangs who supply organs for them. Let's think about individual acts designed to give help or protection. In the first instance there is a belief in sacrifices made to a local god, in order to win some good fortune or to prevent some disaster. Contrary to the belief that this happens only in the southwest, Iyke assures me that it happens all over the country, and indeed all over Africa, or at least, he had heard of cases in the east and in South Africa and in the Congo. Then again, there is some very non-religious reasoning by some superstitious and un-educated people that the simple possession of these organs may rectify a problem or confer a fortune upon the owner. Failing eyesight and failing potency are clear examples of the first: having a heart or lungs or kidneys creates for some people, apparently, the belief that they are about to receive millions of naira, for which they are quite prepared to pay thousands of naira to a head hunter or to go out and do the job themselves."

There was silence for a good while after this. I for one found it very hard to digest this and relate it to Marcus.

"Surely, these cases must be most uncommon?" I said.

"Iyke says that they have done some research on this at the University of Ilorin and there are apparently around 200 cases a year in Nigeria all around the country, growing by between eight and ten per cent each year since the civil war ended in 1970."

I was amazed by the number and Philip plainly saw that.

"I'm sorry to shock you, but we are in the education business because we are trying to cope with the primitive beliefs that still afflict so many. But I think you will agree that we have a real problem. It is getting harder and harder to argue with a narrative that says that after his quarrel with his brother, Marcus was murdered in the bookseller's upstairs room, dumped in the alley, and then became the victim an opportunist assault, possibly performed to secure some imagined benefit, but not completed. Then the perpetrator forgot to take away the spoils of his activity. Henry, my friend, this just does not hang together."

I had to agree that he was right, and we sat together in silence for some minutes before, clutching for straws,

I asked if his expedition had provided any other information.

"Well, not really," came the reply. "Iyke is a psychiatrist and we talked for a bit about his work. He contributed to a major study after the war comparing schizophrenia in Africa to similar conditions in Europe. He said that his European colleagues thought of the condition as a lifelong state of mind, where practitioners in Africa saw evidence of schizophrenic breakdowns or seizures that often did not repeat for the rest of the life of the individual concerned. I could see he wanted to talk about it, and I humoured him: I did not want him to think that I had launched myself at him in the early morning after years of not being in touch, and was running away after making my quick enquiry. Fortunately, he had to go on duty, or I might of learnt much more about his research!"

As we left the room and crossed the compound Philip put a hand on my shoulder.

"I suppose, Henry, that you would like to know why the chief really does not like Fela very much?" I nodded and he continued "Like everything else here, it's all about language. You see, Fela, since the war, has increasingly begun to write his songs, and to sing them, in pidgin. First of all he deserted Yoruba, and now he has given up on English. He says he wants his songs to be heard by all of Africa, and the language which all of Africa speaks is the one which they made up for themselves when they tried to interpret English in their own context. He says that pidgin is an African language of the oppressed, none of which impresses the chief at all. He thinks you speak proper English or proper Yoruba and you buy the books from which to learn those languages properly. You do not learn a grammar-free corruption of one of those

259

languages! He is a bit of a stickler, is our chief! I don't suppose he even knows how to say "I wan chop" if he is hungry."

"Neither would I," I laughed. "That reminds me, I thought that pidgin was Chinese."

Philip turned to me. "It once was in the early days of Empire, but it travelled to British seas with the Chinese crewmen, and conquered Africa like a virus. They say there are 75 million pidgin speakers around the Gulf of Benin – what the British used to call the "armpit of Africa."

Philip went to his quarters to work and I went over to the car, where John was waiting for the chairman. I was about to speak when he came bouncing out of the bungalow, climbed aboard and we sped off for the Ministry of Education. While we had had a time extension to the Kanuri language project, we needed to put in more resources. The chief was anxious to increase the contract value and I could see where he was going, but the ministry officials were very resistant. The permanent secretary was adamant. He had given selected headteachers from government schools time off to work on the language councils with our editors, he said, where they were joined by headmasters from the mission schools. These were the resources we needed, not more money.

The chairman raised his eyes to the ceiling as if in prayer, and then shot back, "If any two headteachers from any type of school in Bornu could ever agree on the spelling of any single Kanuri word, then we could get this job done tomorrow. No wonder nobody ever wrote this language on paper before."

As I've said before, the chief was a well connected man, and the permanent secretary was soon calming him down and offering him more coffee with a discussion which seemed to revolve around not paying more money, but paying the money up front instead of on completion.

I tried helpfully to suggest that, if it gave a neutral element to the discussions, I was prepared to go to the north myself and help to chair the meetings.

Both men broke off and turned on me instead. After what seemed to me a very long time, the permanent secretary said, "I don't think that the man dropped in from Mars would really help resolve the issues."

"This is a land on the edge of the Sahel, Henry," the chief said. "You would only stand a chance if you spoke Arabic, since that is the lingua franca up there, rather than English."

I decided discretion was the better part of valour and made no further contributions to the meeting.

When it was over, the chief looked weary and I was very happy to go along with his suggestion that we go to his club for a drink. Once we were in the lounge and he had conveyed to the barman his need for "two fingers of Talisker," in a tone of voice that indicated that the man was in attendance at a medical emergency, he began to relax. I recounted my discussion with Philip in the morning, and he said that he broadly agreed. Then, when I had a cold beer and half of his whisky had been consumed, I felt brave enough to ask him about his argument with John.

"Oh, Henry, take no notice of it. The old and young are always doing that. To tell you the truth, it is good, to my mind, for John to find some resistance, and to have to encounter it. I think there are some real dangers, but obviously, since you are all going this evening, I do not think that they are insurmountable. However, the man's music is not for me, nor is the fact that he keeps on picking up wives at each concert and adding them to his private harem. Hold on tight to that beautiful young woman that you have with you: she may be in more danger from the performer than she is from a crazy gunrunner."

Then he clapped me hard on the shoulders so I almost choked on the beer that I was sipping at the time, and roared with laughter.

But his mood changed abruptly when the club secretary came into the lounge. The chief beckoned him over with an imperious forefinger.

"Further to my enquiries of a few weeks ago, Mr Secretary, have you seen Ibrahim on the premises since then and where do you think he is now?"

"Oh goodness, chief Sam, how I wish you had been in here last week. First we had policemen looking everywhere. Then we had the army looking everywhere. I have been questioned and questioned. All of our quarters have been searched. I tell them that I am only here in the club. I do not know if he went to Europe. The captain of the British Caledonian flight to Gatwick was here and he said he had been questioned. I do not know if he went to Abuja, although I know that his late father had land there. In short, sir, I know nothing. I know less than the taxi driver who the army people were speaking to, and who said he took him to catch a plane to Zaria. So please sir, please go and ask somebody else!"

The chief and I looked at each other. Zaria? Place of refuge for an on-the-run ex-army officer turned businessman, or another false alarm?

CHAPTER 17 PHILIP

PHILIP WAS OUT on the veranda of the bungalow when he first heard the noise. It might have been an exceptionally heavy vehicle grinding its way around the raised arterial expressway, but then he saw the steward and the security guard running towards the compound gate. He looked in the direction towards which they were gesticulating. Coming down the slip road was a surprisingly clean and shiny Mercedes limousine, with the Nigeria pennant flying on each wing. Behind it, moving more slowly, came the source of the noise. A half-track armoured personnel carrier was following the limo from which soldiers with rifles and submachine guns emerged as the Mercedes approached the compound gate. Philip ran back into the bungalow to warn his colleagues.

Everyone was still in the dining room, but hearing the news, the chief simply said, "I shall be here if anybody wants to speak to me."

He went into the sitting room and placed himself in the centre of the sofa.

"I have suspected that this might happen, and perhaps we should welcome it. An open and frank conversation with our friends in military intelligence may well be overdue."

Before Philip could fully appreciate his chairman's composure, he saw soldiers around the bungalow standing in the yard at each corner of the building with their guns raised, pointing at the windows. The Mercedes had come to rest in front of the door, and a tall, languid figure in full uniform climbed slowly out. Baban seemed to shake himself, took in the whole scene and then moved up the steps to the front door. A sergeant in fatigues kicked it open, and the head of military intelligence ducked slightly as he came in, making Philip even more aware of how tall the man was.

The director of military intelligence surveyed the room. Philip followed his eyes. Standing behind the sofa, he, John and Henry must have looked as if they were taking cover behind their chairman. Bimpe could be seen through the little window in the door that led to the kitchen.

Baban took it all in. "Good morning, chief. Do you mind if I join you and your colleagues? I had not realised that you were based so far out in the suburbs or I would have brought my own refreshments!"

"John, please go to the kitchen and procure some coffee for our visitor, that is, of course, if he has not frightened our staff to death."

Baban nodded and sat down in an armchair. He pointed Henry and Philip to the other chairs, and while he waited for his coffee Philip had a chance to observe him more closely. Of course he had seen him on state occasions, opening schools and colleges, laying the foundation stones and other activities which all of the military junta performed.

Philip read the newspapers. He knew that this was the man who was said to be the power behind the throne in the last two military regime changes. This was the great facilitator, beholden to nobody, who was able to put people into power and keep them there. Philip saw a thin gaunt man who he guessed might be six foot five or six in height, a truly abnormal height in Nigeria. You did not look at this long lanky body because you were transfixed by the head. The rocky cranium was completely shaven, even the eyebrows had gone. The head was oiled and seemed to glint. The cheekbones were high and the nose, was quite unlike his own. This was not the fat, pudgy nose of a southerner: this was a thin, high-bridged nose. Philip tried to find the right word. Nilotic? Certainly the sort of nose that came out of the desert and not from the forests. Then the man's eyes rested on him for a moment, and he felt himself looking away. There was no light in those eyes. They were dark glittering fragments of coal. Philip shivered, and wondered how the chief was going to cope with what seemed likely to be an interrogation.

Baban took a sip of his coffee, nodded to the chief in appreciation, put his cup down on the coffee table and began.

"I think, gentlemen, that we share the same objectives, although for different reasons. You seek the murderer of your friend and colleague, and I quite understand that. I even respect it. I, in my turn, seek people who have smuggled guns, have illegally exported antiquities and artworks, and who may even have been planning an attack on our government, although I'm not quite sure of that at present. I think that I know many of the things that you have discovered during your enquiries. I started today by speaking at length to Detective Inspector Fagunwa of the Lagos police. We had a pleasant and informative meeting. I was pleased to find that his opinion of the police commissioner and the detective chief superintendent is as low as mine, and I suspect yours as well, chief?"

The chief nodded gravely. Then, all of a sudden, Baban was on his feet and shouting at them. The guns surrounding the house clicked audibly as the safety catches came off. Philip could have sworn that the words were addressed to him personally, and afterwards everyone else said the same.

"You will not evade my questions or lie in your answers. I do not need to prove that you have tried to mislead me. A slight suspicion crossing my mind is quite enough. People who lie to me do not do it twice."

He stared at them in silence for a moment, and then resumed his seat. "I was able to clear up a little mystery for the inspector this morning. He said that he was looking for a Lebanese citizen who smuggled Mercedes cars. I told him that my men had found someone answering that description floating in the lagoon this morning. Crocodiles are such a messy eaters."

Another silence followed. Then, he said, "I suggest, chief, that you might instruct your people to tell me everything that they know, one by one, until I am satisfied that I have heard everything."

Philip felt a momentary spasm of worry that the chief would lose his cool with the intruder, and they would all end up in the lagoon. He need not have been concerned. The chief took his time and then answered in a cool and collected tone of voice.

"Director, you are welcome in my house. I hope that you enjoyed my hospitality." He nodded towards the empty coffee cups. "As you know, the laws of hospitality in a Yoruba household are very important. We must make our guests comfortable and we must treat them with a respect that includes not deceiving them, and telling them the truth. My colleagues and I only started to collect information which might lead to the unmasking of the individual who killed our dear colleague, Marcus Diello, when the inspector's investigations were halted from above. You need to tell us, if we are to take your instruction seriously, whether you were the person behind the moves to prevent the inspector from doing his job. The way you answer this question will dictate how I instruct my staff here in my house."

"Answering a question with a question, chief? Do you know who you are speaking to, do you really know how easy it would be to remove all evidence that this compound and its occupants ever existed?"

Philip found that he was holding his breath, and he imagined everybody else was as well, except for the two combatants.

"Oh yes, director," the chief continued calmly, "you certainly have the power to do exactly what you have described. The great mass of Nigerians would not notice our departure. But, as I'm sure you are aware, Mr Kettering is a UK citizen, and one with close associates in the US Embassy and the British High Commission. I think that they would notice. At a much lower level, I have to remind you that I am the peacemaker of the Yoruba people of Old Oyo, a hereditary office we believe to be 600 years old. Amongst those who would be surprised by my sudden disappearance would be our paramount chief, the Alaafin, as well as our revered and honourable vice president of Nigeria, a member of our tribal council, and my good friend and companion since our school days at Abeokuta Grammar School. Killing us all would be quick: the explanations afterwards would take you quite a bit longer."

Philip realised that he was still holding his breath, and he did not release it until he saw a small, sly smile cross Baban's thin lips. The tip of a pink tongue flickered after it. Philip thought the man looked more like a lizard at that moment but he was relieved by the softness of the reply.

"Well, chief, I always knew that you were a brave and resilient people. I agree with you. We should put our cards up on the table, and tell each other frankly what we have discovered on our journey. So let me begin by addressing your question. Yes, I did halt the police investigation. I was worried that an attempt might be made to overthrow the government. If the plotters were disturbed too early, then my ability to frustrate them might be compromised. Having the Lagos police blundering around would, I thought, be a hindrance rather than a help. So I called the police commissioner, who is I think one of your huge group of tribal school friends, and I gave him instructions to desist. I had not reckoned, however, that the friends of the deceased man would become as formidable a detective force as the Lagos police."

The answer left Philip wondering. He had formed the view that Baban tracked coup attempts and their instigators through the planning stages, formed a view on whether they were likely to succeed or not, and then either threw his weight behind regime change, or arrested and shot treacherous elements. Baban was obviously a shrewd observer and he knew just when to commit or arrest.

"So here, by virtue of my telling you this, is evidence of my good faith. Now, chief, if you are happy, I would like to start with Mr Kettering. I have to tell you, Mr Kettering, that I spent last night speaking to those people that your chief calls your "associates" in the diplomatic missions in Lagos. I think we had a fairly good exchange of views, although , of course , you never quite know with them. So please, Mr Kettering, tell me what you know."

After a nod from the chief, Henry began, and Philip and John joined in to round out the story where needed. Then Bimpe was coaxed into the room, and with John holding her hand she told about her struggle with Holgar Pipek. When she had finished, Baban looked extremely interested and turned and said to his sergeant: "This is him, this is the man we need to get."

He leaned back in the chair and seemed lost in thought for a moment. When he spoke, Philip thought that his voice sounded slightly different, less the interrogator and more the contributor.

"We have been following the same trail in different ways. I have to congratulate all four of you. You have discovered far more than either my men or the police, and your account today has filled out my picture in some very material ways. I am particularly interested in the reading group that convened in the old gymnasium room above Oladipo's bookshop. Let me now fill out your picture from my perspective. I knew of this group and their meetings long before you. As you may imagine, I was always sceptical that this was a group of young officers who wanted to read works of Nigerian literature. I felt that the world had changed radically from my own youth if young officers read anything at all. So I sent a man, an agent of mine who owed me some favours, to investigate and, if necessary, to take charge. His name was Ibrahim Kabeysi. I had met him some years before when he was facing court-martial for some matters that are not strictly relevant here. I got him an honourable discharge and the hotel kindly cooperated with me to give him the retail concessions that you know about. He was to be my eyes and ears in the hotel and the club. It seemed natural to extend this to the young officer reading group, since many of its members were known to him and were users of the club as well."

Baban was looking at the ceiling and Philip wondered if he had wandered off on a line of thought of his own. Or was he, perhaps, thinking about how to tell the story while diminishing or white-washing his own part in it. When he resumed, Baban addressed the chief. "You are aware chief, I well know, that your young colleague Marcus Diello had two elder brothers. One, a young tearaway in my view , was closest to your Marcus in age. His name was Samuel, named, I think, for you, chief. He was two years older than Marcus, and the younger boy loved him dearly. You are right, Mr Kettering, in your suspicion that the journey Marcus made with Ibrahim to the upstairs room at the bookshop that evening was to warn his brother that he was hearing rumours that Samuel was part of the plot. He wanted to try to persuade him to disassociate himself from the plotters. Indeed, I know exactly what took place in that room that night. You see, gentlemen, I have Samuel Diello under guard at the Dodan barracks and he has felt able, after a little while, to confide in me entirely."

Philip thought that the tone of voice used here sounded almost kindly, until he realised that brute force may have been used to obtain that cooperation. At least the young man was still alive. Philip now wanted to know more about the elder brother, and he did not have to wait long.

"For myself, conspiracies have become so regular as to be boring. Get a group together with tribal or ethnic affinities, foment discord in different regiments in different parts of the country, seize the radio stations and the power plants et cetera et cetera. Ideology rarely plays a part. The plotters, whatever their press releases say, rarely have the good of the people in mind. What they want is power, and they imagine all of the advantages that go with power. It bores me and it disgusts me, but the other Diello brother was totally and completely different from this. He was a man of ideas and ideals. Did any of you know anything about him?"

Philip noted that everybody shook their heads. Shehu Diello was not a known quantity.

The chief commented, "I knew that he existed and that he was a more senior army officer, but I did not even know his name until I heard that he was dead. Did he commit suicide?"

"I am not sure that we can really say, yet. My men in Sokoto are working with the local police and I await the report. However, I do know that his extraordinary plans had been discovered, and that he was aware of this. This may have been a factor. I can also say that we raided his house in Sokoto and brought away a huge collection of documents and correspondence that points not just to an attempt on the Nigerian state, but an attack upon the stability and governance of Africa as a whole!"

This dramatic statement silenced everyone, and Philip wondered what on earth might possibly come next.

"Gentlemen, in order to explain what has been going on I have to give you rather more background on Shehu Diello then you might have thought necessary. He may be the elder brother of the two other boys, but they had different mothers and he was about six years older. Of them all, he was probably the cleverest. He rose rapidly in the post civil war army. We were short of officers, and he was selected for Sandhurst and then for advanced technical training with the British Army at Shrivenham. Did he develop his ideas there, I wonder? He certainly lost his faith, although he skilfully disguised that from all of us. He became – and I think that this is a term of abuse amongst the English, but not here – an intellectual. He would have made, I think, a good imam. As it was, he fell captive to another religion, the pan-Africanism of Kuame Nkrumah. He began to believe that the borders and the states left behind by the European colonial powers were meaningless. He wanted an Africa where nationhood was based upon ethnicity, language, affinity, even economic logic, but not upon the European power struggles of the 1890s. I understand this viewpoint, although I cannot condone it. In his rooms in Sokoto we found the whole library of Panaf Books, from Nkrumah to Frantz Fanon.

"He moved then from a belief in the self-determination of African peoples to doing something about it. He needed resources to accomplish anything, and my man Ibrahim effectively did that for him. He discovered that Ibrahim was smuggling antiquities, and diverted that flow of illegal activity into buying weapons from gunmakers in the Soviet bloc. Ibrahim protested and tried to get out, but was kept in the group by fear of exposure. Shehu established correspondence with dissident groups all over the continent, and had begun to supply them with guns, hence the strange appearance of cases of weapons in all sorts of places outside of Nigeria.

"What his plans were for this country, I am not sure, but this is not a country that can contemplate another ethnic civil war because some ideologue thinks that all of the Hausa people of the Sahel, now living in Mali or Senegal or Chad or Niger or Nigeria should be reunited in some 13th century empire to which they once belonged. Army command feared that he was going slightly mad and they did not then know anything of this. They posted him to a purely nominal position in the court of the Sultan of Sokoto, hoping to keep him out of trouble in a remote place.

"In fact, they did the opposite. They put him in a place where he could plot quietly, coming down to Lagos at regular intervals for meetings with his co-conspirators. I've now rounded up most of the other officers, and like Samuel they are proving very cooperative. I suspect that they did not want to see the kingdom of the Zulus rise again, or create a Matabele state, or a kingdom of the Luo in east Africa, or of the Ashanti or the Twi in west Africa. Nor, my dear chief, are they concerned to reunite the Yorubas of the former British province of western Nigeria with their fellow ethnic kinsmen next door in the former French colony.

"In short, this madman was planting arms dumps around Africa in order to allow Africans to decide for themselves which country they wanted to belong to, and this madness had to be stopped. I have stopped it."

Now Philip had twenty questions that he wanted to ask, and he sensed that everybody else did as well. Henry was the first to get a word in once this tirade had ended.

"So is it clear to you that it was one of the officers who killed Marcus above Oladipo's bookshop? And if so, do you have him in custody? Which one was it?"

"Well, I do not think it was any of them. There was someone else at the meeting that evening. Holger Pipek was there. He had travelled to Nigeria for reasons of his own. Did your intelligence colleagues tell you this, Mr Kettering? Pipek is a full colonel in the Stasi, the East

German secret police. While they were working to supply Shehu, and made a number of deliveries, they had never met him and were not sure that they could trust him. They wanted to know a lot more about the status of the conspirators in each of the countries to whom they were supplying arms. They were happy to start fires and keep the security forces across the continent in a state of alert, or in some places, panic, but they wanted to know who they were backing. Only Shehu could tell them that. And they were also having a small money problem. It was proving more difficult than they thought to sell the artefacts, and the dealers in the west were taking big commissions off them for doing illegal trades. It seems to me that we have heavy dash in every culture."

"So you think that this man Pipek was the murderer?" Henry pressed on.

"I'm pretty sure of it. I think that he was appalled that Marcus was going to leave the room and would betray them all to save his brother. Samuel says that Marcus got angry and demanded that he and his brother should go, but when he got up to leave, Pipek pulled out of stiletto and cut his carotid artery. He was dead in moments. Samuel was frantic. All of the other officers fled and, as Samuel testifies, Marcus bled to death very quickly."

Philip was next in line. "Marcus's body wasn't found in that room, sir. Do you know who moved it, and was the ritual murder a way of disguising what had happened?"

Baban allowed himself the thin smile once again. "You are going well beyond me, I am afraid. My interest stops with Shehu and his conspiracies. One murder more or less in this country is of no great moment. I will continue to interrogate my prisoners and if I gain further intelligence then I shall, of course, let you know. You, meanwhile, must help to find this Pipek character. He can hardly hide in a crowd in this country. I imagine that he will find it fairly difficult to get out. He is the person of interest that you should concentrate upon, gentleman. Leave the rest to me!"

With this, he got up and it was clear that he was not going to entertain further questions. He strode over to the chief, shook him firmly by the hand, and strolled out through the door, which the sergeant held open. In a few moments, the Mercedes was disappearing in a cloud of dust and the armoured personnel carrier, now replete with his armed guard, was following slowly up the slipway onto the expressway.

CHAPTER 18 CYRIL

CYRIL WOKE UP feeling stiff and sore the next morning. He guessed that he had slept in an awkward position. He was a bit later than usual and he ate his breakfast quickly, some fried plantain that he had cooked at the weekend. As he drank his coffee, his mind went back to the long interview the previous evening. Being interrogated by Baban was like being in a ring with a prizefighter. No wonder he felt stiff and sore. Henry, Philip, probably their chairman and John, the driver, would be undergoing much the same treatment today. He vividly recollected he had promised this intimidating man that he would be single-minded in his pursuit of Marcus's killer from first light this morning.

He was not reluctant to admit that the director of military intelligence frightened him. While he was quietly pleased to know why he had been taken off the case, and even more pleased to be put back on it, he really had no idea where to find the German or Czech fellow Baban was convinced was the murderer. He cheerfully admitted to himself that the culprit would stand out in a crowd - but if the culprit had any sense, he was lying low and it was not at all obvious where to start looking for him.

When he left the house he found an empty taxi parked in the endless line of vehicles waiting to go over the bridge onto the island. On the other side of the road, a group of traffic policemen were sitting on their morning break, taking refreshment. Cyril impatiently left his stranded vehicle and its protesting driver, and marched in a huge crowd of commuters across the bridge and down to police headquarters. He was running with sweat, the dust of Lagos powdering him all over, when a young woman constable grabbed him as he passed the reception desk on his way to the lift.

"Inspector? Inspector Fagunwa?"

Women police officers were new to the Lagos force, and as far as Cyril was concerned there was a regrettable tendency for them to be used as a substitute for the internal telephone system. He listened sympathetically.

"Detective chief superintendent say he want you in his office immediately, soon as you arrive. I am posted to catch you. Please follow me."

She marched to a lift, and as they rose to the top floor, Cyril's morale sank back down the lift shaft. Inevitably, he thought, Baban had spoken overnight to the police commissioner. Probably he gave orders that Cyril should be put back on the case. Probably they were forced to do that, but as soon as the case was over, he was sure that he would be demoted for disobedience and sent to be a traffic policeman under the same awning as those poor fellows who he had seen on his way in. Imagine that! Cyril would rather return to Benin any day of the week.

The detective chief superintendent was a large, corpulent man. His double chins rippled around his collar. When the constable knocked on his door and then showed Cyril in, he leaned back in his chair and pressed his fingers together in a little cage, through which he viewed the man standing in front of his desk.

After a moment of observation, he sat up and said, "Well, sit down, man," and pointed to a chair. Then he slowly began what was obviously a preprepared statement. "Inspector Fagunwa, I have called you to my office today to talk to you about a murder case that you have been working upon. I might remark now that this is a case that both the police commissioner and I myself forbade you to proceed with earlier. The fact is that you disobeyed us. The fact that this action of yours earned the commendation of the director of military intelligence in a military government, does not in my mind excuse the flagrant lack of police discipline and wilful evasion of police procedures that you have shown. However, the director is certain that you are close to solving the case, and has asked for you to be given all the resources that you need to do so. The police commissioner has asked me to ensure that this is the case, and I of course shall do so."

So far things were going just as Cyril had anticipated. He looked at the man's piggy little eyes squinting hatred at him and he saw himself issuing parking tickets. But there was more.

"As you know, inspector, I have never had a high opinion of your capabilities. People from your part of the country seldom show skill in deductive work. Add to that, you have shown a marked reluctance to work within the systems and the culture of our headquarters force here in Lagos."

Yes, indeed, Cyril thought. He had shown not only reluctance, but he had refused to join 'the system'. In this so-called system, police officers legitimised the bribes they took by passing a percentage of the bribe up to their immediate superior officer, who in turn passed a percentage up to his senior officer and so on. This income stream, added to dash received for turning a blind eye, obtaining a permit, or simply for giving ample warnings of when raids or arrests were about to take place, made many senior policemen very wealthy. When asked to join the system, Cyril had said that since he did not take bribes he could not play, an answer that endeared him to no one and made him an object of ridicule in senior police circles.

"Let's make no bones about it. We tolerated you here because the federal government wanted a showcase for diversity. You were an advertisement for nation building, for mixing us up so that we were first and foremost police and not easterners or westerners or northerners. In my view, it does not work. The police commissioner was right to take only one exchange, as an experiment. You were the exchange, and I think it is clear that it has not worked."

Cyril was beginning to feel that this conversation had run its course. His worst fears were realised. He cleared his throat and said, "If that's all, sir, maybe I should now be getting on with the task that the director of military intelligence has agreed with the police commissioner?"

"Unfortunately, inspector, it is not the end of the story. I have a further communication to make to you. And when I have made it you will realise how difficult we all find this. After his discussions with the director of military intelligence, the police commissioner has agreed to enable some further provisions with regard to your work here. He has decided that you should be promoted to Detective Chief Inspector, with immediate effect, and with your salary backdated to the day when this fellow Marcus Diello was killed. He has furthermore agreed that your office should be moved from the second floor to this floor. Since this floor is full it means that one of your other colleagues will have to be moved down to your present accommodation. Furthermore, as well as your sergeant, you will have two constables permanently assigned to you. And a telephone."

There was a silence while this sank in. As he struggled to grasp it, Cyril said the silly thing that came into his head and he instantly regretted it.

"But, sir, I already have a telephone."

The detective chief superintendent blew out his lips in a gesture that demonstrated the impossibility of dealing with small children or country idiots or both at the same time.

"I thought I was being obvious, but now I see I must be explicit. You already have a telephone for internal and external calls. You will continue to have that telephone. You will however have an additional telephone. Only the police commissioner has a telephone of this type. This telephone will connect you with the office of the director of military intelligence without going through a switchboard. And if you think that having this telephone will make you any more liked or respected in this building than you are already, then I will have to assure you that you are quite wrong. Now, inspector, please go about your duties."

Cyril left his superior's office in a great rush with no ceremony. He knew that, while Baban's provisions made life easier in the short term, they were not a long-term solution. As he went back down to his office, the thought struck him that he himself now had a vested interest in there not being another military coup, since that might be as likely to remove the director of military intelligence from office as to increase his power and influence in the affairs of the military government. It was all too confusing. A decent murder would be far simpler.

Just as he came along the corridor to his office, he met his highly excited sergeant coming in the opposite direction. "Inspector, boss, I think we got him."

Cyril went into his office, pointed his sergeant to a seat, and asked him to recount slowly what had happened.

The sergeant's eyes were rolling. He kept on starting and stopping and beating his palms against his knee in excitement.

"Now, sergeant, go back to the beginning and tell it to me as it happened."

"Well, sir, last night when I took you home you were so sad, I hate to see you so unhappy so I thought, get up early, go and take the car and collect the inspector and give him a ride to the office. But I am too late. It is the traffic. And then, you know, inspector, there is a delivery vehicle outside Marks & Spencer. Just put his flashing lights on. Open the doors , carrying in goods. Is there no traffic policeman left in Lagos? We are all waiting there, blowing our horns and I am thinking of you."

"Well, perhaps sergeant, we don't need every exact detail. I thank you for your concern. What happened to make you so excited?"

"Well boss, so I am crawling along in the car, and I have the police radio on, of course, and I'm just coming onto the island, past the hotel, when I get an emergency call. Nearest vehicle. Well, this is not for us normally. Nearest vehicle, in this traffic, is hours away. And then I hear it is a man in the hotel believed to be armed with a knife. Well then, I know that my inspector would want me to look at this. So I pulled into the hotel car park and go into reception. That stupid clerk is on duty. You know, sir, the one who thinks he is such a big noise, and he asks to see my ID, and I am shouting at him that someone here called the police and we are all shouting louder."

"So had they called the police?" Cyril was trying as hard as he could to keep the younger man on the story.

"Yes, indeed, sir, in came the manager and told the little clerk he was such a foolish fella, and told me the story. And I asked him to show me and he would not go, so I went and got my gun from the car and then I investigated, sir."

"Okay, Maro, what was the story that the manager told you?"

"Just this, sir, that his kitchen staff had reported a terrible riot in the backyard of the hotel. Banging and crashing and shouting and screaming. They say to him that murder is taking place. So he took immediate action."

The sergeant had paused, whether for dramatic affect or lack of breath was hard to tell. Cyril felt the need to prod him forward.

"And then?"

"As I say, he is one brave man. He stay behind the desk and call the police, and send the clerk to investigate. When this clerk came back, he say that he see a white man being eaten by monkeys. So the manager, he got angry, and he hit the clerk hard and now the clerk has a black eye. He showed me, and it looked very sore to me."

Cyril felt that he had embarked on a long journey when all he had required was a shortcut. "So what had really happened in the hotel backyard?"

"One of the hotel European guests was being eaten by monkeys. And, lucky for us, sir, these monkeys had caught the very man we were looking for. Maybe they should be enrolled in the Lagos police. They are certainly smarter than some of our people, and it would be cheaper to bribe them with a jackfruit than naira."

Cyril resigned himself to hearing the whole story in the way that the sergeant wanted to tell it. He sensed that this was the sergeant's moment of triumph, and no promptings from him were going to stop that happening.

"So, sergeant, tell me in your own words what you have found out in the course of making this arrest."

"Well, sir, I proceeded into the hotel and followed the principles of interrogation that you have laid down for me so clearly. So, in the first instance, I did not shout at witnesses or hit them, but simply listened to what they had to tell me. They told me this story about the monkeys in the yard. So, sir, I proceeded in the direction of the yard. There I found a European individual lying on the ground. He is bleeding from many cuts and bruises and his clothes are in tatters. He has lost chunks of hair and one of his ears has been badly bitten. Also, I think he may have a broken wrist. I find out later that he cannot put weight on one ankle. He is very distressed, and when I approach he points towards one of the big waste food bins in the yard. I stand by the bin and there is noise inside, so I am glad that I went back to the car for my handgun. Then I stand by the bin and slowly open the lid, and nothing happens. So I fire the gun into the air and out from the bin come five or six monkeys. They move so fast I cannot count. In a moment they are all gone away.

"I thought a bit, sir. I know these monkeys. They are the same monkeys we have in Cross Rivers. They used to live in the bush, now they like to scavenge for food around the houses. Tantalus is what they are properly called. You know them, sir, surely? Big white eyebrows?

Tantalus is the official name, and I think it means they can't get into anywhere, which is true, but down in Cross Rivers we call them "blue balls," and you know why that is!"

The sergeant was now giggling and Cyril felt that redirection was required.

"So, sergeant, stick to the facts. How did you find out who the man was and what had happened to him to put him in this position?"

"Well, sir, after I find my gun, the manager and the clerk were brave enough to come running out because they thought I had shot him dead. Then I asked them who it was, and they said it was the German guest that everybody was looking for, so I pointed the gun at him and told him he was under arrest and he looked quite happy. But he could not get up. I just wanted to get him to the car, but when I got close to him, oh sir! He smelled so bad. I cannot say if he smelt more of rotting food or of monkey, but either way, you would not have been pleased, sir, if I help him into the back of the car. So I ordered the manager to have him showered and cleaned, and to get the nurse. Sir, did I ever tell you they have a nurse? I once went on a date with her, sir, she is one impressive lady. I thought she could put some antiseptic on his wounds and some bandages where he was bleeding. I am not afraid of him running away, sir, so no handcuffs. But inspector, can I say, I am most upset with that manager. He and the foolish clerk will not touch the man, but call for the kitchen porters, and they come out and have to carry the man into the hotel. They work out what happened to him. They are smart guys, those kitchen boys. They are a lot smarter than the manager. One of them ask if the man came out of the waste bin where the monkeys were. Another one laughed and said that if the man was hiding there, they would have covered him with jackfruit waste because they had dumped a whole vat of it into that bin only a few moments ago. And so we pieced it together. The man was hiding in the bin, they covered him with fruit pulp and rubbish, he tried to climb out, that let the monkeys in, they all fell down to the bottom of the skip and the lid closed on top of them. Case closed, as you would say, inspector."

"Not closed at all, I am afraid, sergeant. I still do not know why the man was hiding in the backyard of the hotel in the early hours of the morning."

"No, sir, you do not, and at this point neither did I, but you know, that nurse is very thorough. She took a long time patching this man up after they had cleaned him off in the staff changing rooms. I went back to the car. I hate walking around with the gun, because I am always afraid it might go off again. Also I needed an evidence bag to put all the man's clothes in. I thought if I sealed this up it might help to keep our car from smelling so bad. So when I walked back to the car there were all the taxi drivers from the hotel taxi rank, and they all want to know what the shooting was about. So I told them. And it turns out that all of these men know my prisoner very well. One of them said that he drove the man to the airport, but when the man saw that there were security checks and army road blocks on the airport road, he asked to turn back and come back to the hotel. Then the other fella tells me he took the same man to the docs and same thing happened. Turn back. Come home.

"So I took details from them both and asked them

to report to HQ to make statements. Then I went back into the hotel. My prisoner is sitting in the kitchen on a chair wearing a bath robe and smelling much better. Beside him is that wonderful nurse . So I put all his possessions into my evidence bags and sealed it up. I handcuffed him, just to show he was a prisoner and under arrest, you understand, inspector, and pulled and pushed him out to the car and put him in the back. I could tell he was feeling better because he started to chatter to me in his own language.

"I thought it was Kanuri at first, and then pidgin, but of course we were now in the really heavy traffic hour, so we had plenty of time. Eventually I realise he is speaking English, put in a very strange voice. and he is trying to offer me some heavy dash to drive him to the docks. Apparently there is a boat there going to his own country and he must get on it before it leaves. Aeroplanes are no good because they do not go direct to where he lives and he has to change planes in unfriendly places. I tell you, sir, we are getting along like a house on fire. He is still anxious to give me his wallet, which is in the evidence bag, if I help him. But, you know what, inspector, I have seen that wallet. It is looking a bit damaged. Somebody has bitten through the lining at the back. All the notes inside are in two pieces. We have a saying in Cross Rivers, 'If you have to take dash make sure it is clean money.' If you follow my joke, sir, someone had been monkeying with this money."

Cyril groaned. So far he had been spared too many examples of the sergeant's wit and he realised that he should have been grateful for that. He still had not got, however, the answer that he had sought.

"Yes, I think that you acted honourably and well,

sergeant, and I agree that you have followed my advice and instructions to the letter. But why on earth, man, was this guy hanging around the backyard of the hotel in the early hours of the morning?"

The sergeant was slightly taken aback. "Didn't I tell you that already, sir? Well, it appears that when he went to the docks and had to turn back because of the security checks, the truck in front of the taxi was carrying waste. He asked the driver about it and he said that this was waste from all the hotels on the island, and that it was dumped into a freighter in the docks, and then carried out to sea and dumped in the gulf of Benin. I ask you, inspector, no wonder they call it the armpit of Africa. Yes, that is what they do in the Gulf of Benin! Anyway this stuck in the man's head, and he thought if he hung around waiting for a waste disposal truck, he could buy the driver and get into the docks hiding in the vehicle. But as he waited people started to arrive for work in the hotel, so he had to hide."

"And he hid in the food waste bin?" Cyril felt that he could now comfortably complete the story.

His sergeant smiled broadly. "I knew that you would see it eventually, sir. As a detective you have taught me everything that I know."

"And you do know a very great deal, sergeant. I do commend you on this excellent work, and I can confirm that you will soon be able to tell your family that you have risen to the rank of inspector."

His sergeant's happy composure disappeared and his jaw dropped. "But the exams, inspector, I have not even started to work on the exams."

"Well," said Cyril, "I have just become a detective chief inspector without taking any examinations. I shall need an inspector reporting to me, and it may be that you will have the same good fortune. In the meanwhile, tell me where you parked your prisoner."

The sergeant looked slightly apprehensive. "Well, sir, I put him in the interrogation cell, along with all the rapists, murderers, robbers, pickpockets, drug dealers and everyone else detained overnight. You cannot miss him, sir, the only European there wearing a hotel bath robe. But now that you mention it, I'm a bit scared that I might have put him into another bin full of monkeys."

The two men hurried downstairs and found their worst fears were unfounded, although the German did look distinctly uncomfortable, and as the sergeant pulled him out of the cell, someone in the crowd murmured, "That's disappointing, inspector. We thought you left him here for our use and pleasure!"

Cyril had the man brought to his office and after a brief effort of trying to be Bruno Teitelbaum, Holgar Pipek confirmed his identity and claimed diplomatic immunity. Cyril was not quite sure what that meant, but said that he would put the man in touch with people who did. He then telephoned military intelligence, cursing the fact that his special direct line was not yet installed, and gave the news to one of Baban's assistants. Despite the traffic, two military policemen arrived within half an hour, and signed a receipt and took the prisoner to the Dodan barracks. As he watched them depart, Cyril reflected that this was a case that would never come to court and that his involvement in it was probably now over. If he had real satisfaction in it as a case, it was that the murderer had now been uncovered and would be known to everybody. Or at least, to those who had struggled so hard to find his identity.

CHAPTER 19 HENRY

AND SO BEGAN my Kaduna days. I reflected later that my life in Nigeria fell into distinctly different phases. The intensity of the work with Marcus in Ibadan on printing and distributing millions of books was one clear period; the murder of my friend and three furious weeks of Festac in Lagos, dominated by the hunt for his murderer and the great festival were another; and then Kaduna, with the rich ceremonials that ended the festival marked the beginning of the end of my turbulent time in Nigeria.

I had been frantically busy during Festac and I knew that I needed a change of pace. Quite apart from the events recounted here, I had tried, most days, to attend the morning colloquium. The chief had secured the contract to publish the African New Writing book of the festival, and I was working with the editor, Cyprian Ekwensi, and Philip to collect contributions for Cyprian to review. I also needed to promote it alongside our other African New Writing books. Then there was the music, both formal sessions in the new National Theatre and in the city squares, and the impromptu concerts which began like forest fires in the festival village every night. Music and dancers merged – the Efik dancers remain etched in my mind. Like the Fela gig, nothing ended until it blew itself out, whether that was at midnight or dawn. The heat was sapping, as was the cumulative effect of alcohol. Now we faced the regatta

Every state had a boat, and every boat had a band. By the time Philip and I arrived at Ikoyi, where he was going to be honoured and installed on the Imo state boat in recognition of his mother (several of the bandsmen had formerly been amongst her orphans), I wanted to sit down somewhere cool and quiet. I found a place of relative shade under the palm trees, and Philip sat beside me while they got the boats ready.

"So is it all over?" I remember asking my friend.

"If you mean the festival, yes, it is almost gone. And if you mean the murder enquiry, it has also been wrapped up to the great satisfaction of some of the participants, but it leaves me with a distinctly uneasy feeling."

"You mean, you wonder whether we have the right man?" I was voicing fears of my own.

"Well, I would not quite say that," said Philip. "But I am left with some very serious questions. Let us suppose that this East German agent committed the crime in order, as has been suggested, to prevent Marcus from leaving the meeting and revealing their secrets. What happened next? Who moved the body and why? Was the body of Marcus desecrated, as we saw it in that lane, by one of the plotters? And why? And who moved it to the lane?"

"I share all those questions. And I also ask what has happened to his brother Samuel, and what did happen to Shehu Diello in Sokoto? And what was the East German man doing in Nigeria anyway? And what is going to happen to him? Will he be tried for murder?"

"Or extradited to his homeland?" Philip added. "Let's imagine that we do have the right man who did the murder, we still do not have the murder story!"

When he came back from his boat trip, he found me fast asleep under the same tree, the object of attention and adoration of every stinging insect of the shoreline. We took a taxi back to the compound and the calamine lotion. In the car I told him that I was leaving for Kaduna in the morning and he looked slightly surprised.

"Well, I wonder that you are bothering with that – your friends in the CIA and MI6 probably have less interest in what is happening there than amongst the 15,000 so visitors that we have had down here in Lagos, surely?"

"Well, I'm not sure. For a start, I have not been in touch since our last meeting so I do not really know what they want. Then again, a big chunk of the visitors are going up north, over 500 miles to Kaduna and the government have chartered 2000 luxury buses, as it says in the press releases, to take people out there. I am sure that the chief wants me there, however, and that is really why I am going."

"You bet!" grinned Philip. "I am sure you're right. He certainly does want you there. What better opportunity to show off his deputy chairman, MA (Oxon)?" Then he raised his hands and paused in mock humility. "Or have I got that wrong? Perhaps you have not bought your second degree yet and are still simple BA? So Nigerian, your universities!"

Both of us roared with laughter, and I confessed that I had to wait a couple more years before I was entitled to buy my further degree. I did however point out that it would cost at least 15 naira and I would have to pay the rental fee for my gown as well.

"But, yes, the chief does want you there, and he certainly deserves that. Please go along and look after him. But it will be a long and tedious drive for all three of you. How are you are going to keep John awake while you two are asleep in the back, I would like to know?"

"No, I am not going with them. The chief has to resolve a land dispute in a village in northern Oyo on the way and thinks my face would not be quite so appropriate there. He wants to send me ahead to secure the hotel rooms and sit in them until he arrives. Apparently, there is a tendency for receptionists to sell rooms to the highest bidder regardless of previous bookings."

"Our chief is a very wise chief, Henry, and that is a sensible policy. So I guess you are going to fly?"

Well, yes, he was right, it had been arranged that I was going to fly. The chief's office booked me a seat – "the one we normally book for the chief" – and John drove me to the airport.

As I waited in the lounge, Philip's disparagement of the durbar rang in my ears. "Why on earth the Nigerian government are aping the previous practices of the British I cannot tell! This is what we did in the early years of the century. Get all the northern tribes to move onto their horses and see how they parade in front of the British governors. Just like the great durbar in Delhi for the Queen Empress of India. We have had a great cultural festival here in Lagos, and now we end it with an imitation of trooping of the colour in Kaduna."

Yet despite Philip's condemnation, I was rather looking forward to it. It was a complete change from all the things that I had encountered during the last three weeks, and in a different part of the country. I looked forward to it.

When we boarded, I was delighted to see that the chief's usual seat was seat 1A, and that the seat next door to it was empty. The cheerful steward brought me a glass of champagne.

"I know your chief."

As the doors were about to shut, the steward struggled through them with a heavy piece of baggage. This was thrown onto the empty seat next to me and strapped in. My new companion, looking sideways at me with distant and slightly forlorn eyes, and dressed in a tight string bag, had an apple in his mouth. A dead goat.

"Sorry about this," said my friendly steward. "But they did book a full ticket for him and you cannot say no to them." He leant down and turned the label on the goats collar towards me. "Department of military intelligence, to be collected in Kaduna."

The flight passed quietly with neither I nor my companion having much to say to each other. The goat got off first and I followed, taking care to follow the chief's instructions, going into town immediately to secure the hotel rooms. I was in occupation when he and John arrived. We were reunited over dinner in the chief's room. John said that the chief was received in Oyo like the old Testament judge Solomon.

The chief said that for a chauffeur, John was becoming far too cheeky and knew too much. "Soon I will have to send you away to discover how to earn a living, instead of riding around in luxury in my car."

The next day was the durbar. Despite Philip's criticisms, once it was all over, and I was looking back on it the truth was simple. I loved it. The kings and presidents and ambassadors of the fifty-six countries taking part in Festac sat in the grandstand. The chief and I were in a smaller stand on the other side of the parade ground. The parade was opened by the Sultan of Sokoto, his retainers and bodyguards, followed by the emirs. Kano was followed by Katsna and then by Kaduna and Zaria, dignified men of the semi-desert mounted on beautiful horses, groomed and oiled until they shone. The bridle work and saddlery was equally polished, and studied with sparkling gold for the leadership, and shining brass and bronze elsewhere. Then came the Fulani horsemen, charging at speed, mounting and dismounting in a single bound, and charging imaginary enemies with bloodcurdling cries.

The parade and demonstrations lasted three hours, but the spectacle kept you in your seat, eager to take in the next display. Then came the mounted troops of the Nigerian army, and at their head a tall man riding a black horse as spectacularly turned out as everybody else. As he passed the grandstand and saluted his face was turned away from me, but as he turned back I saw the unmistakable profile of Baban. He held the reins lightly in one hand above the pomel, but he held the horse as if it was possessed by an electrical force that ran from his body into its beautiful, delicate frame. There was no more impressive horseman in sight, and the chief and I turned and looked at each other in mute recognition of that fact.

As we were leaving the stand and walking slowly across the now emptying parade ground – slowly because the chief seemed to recognise someone every ten feet, and elaborate introductions had to take place. His deputy had to be introduced and other formalities observed. While we were seemingly meeting the whole world of Nigeria in this way, a young army officer came panting up at a run and planted himself in front of us.

"Compliments of His Excellency, the director of military intelligence, but you are both required immediately and I am to lead you to him." He must have caught the look of alarm on our faces, because he quickly said, "You are not under arrest, gentleman. The director just wants to talk to you for a moment."

I glanced at the chief and he shrugged.

We followed the officer behind the grandstand and into the cavalry lines, past some very wonderful horses until I saw the striking 18 hand gelding upon which Baban had been mounted. Just beyond it, in a small sideless tented pavilion, was the great man himself. He stood when he saw us approaching and greeted us affably. His demeanour was totally different from the way that he had started our last meeting and I was quite shocked at the change. He beckoned to aides to bring up the chairs and we all sat down to drink what turned out to be iced coffee.

"Do you like it? I saw it first in America. Never saw it here. Now we have it regularly!"

If he had something on his mind, as his messenger had indicated, he was in no particular hurry to share it. He certainly did not agree with Phillip's view on the durbar.

"This is Nigeria at its best, don't you think, gentlemen? I am sure that the writers and musicians and the dancers are all very well and good, but it is here, today, that you see something of the essence of my Nigeria. I was brought up to this. Did you know that my father managed the horses of the Emir of Kano? We were not important people, from a small tribe on the plateau and as a boy I spoke neither Hausa or Fulani. My father had great skills and was very valuable to his master, and he raised our status, so much so that today many people think I came from some important northern family."

The last sentence was spoken almost introspectively. Almost as if it was not addressed to us at all, and the next sentence had a similar quality.

"Like the Diello family. How we looked up to them

- they were really important. Rather like your English aristocracy, Mr Kettering. I learned all about that at Sandhurst."

Now he was looking at me closely, and I felt an urge in him to explain something to us without giving anything away.

"Yes, Sandhurst was very important to me. I know that you are familiar with Britain in a way that I will never be, chief, and that you visit London often. Mr Kettering, I can never know what you know about your own country. But I have tried to mould many of the ways in which I behave on the things that I learnt during those years. In particular, my patriotism. I love my country, gentlemen, as the English do theirs. And if the Welsh and the Irish and the Scots try sometimes to get out, it is you English, Mr Kettering, who bind them all back together and make them feel how important it is to be British!"

Nothing, it seemed to me, was more bizarre than a talk about patriotism from a Nigerian general shortly after a dreadful civil war, but I could see that I was not there to voice an opinion but to listen to a great man's soliloquy.

"That generation who went to Sandhurst with me, and I remind you that it has included three presidents of our country so far, then found itself subjected to the test of secession and war. Using all that we had learnt at Sandhurst, we joined the peacekeeping force and went to the Congo, gentlemen. Few people realise how important it was that we all saw service in the UN peacekeeping forces. Mr Achebe, who everyone says is the most important writer, although I have not read his books myself, writes of how 'things fall apart.' Well, I saw how things fell apart in Katanga andI determined that they should not fall apart in Nigeria."

Although it was clear that he had not finished, he paused here for breath. He looked about him and called an aide over to his side. After a whispered conversation he turned back to me.

"I am told, Mr Kettering, that your father is a farmer. You will be the first to appreciate that this horse" – he nodded towards his magnificent charger – "must be properly rubbed down after exercise, and while he must have water he must not have too much."

I nodded my agreement and I would have added a compliment on the superb beast had he not immediately continued. "That aristocratic Diello family. The ones that you know, chief, are only a branch of that noble tree, but the inheritance of intelligence runs to the very tips of the branches. I understand that the young man Marcus was very bright. I cannot speak of Samuel, your namesake, because I never met him. But Shehu, whom I met several times, was a brilliant man. He was a student of African politics and literature, and although I fundamentally disagreed with him, I had to admire his arguments and the intellectual force behind them. When I first met him I thought that his first concern was language and culture . He kept talking about people having the right to decide which community they belonged to and how that community expressed itself.

"Then one night I heard him speaking to a group of officers at the training school here, in this town, about restoring the great empires of the Sahel. When I heard him speak about the empire of Songhai I thought I was dealing with another fanatical regionalist and I began to prepare myself to stop him if he became dangerous.

Then I heard that he was exporting antiquities and buying arms, and I knew that it would shortly be time to act, so I planted a man loyal to me in his midst. As I told you when we last met this was how Ibrahim became involved."

Both the chief and I nodded. We did not want to interrupt but to hear what came next. Baban cleared his throat and looked from one to another.

"Here it appears that I might have got things slightly wrong, or at least, I might be guilty of having misunderstood things a little bit."

The man was clearly having difficulty in recognising that he could have made a mistake. I watched as he tried to reconcile himself to what he had just said, and then he hurried on.

"I thought, you see, that he was intending to bring arms into Nigeria, perhaps to try to overthrow the government and start another civil war. This would not be so unusual here. As you will know, chief, when we have had regime change, it has usually been because the army itself has decided that we need to change. A provincial revolt with guns coming in from outside would be a grim reminder of Biafra and I determined that I must act against it and nip its bud, as the English say. Accordingly, I instructed my man Ibrahim, who by this time was so much in the confidence of the plotters that he had become their business manager, to stop the guns being purchased and close things down. I thought I had done enough, but I had misunderstood two things."

I could see that this conversation was getting tough for its main participant but I could equally see that he was determined to complete it. He felt compelled to tell us all of this. His hands were gripping the arms of the folding campaign chair in which he sat so tightly that I thought he might pull it apart.

"It is important that these things are known to you, chief. You have to comfort the father and the family that produced these three boys. What you do not know at present is that, last night, young Samuel most inadvisedly tried to escape from the Dodan. He was seen by a perimeter guard who commanded him to stop, and, when he didn't, shot him. The young man died of his wounds in the infirmary. The report will say that this was a tragic accident. Meanwhile the official report on the death of his brother Shehu, in Sokoto, will say that he was killed by intruders while he was trying to defend the sultan."

Both the chief and I were now watching him intently. The hands had come off the arms of the chair and were now twisting and turning on his lap. He did seem very genuinely agitated, and the next words came in a whisper.

"Please, chief, do your best to assure the family members and the father of these boys that they all died honourably. I cannot do this myself. You are their trusted friend – please do this for me. No one else knows the story as you do. The other officers involved in the plot, two of whom were in the room when young Marcus was killed, were tried by military tribunal this morning and shot at lunchtime on Bar beach by firing squad. This could have been so different. If I had known in time that Shehu planned his revolutions to take place in other African countries and not in Nigeria. If I had known in time that the people that they were buying guns from were really the Stasi and the KGB. If I had known that stopping the pattern of purchasing would send somebody from East Germany to find out what was happening. If, if! But I didn't, and I blame myself because my intelligence should've been better."

He looked up again, and this time I read in his eyes a plea for some form of forgiveness. It was almost as if he expected us to chorus, "Oh, no, you were not really to blame!" Both the chief and I were silent, however, absorbing his story, and the ruthless violence that he had used to bring it to its closing point.

The chief broke the silence. "And why, director, do you imagine that neither Mr Kettering nor I myself will keep your secrets?"

The sinister, thin lipped smile reappeared. We were back to the old Baban. "You, chief, will be absolutely silent. You have too much to lose. Your family, your status, your company – all at risk. And your Ibo friends, like your publishing director and even your driver, what crimes did they commit during the war which we have not yet discovered? And you, Mr Kettering, could face a prison sentence for breaking the Official Secrets act if somebody spoke the wrong word in the wrong ear. Besides which, you would want to protect your chief. And both of you would prefer the Diello family to cope with the sadness of their loss knowing that these three died in honourable circumstances."

The lizard eyes flickered and the little pink tongue slid across the thin lips.

"Now, do either of you have any questions? I can answer one each, and then I have to accompany the president to the reception for heads of state."

The chief beat me to it. "I can hardly bear what you are asking me to do, but of course I have to do it. Personally, I think that your man Ibrahim must share the blame. What has happened to him?"

"Well, chief I am glad you have the good sense

to accept the fait accompli. And the Diello family will continue to enjoy your support and friendship. Ibrahim has come out of this really quite well. He did not know of course where the guns were going, only Shehu knew that. I do not know whether you were aware, but Ibrahim comes from Abuja. Next week there will be a federal decree concerning the new capital city of Nigeria. Like Australia, and Brazil, and indeed the United States, we are building a new capital outside any state boundary. The new federal territory is in Abuja. Ibrahim will be silent and discreet as long as his father's land is included in the designated capital territory."

It was my turn now, and I had at least two questions, but Baban stopped one of them in its tracks.

"Mr Kettering, if you were thinking of asking about ritual murders, then I have to say that I know nothing, and everyone who might know something seems to be dead. Anything else?"

"Yes, I would like to know what happened to the actual murderer. Where is this East German and what are you going to do with him?"

Baban gave a most inappropriate laugh. It sounded like a tin can rolling down a windy cobbled street. "I should have told you, it is the most delightful story."

He brought us up-to-date in terms of the capture of Holgar Pipek, adding, "Of course he is no longer in my hands. I cannot shoot him or put him on trial or do anything else to him, since he is not a Nigerian citizen, so I have handed him over to your British and American friends, Mr Kettering, and they have flown him home to his native land."

"So he is the one who gets away scot-free?" I could not help saying.

"Not at all, Mr Kettering, not at all. I understand that the British and the Americans have swapped him for another spy, one of theirs. I also understand that his masters in the Stasi and the KGB get a bit suspicious about captured agents who might have been, as I think they call it, 'turned' by the opposition. I do not imagine that he will have a comfortable time at all."

At this point he unwound his long body from the chair and prepared to leave us. He shook the chief by the hand and told him that his work on the schoolbooks programme was of vital national importance, and then he turned to me.

"I am pleased to have met you, Mr Kettering. You have, I think, only a few weeks left in Nigeria. At least, that's what your visa says! I hope you have an enjoyable time. I have to say, truthfully, that having watched your efforts since your arrival, I conclude that you were not cut out to be a spy. You have been lucky that this turned out well for you, since it could've been a disaster. My advice, for what it is worth, is to steer clear of espionage in the rest of your life. Stick to books, Mr Kettering, they contain the only secrets that you will ever need to know!"

With that, he was gone, and the chief's arm was round my shoulder.

"Come along, Henry, we have some sad things to chew over, and then we need to restore our spirits with a good dinner!"

CHAPTER 20 EPILOGUE

'THE PAST IS is another country.' The dictum is so well worn that it is almost a cliche, but it keeps coming back to me as I retrace my steps of 45 years ago. At times I find myself so full of remorse and shame about the idiocy that took me to Nigeria in the first place that I can scarcely think or write. At other times I glorify those months in 1976 in 1977 as my 'university of life.' I can speculate for hours about the life of Marcus, which we were denied, and then again there are periods when I simply rejoice in my great good fortune in meeting such wonderful people with such real values, although in some fairly strange circumstances. Now, as I stand on the brink of my 70s and have a little more time to look around me, I find that the people that I want to celebrate the most, my friends from that time, were not great correspondents. In the years following my departure, there was no great and continuing flow of letter writing perpetuating our friendship. Rather the reverse.

Indeed, for the first decade I heard very little except for the odd, quirky communication from Philip. One, I remember was a note on Ikoyi Hotel notepaper that read, "Henry, we never solved the mystery. Tell me if you think that Baban's explanation was correct, and, if so, why was the death of dear Marcus presented as a ritual murder?"

I replied, of course, giving my thoughts at that time as best I could, but I have no means of knowing whether it reached him, because there was no reply. When we eventually met again years later, I completely forgot to ask if he had received it

The whole pattern of events that took place in those

303

last weeks in Nigeria after the durbar and in the next 12 months back in England is pretty hazy in an aging memory. I do recall a trip to a teachers' conference in Port Harcourt, where the bidding on hotel rooms went so high that I was forced to sleep in one of the cabana beside the swimming pool. Going up to Enugu with Cyprian Ekwensi to finalise the contents of the Festac African New Writing book was a highlight, especially since it allowed me to spend time with Philip in his village, and get acquainted with his mother and the orphans. I was also able to spend time at the University at Nsukka and meet Chinua Achebe, and I regard this as one of the greatest privileges of my life as a reader. I recall rushing with Philip to Maiduguri to do what we could to help finalise the last stages of getting the Kanuri language written on paper. I have heard my children groan when I begin again on the old story of my visit to the court of the Emir of Kano to petition the ruler to allow our technical drawing handbooks to get the imprimatur of his royal highness in order that they could be used in Islamic schools and technical colleges.

The most important meeting for me personally during this time took place at the US Embassy in Lagos shortly before my departure. I really did not know what to expect. I had heard nothing since our last meeting, when my two colleagues had run off delightedly to report to London and Washington on their successful work in blocking Soviet influence, curtailing gun smuggling, thwarting rebellion against African rulers under British or American influence, and no doubt other good things that they found themselves able to include in their dispatches. I imagined that this meeting was going to be "your contract is at an end, thanks a lot and goodbye." If so, I was in for a shock.

The meeting convened in our usual place in the embassy. Cy, as usual, was late, and as usual, set the tone and agenda for the meeting. His opening line was indicative.

"Now, Henry, sorry to put you in for this. But I have to tell you formally and officially, you are fired."

George chimed in. "Well, Henry, Cy has said what he has to say, and given the recording devices here, that is now all on the record. No doubt he will send you a note in writing. For me, it's a little more complicated. I need to ask you to sign a letter to me confirming that you were never employed by any British agency, at any time, and that while we may have paid you for information provided, on occasion, we entered into no agreements and have no formal or legal relationship with you."

I was dumbstruck. I can recall stuttering something like, "Well, why has this suddenly happened?"

"It's all a question of deniability, Henry," George replied. "Delighted as they are with the information we sent them, and the actions they were able to take as a result, both the boys in Foggy Bottom and our friends on the other side of the Thames in River House, have asked about the information trail, and when it comes up to you, they have asked that your role in all of this be deleted. I suspect that there may have been sensitivities in the Nigerian government about covert intelligence gathering in a now independent nation. Certainly, we are all agreed, on all sides, the record must show that you never existed. So I have drafted a note to cover that."

He pushed a piece of High Commission notepaper across the table towards me.

"If you would kindly sign that this, it will bring our relationship to a satisfactory end."

Both men looked a little bit embarrassed. When I read the note, it said exactly what George had intimated. If Nigeria had been for me a process of reaching maturity, then this was the point at which I realised that the process was beginning to yield benefits.

"No," I said.

The effect on both men was hugely satisfying. I could not have done better with a stun gun or a taser. After a recovery period, Cy said, "You know we can make you sign that, don't you?"

Offering resistance to his colleague's view for the first time in my recollection, George said, "No, Cy, we can't. Henry, why can't you sign it?"

"Well," I remember saying, "I can't sign it because it is not complete. When I entered into this agreement with you, I was also required by you to sign the British Official Secrets act. If you now wish me to say that I did not sign the agreement, then you must also say that I did not sign the act. I cannot do one without the other."

George looked at Cy, who started to say, "But that means that you can tell…"

Taking out his fountain pen, George added the necessary words and shoved the document back to me.

"Now, gentlemen, I need your undertaking that the original papers that I signed in London have been destroyed, and I need a copy of this document with both your signatures upon it before I sign the original."

George did as requested without further reference to his partner in arms, and we accomplished the remaining business. Cy abruptly said, "So long" and left the room. As George and I went downstairs, George said that he felt that that was really the best conclusion for both of us.

"We were not so fussed but the Yanks were really anxious to cover their tracks. So, very sorry, old boy, no OBE for you! One thing did strike me, though. Shan't be needing my informants budget for the rest of the year now you will be gone! So I've emptied what remains of it into your bank account, dear boy. Hope that recompenses for not being able to offer further services to Queen and country."

We shook hands and went our separate ways, not thinking, on my part, that I would ever encounter him again. Since I was going home to unemployment, I knew that I would be grateful for any further cash support that my Queen and country could provide for me.

I was really surprised when I returned to London and checked my bank account. That last contract payment was double the value of the original contract. Since I had lived entirely at the company expense while in Nigeria, for the first time one my life, I had a small capital sum at my disposal. On the other hand I had no job. Although, in my ignorance, I thought that I was reasonably well educated, I had no training for any sort of job. I remember going up to Shropshire to see my mother, and mooching about in London where I took a small flat in Bayswater. Eventually I determined to do a training course that fitted me for something, and in September I moved to Glasgow and enrolled on the Strathclyde University librarianship diploma course. The year that followed fulfilled all of my expectations. Although I never did get to write my seminal thesis on 'The role of single malt whisky in the literary development of radical writing in Nigeria and Scotland: a study of Wole Soyinka and Hugh McDiarmid,' many other life changing events occurred.

First amongst them, I met Lydia. After the course we settled in London, and eventually married and brought up a family. During those early London years I cannot recall too many reminders of my peripheral dabbling in the world of espionage. But there were a few. In the first instance, I had applied for a job as a junior librarian at the House of Commons. I was pleased and gratified to be called for interview, and then to be shortlisted. When I turned up for the final interview, the chairman of the interview panel took me to one side and said in that English intonation that implies that he knows something about you that neither of you can discuss, "I asked our people if you would need full security vetting if you got this job, and I was gratified to hear from them that after a background check, they had established that your vetting was already in place, and that certain parties vouched for your 'integrity, dedication and discretion.' Good for you. Nod, nod, wink wink, as we say!" I have to say I found this very unnerving.

The second occasion occurred a few years later. Lydia and I had been to the theatre and had called in at my club for a drink on the way home. As soon as I saw him there, I recognised him. Hunched on a bar stool, older, greyer but unmistakably George Mainbrace. I settled Lydia at a table and went up to order our drinks. He looked up and recognised me.

"Hello, dear boy. Had no idea you were a member here. I am next door, but our bar is closed tonight. Leak in the ceiling. So doing the old reciprocity thing."

I explained that I was with my wife and must take her a drink but hoped we could have a brief chat before he left. And we did. He claimed that life had treated him well, though to my eyes he seemed rundown and depressed. He told me that he had left Nigeria to become military attaché in Tirana.

"My lady wife loved it. Bought a little place in Tuscany for our retirement. Just me now though. She left me. Cancer. Seldom in London these days. Have to look after the vines and the olives, don't you know? Only me to do it. And the dog."

I asked after Cy. "Went to Costa Rica as first secretary. Promoted, just like me, after a great success in Nigeria. Silly sod died of aids. Never saw him again."

I found that I had one final request. "George, are you absolutely certain in your own mind that the Stasi colonel killed Marcus Diello? It is very important to me, and I can never get it out of my mind. I thought it might all have been a manipulation of Baban."

"Absolutely certain sure, dear boy," came back the reply.

I can see him now. My question had caused him to draw himself up and compose himself. I was sure that he had consumed a drink or two that evening, but his reply was straightforward and direct.

"Do you know, we interviewed Pipek directly before he was deported. He said that he had no option. He asked for our understanding as fellow intelligence officers. Once he had gathered that Marcus knew all of the details of the plotters and the plan, and that he was about to leave the meeting and communicate this to his father and others in an effort to stop the work that Shehu and Samuel were doing, then this breach of security had to be curtailed immediately. He said that he hardly thought before he had acted, but as soon as he had done it, he was really scared because he thought that his own life was in danger in that room. For that reason he left immediately.

"He told us that he hid outside in the square, and saw some people – who they were he did not know, but it could have been some of those who were at the meeting or possibly some of Baban's people – moving the body. His story was that as soon as he had left the meeting room, Baban's people came rushing into the room and arrested everybody. Colonel Pipek was relieved by this, since he felt sure that Samuel Diello would come after him and try to kill him."

George sighed. "This part was a bad business, don't you think? I mean, quite apart from killing your friend, we missed the opportunity here of running this thing on for a few months and discovering a lot more. It was a bad show for Pipek himself. As you know, he spent the next 24 hours struggling to get out of the country. The Americans swapped him for two of their people that they wanted out of Moscow, but of course if you go back on a swap deal then your ultimate KGB masters get very suspicious about you. He resumed his Czechoslovakia job, but a year later got a posting to run a hydroelectric generating plant in Tomsk. Or was it Omsk? Memory not entirely reliable now. But rely upon it, old chap, he did the job. Had it from his own lips. Probably drowned in vodka at his hydro plant, just as I am in San Giovese in Chiantishire."

With that, George crashed through the club swing doors, staggered down the steps signalling for a taxi, and disappeared into the night. I never saw him again, but I took good care to report his verdict to my friends in Nigeria.

As always when time has passed, they took the news in very different ways. The chief, for example, was grateful for confirmation of what he felt that he knew already.

Our conversation with Baban in Kaduna had convinced him. Now somebody had independently confirmed it. At the other extreme, Philip always pushed back, asking what the motivation was for anybody saying anything. Just as he had been worried that Baban was selling us a story to disguise his own encouragement of a putative coup that he had abandoned before it got underway, so he now sent me a note asking what I thought the security forces were trying to hide by telling me this.

I must admit that I always felt slightly aggrieved when I sent him what I thought was an answer, and he, after a while, replied with further questions. Perhaps I was still hoping then that life resolved itself like detective stories on television: you end up with a real conclusion that everybody accepts, and then go on to the next episode. I was learning slowly that the guilty verdict may be different for each observer, and that perhaps what is most interesting is the impact of the deaths of three brothers on their family and their society, as significant in its way as gun running and antiquities smuggling. My mind was turning from solving a crime to seeing how a whole society was changing and reshaping.

I was thinking this way when on my social media an image of two panting dogs appeared. Mongrels of uncertain patrimony, I thought, but certainly bright and hungry looking. The accompanying message named them as Henry and Philip, "completely clueless, capable of following a trail if given enough help by their owner, Cyril Fagunwa."

I messaged back immediately, and discovered that Cyril had retired from the Lagos force and returned to Benin, where he was promoted to chief superintendent of detectives.

"It's a small force, but I'm back with my people, and I now know how much my wife and children have missed me."

I told him about my talk with George, and I could not resist asking him for his conclusions. Here is his text:

"I am quite sure that we got our murderer. There were four people in the room besides Marcus and Holgar Pipek. I was never allowed to interview the three army officers, including Samuel, and then they were dead. But I did catch up with Ibrahim and his story does confirm what you know already. He said that Pipek acted in a moment, before any of them realised what he was about to do. Samuel was distraught and kept trying to stop the bleeding by pressing on the archery with his fingers. But it seemed only a few seconds elapsed before they became certain that Marcus was dead. When they looked up the East German had slipped out, and Ibrahim said that he had insisted that the body could not be found where it was known that they were meeting, so the other two officers wrapped Marcus up and carried the body into the square. Ibrahim said he did not know where they left him."

In response to some further questions from me, he replied that Ibrahim was a naira millionaire property developer, having made a fortune from the development of the new Nigerian federal capital at Abuja, large chunks of which were built on the family far, and Cyril's belief was that what we had thought was a ritual murder was in fact a clumsy attempt to disguise the crime and to distance it from the military. He concluded that perhaps we would never now know more than this.

Ever since I had left Nigeria, I had seen the chief at regular intervals. He came to London for meetings of the supervisory board which owned the Nigerian company as well as companies in Canada, Australia, India and the UK. When our first child, a baby girl, was born and I sent him a telex, I received a very excited message back about the urgent need to perform Yoruba ceremonies to bless the house. Fully attired in his ceremonial cloth of gold agbada and carrying a bottle of Highland Park single malt, he carefully poured libations into each corner of the main rooms of the flat, including Kate's bedroom, while her mother looked on in some distress. Verses were read from 'The Forest of 1000 Daemons', before we settled down to enjoy what remained of the whisky.

Ten years had now passed, and the chief had no more questions about the murder. His mind that night was upon other things. He had recently been awarded the Order of the Federal Republic (MFR) to add to his Order of the Niger. These honours marked the completion of the initial Universal Primary Education plan, but also heralded his retirement from the company. The huge commercial success that he had created heralded the gradual nationalisation of the company, and the replacement of people like himself with political appointees.

Some weeks later, when the awards been announced publicly, I sent him a note congratulating him on his achievements and he responded with his normal mixture of pride and irony.

"It is a normal mark of respect, Henry, that in our tribe we give a live turkey to our friends at moments of high achievement. I now have 103 turkeys in my garden in Ibadan, and they have eaten all of my wife's roses. She suggests that I retire immediately and become a turkey farmer. What is your professional advice?"

The last time I saw the chief, he looked tired and drawn, and if he had not already announced his intention, I would strongly have advised him to retire. But as is often the case, retirement was also a death sentence. I had reports of continuing health difficulties, not least of all from Bimpe, who now was becoming my chief Nigerian correspondent. The age of letters and the age of telex are now well past. We communicated first on email and then on text, and direct message and Instagram and WhatsApp.

Bimpe quickly became an expert in instant communication. She kindly included me in her family communications, as John, with her help and support, built a taxi and freight transport company in the east, helped initially by contracts to deliver books for the chief. John's passion and marketing flair soon turned his enterprise into a great success as the economy, and the roads and petrol supplies in the east at long last returned to normality after the war. They named their first child, a daughter, for me, despite my protests. As it has turned out, Hen has now become my chief Nigerian correspondent. She went to Calabar to study and she is now an agronomist working for the Anambra state government.

It was Bimpe, though, who told me about the chief's last great tour of the eastern states. John had driven him "in a brand-new luxury Land Rover called a Range Rover. He was like a great Oba in his state carriage. He was received by headteachers and state education ministry officials everywhere. John said that it was like a football team touring the town after winning the cup."

Sadly, within a few weeks of this I was receiving obituary notices. Amidst the grief, to my huge satisfaction these seemed to see him largely as I did: a man determined to do good for his fellow man, whether at a personal, regional or national level. Not a very political man, and not a hugely commercially motivated man either, but a man driven by what he saw as the need to break the logjam of history by adding educational development to the skills and ingenuity and imagination of the people he saw around him. It is sad that people have to die before you realise what the real impact was upon you, and my sense of what I owed to the chief increased in the months following his death.

When the call came from the Nigerian Embassy in London, it fell on fertile ground. Would I be interested in helping to organise a meeting in London to celebrate the memory of the chief and of his achievements? I jumped at the opportunity. They were planning to hold it in the School of African and Oriental studies (SOAS), and I undertook to invite various educationalists and publishers who could testify to that achievement. My wife, Lydia, was by this time a recognised authority on the economic and social effects of mass literacy, and we agreed that she should speak on the context of Universal Primary Education and its importance in the development of the federal Nigeria of today.

I immediately got in touch with my Nigerian friends to tell them what was happening. I did not expect any of them to travel. Communications from Philip were, to say the least, "occasional." I had a photograph from the Marilynn Nance collection – she was a wonderful American photographer who took pictures throughout Festac— in which she had captured a crowd in the village listening to Mighty Sparrow, the celebrated Trinidadian calypso singer. Since I was slightly taller my head is clearly visible, and we were sure that it was the back of Philip standing alongside me. Henrietta sent it back with Philip's caption: "Oxford men stand out in a crowd, even in Nigeria."

I have an album of photographs of a visit that the chief and I made with Philip to the palace of the Alaafin of Oyo. It shows Philip and me being presented with a live turkey, which we are holding gingerly in case it showed resistance. I captioned it : 'Turkey competition: Chief – 103, the rest – 1.'

I knew from Bimpe that when Philip's mother died it was a shattering blow to both John and Philip . At this point, Philip had decided to leave publishing and move back east. He felt strongly that he should always support the orphanage in her memory, and he settled down to do that, as well as rebuilding and extending the empty homes in the village that his mother had taken over at the end of the war. I know that the chief made contributions, and did fundraising, but from what I have learnt from Bimpe and Henrietta, John was the chief source of funding. Eventually John was able to sell his business for a good price to a branch of the Mbanefo family trying to rebuild their dominance in transport services in the east, and some of this capital was used to set up a trust fund for the orphanage and support Philip in his old age. I had no idea as to Philip's state of health, but I knew that he must be in his late 70s or early 80s. I also knew that during the last decade he had not travelled further than one of the regional towns on the other side of the great river.

So, I was shockingly unprepared when I had a text saying that Philip and Bimpe would be attending the chief's memorial celebration. Could I meet them at Heathrow and arrange hotel accommodation for them?

I recalled that John had a fear of flying, helped, no doubt, by his memories of being bombed by the federal air force as a child. Henrietta apologised on his behalf and said that it was important to him and Philip that things were properly managed in the village while Philip was away.

For a day or two I was confused by the prospect of the sudden reunion. How should I entertain Philip? Should Lydia and I put them up at our house, now some 50 miles from central London, or should we find him a hotel near the venue? How mobile was he? I recall that I bombarded Bimpe with questions, and then received a firm reply saying that Philip would like to stay in the Hotel Russell in Russell Square, where he had once stayed before and which was very close to SOAS.

She said that they were both fit and healthy, and that if I could meet them, we could decide how to proceed as we went along. "No plan, Nigeria style," she put on the end of her message.

Then came a WhatsApp from Henrietta: "Mum and I put all your questions to Philip, and he has replied that when he was next with you, he would talk. Then he told me to tell you that he is really coming to London to collect the shoes of Chief Taiwo, which you took for repair at his favourite shoe repair shop in the Strand in 1977, but it appears that you never collected them or returned them to the chief. The chief's son, Michael, thinks they should fit him and would like them back."

I did remember this very well, and felt a sudden and urgent flush of guilt. This chief had been an elderly board member. He was a judge in the High Court of Lagos state, called to the bar in Middle Temple - and very fond of his black brogues. It was true, I had consented to take the shoes to be soled and healed. In the rush of events after my return I had completely forgotten. A quick check showed that the shop was closed 20 years before. I made sure however, before Philip arrived, to equip myself with a brand-new pair of size 11 1/2 black leather brogues for transport back to Nigeria.

As we approached the commemorative event Nigeria was back in my mind in a way that had not really been true for much of the intervening forty years. I had flashbacks of events and people, and a desperate anxiety to ask Philip what happened to various colleagues in the company and elsewhere. Realistically, I knew that domestic trivia, 'whatever happened to A N Other,' might not really engage him.

I was about to compile a list of such questions to send him before he left Nigeria when a message from Henrietta drove all other considerations out of my head. It simply said, "Sending urgent document to you at the request of Philip. Look out for a UPS delivery on Thursday and confirm you have it. Philip says this very important."

You can imagine what it was like waiting for Thursday. Eventually the day and then the delivery came. I signed for a slim envelope and opened it on tenterhooks. Inside was another sealed envelope, and a note from Bimpe I glanced at the envelope, which merely said, "What do you think of this?" in Philip's unmistakable scrawl.

Then I looked at what Bimpe had written. It turned out that she wanted to give me a factual account of how they had come by the document that Philip had now enclosed for me. She reminded me that her brother Ben was a journalist in Lagos and apparently he was preparing a feature on student life in London and Lagos.

Amongst the different episodes that Ben and his team had researched for serialisation in the Lagos Times had been pieces on student partying, on student poverty, on racial discrimination and stereotyping, and on high student suicide rates. While researching the last named, one of the researchers came up with a social media item from the earliest days of Facebook, pointing to a suicide note written by a medical student at Guys Hospital in London.

When Ben and his people had got back to the original, they found that it was much older than they thought. In fact it dated from the early 1980s, and had been archived in the records of the Greater London Council psychiatric services department, and had become available in full under the 30 year confidentiality rule. The early social media references that quoted it had said that it was written by "a Nigerian medical student in London." She said that the name "Uzman" was used in the text, but it was not signed, and all of Ben's efforts to find the writer's identity had failed so far.

At this point I put Bimpe's note to one side and sliced open the envelope. Inside I found three typed sheets attached to copies of both sides of an original handwritten note. I saw – this much remained of my Nigerian education - that the original had been written in Hausa. The type-written section was headed: 'Official translation prepared for the Metropolitan Police by AfroTrans Ltd, November 1981.'

If you have read this far, then I need you to read the full text of the note in order to appreciate how I felt at this point.

"Our ancestors, before embarking on a momentous journey, either through the great desert, or the inhospita-

319

ble forests, used to wait for a propitious time, or an event which cast a favourable light on their journey. They took care not to move forward unless blessed by a good atmosphere, and with all the sins and guilt arising from those sins of the past, propitiated and washed clean.

"I, Uzman, am here now to testify that these ways were the right ways. I am embarked upon my chosen career with good omens, and then, one night, I committed a sacrilege so dreadful that its dark shadow dogs my ways and prevents me from moving forward. When life is founded upon a lie, then you need to live an exceptionally good life to atone for it. But when, in a moment of aberration, you commit a sacrilege so great that you become a pariah in the eyes of all mankind, then you cannot ever recover. Should my kinsfolk ever discover what occurred, then the stain on our family honour would last in perpetuity. Making an end of myself, if it prevents that discovery, is the best act of my life. I have struggled on for four years since that abominable moment. Next year I will qualify as a doctor: I cannot practice with blood on my hands.

"Nor can I explain the night of my transgression. The strain of study on a night when I had been doing laboratory dissections. The 'Fela' concert that I had attended that evening and the capacity of the music to drive me towards hysterical madness. The alcohol? The ganja? Overwhelming fear of betraying the expectations of my family whose sacrifices had enabled me to reach this point in my studies? Nothing and nobody can explain, least of all I myself.

"When I finished my studies in Lagos and won my place in London, I took my troubled mind to a psychiatrist. One, and then another. They spoke of breakdown, schizophrenic episodes, of "not being in my own mind." But I have never had such a seizure since. None of this touches the torment that I feel.

"Nothing explains why, on my way back to my dwelling in the slums, I saw the body of a murdered man and, with my dissection kit in my bag, decided that the gods had sent him to me. I am starting my work neatly and methodically as I have been taught. I could not finish it. I woke up as if what I had been doing had been done in a trance. But I have never gone to sleep since without reliving this. The face of this young man whose throat had been cruelly cut is in my head and behind my eyes, waking or sleeping, always. I desecrated him. I am untouchable and unforgivable. I cannot be a doctor.

"I plan to slip away soundlessly. No one will know that I have gone. I plan to slip through the gap of life. As I come to work here they say, "Mind the gap" on the tube trains, but I do not mind it. It will be the doorway to my freedom.

"I leave these words with Galen, you great explorer of human anatomy. I know that you dissected Barbary apes, but could not bear to look at their faces. You should have guided my hand. I know I leave myself in yours."

Here it ended, and I realised why the paper had originally been found in a copy of Galen's Anatomy. I also realised that, whether or not it was the answer to our questions about the way in which Marcus had been found and what had been done to him, it spoke directly to my own life. Had I done enough to make good?

If I was thinking of verdicts then I did not have long to wait. Soon Philip himself was in town, an aging Tiresias, losing his eyesight, not the cutting edge of his incisive judgements. I soon realised that he was not a very comfortable person to be with these days. His judgements on London soon fell thick and fast.

"It's a dull grey place with nothing to celebrate;" "the racialist capital of a racialist country;" and "a triumph of man's inhumanity to man" were some early samples. Yet he was quite delightful at the memorial meeting, and with his remarks from the podium reminded us all of the chief's determination that minority groups in tribal terms should not be left out educationally - he used the Kanuri example effectively – and then making us laugh by recounting the chief's love of small children, and how his grandchildren used him as a climbing frame, exploring the deep pockets of his robes for money and illicit food stuffs. He invited us to picture of the chief's wife watching this performances and muttering, "Who diss man think he is? A chocolate bear?"

Towards the end of the week, I was developing a slightly edgy feeling. We needed to talk about the document, yet somehow events and perhaps our own reluctance was preventing this. On the Friday night (Philip was leaving on the Sunday) we went to a revival of Ola Rotimi's wonderful play, 'The gods are not to blame'. This reworking of Oedipus has a crucial relevance to the civil war, and as I glanced at my old friend's face from time to time, I saw that the struggles of 1967 - 70 were close to the surface.

When I got him back to the hotel, Bimpe, who had been out with friends, had already gone to bed. Philip asked if I would like a nightcap. We sat in an almost empty hotel bar. I remember that I was drinking the Highland Park, but he was drinking Glenmorangie. We drank ruminatively, and I thought that he was about to say something about the play when he suddenly said,

"Do you have a clear and satisfactory explanation in your mind for what happened to our dear friend Marcus?"

I should not of been surprised, but I was. I started out with something about it being fairly clear who murdered Marcus and why, but we had to be careful about things like this latest document, since we had precious little evidence to tie this desperate medical student to the events that took place.

He nodded for a moment and then said, "What if we have got it all wrong? I have always wondered if Baban was behind all this. What if he got these younger officers involved in a plot to overthrow the government, but then they did not want his leadership? They might have felt that he was the older generation trying to manipulate them. What if he was the importer of arms and the exporter of the antiquities? And what if the East German was there to negotiate with him, and could be used as a handy scapegoat? What if the attempt to disguise the murder as a ritual killing was just that? For me, we keep on relying on things people said in interviews that were never recorded and we do not have a very reliable set of witnesses.

"I concede that Cyril's view is pretty powerful, but notice how Baban eventually silenced him with a promotion which settled the case. We are dealing here with a major figure of evil and manipulation, but he is somehow anxious to present himself to us as someone who read things wrongly at the beginning of this officers' plot, and then struggled to recover, until the murder took place for which he was not responsible, and after which he could get a better grip on what was happening. I don't buy what he said to you and the chief in Kaduna. John and Bimpe say that I grow more sceptical, more cantankerous and more left-wing by the year. I don't mind dying with my doubts, but I cannot rationalise them into certainties."

I pondered this. I realised that we were all going to see what happened through our own eyes and in our own ways. Speaking personally, I had a story that explained these events, and although it was not a comfortable fit and there were legitimate questions to be asked, it was a reasonable explanation. Yet in the face of Phillip's uncertainties, I still wracked my mind to find ways of demonstrating more certainty.

"I respect your position, Philip, and I do wish that I had fresh evidence to offer. But, you know, only one man can tell us the absolute truth, and that is Baban himself! Why don't we go and ask him?"

The question was asked with a smile. My memories of Baban were very clear and even at my advanced age the idea of being in the same room with him were quite terrifying. I was still shivering with anticipated apprehension when Philip came back with a devastating reply.

"He's dead!"

I was shocked into silence for a moment. We always think that evil lives forever. How? Why? Where? I asked. In what circumstances? Philip explained that towards the end of his career, the director of military intelligence was becoming less and less trusted by his colleagues in the military government. Successive presidents owed less and less to him, and his ability to effect regime change through a military revolt had declined since, as we had seen, he was becoming less influential with younger soldiers. His reputation went before him: every time there was the hint of a coup it was blamed on him.

Yet the men in the Dodan still feared to remove

him, since in retirement he might become an even more potent rallying point for revolt. So, in Philip's words, "They kept on giving him more and more dangerous jobs, designed to keep him away from the centre. He must have hated that. Eventually he was sent to lead a task force dealing with jihadist attacks across the border with the Cameroons in the far north east. His expeditionary force was attacking a Boko Haram camp when they were caught in an ambush."

"This was big news, Philip. How did I miss it? Where were the obituaries?"

"Well, you did not miss anything. It was all hushed up at the time. In fact, I only heard myself quite recently. The official line is that nothing was said because it would have encouraged the enemy. And, strangely enough, it appears that he was the only casualty in this ambush. I remain very sceptical."

There was a long pause while I took stock of this and took a long pull of whisky at the same time. I looked at the tired old man sitting in front of me. I did not know what to say next. Then those broad features broke into a smile and the wise eyes sparkled.

"It's like I told you years ago, Henry. Doubt and uncertainty live in the same house as you. The trick is living with them and understanding what they tell you. Things only get resolved in murder mysteries and detective stories. In life we have to make an accommodation with uncertainty. Rotimi was right. The gods are not to blame. As a lifelong atheist, I forgive them. It is men and women who betray humanity. Marcus died because he tried to protect his parents and his family from what he knew would destroy them. Around him, however , whatever their claims, everyone else was playing the great game of self-aggrandisement. For me now, the important memory is the nobility of Marcus and the humanity of our late chief. I have no more interest in the plots or the criminals."

With this he pulled himself out of his chair with some difficulty, straightened up, embraced me as I stood as well, and made for the lift and his bed

The rest of the visit passed without incident, though I was sad to see them go, since when I said goodbye at Heathrow I was acutely aware that I would never see him again. I was right. About three years later I got a text from Bimpe warning me that he was very ill, and then a few weeks after one from Henrietta telling me that he had died peacefully the previous night. He was surrounded, apparently, by orphans past and present. I mourned a great humanitarian in my own way, reading Achebe's autobiography with a glass of Bunnahabhain in my hand.

THE END